TEAROOM
mysteries

Dear Reader,

Is there anything as perfect as a summer day? The warm breeze, the lazy afternoons, the long, sultry evenings...And then there's the beach. I love nothing more than spreading out my blanket, picking up a good book, and losing myself in the story while the waves lap at the shore.

Though our fictional town of Lancaster is beautiful in all seasons, it was especially fun to write a book set in this town at the height of tourist season. Elaine and Jan are thrust into another mystery when a customer is robbed right in their tearoom, and naturally they are led all over town as they attempt to solve it. I really enjoyed bringing the marina to life, and sending them to the public swimming area on Chickadee Lake and exploring I Scream, the ice cream stand (and it's possible I visited some local ice cream shops as "research").

I also enjoyed introducing a romantic storyline for Rose. The poor girl has been through so much, and it was fun to have her wrestle with her own hang-ups and fears about a romantic relationship. And speaking of romance, Jan has some excitement of her own in this story.

No matter what time of year it is for you, I pray that you will enjoy reading *Mystery and Macarons* as much as I enjoyed writing it.

Best,
Elizabeth Adams

Tearoom Mysteries

TEAROOM
mysteries

Mystery and Macarons

ELIZABETH ADAMS

Guideposts

New York

Published by Guideposts Books & Inspirational Media
110 William Street
New York, New York 10038
Guideposts.org

Acknowledgments

Every attempt has been made to credit the sources of copyrighted material used
in this book. If any such acknowledgment has been inadvertently omitted or
miscredited, receipt of such information would be appreciated.

Scripture quotations are taken from *The Holy Bible, New International Version.*
Copyright © 1973, 1978, 1984, 2011 by Biblica, Inc. Used by permission of
Zondervan. All rights reserved worldwide. www.zondervan.com

Cover and interior design by Müllerhaus
Cover illustration by Ross Jones, represented by Deborah Wolfe, Ltd.
Typeset by Aptara, Inc.

Printed and bound in the United States of America
10 9 8 7 6 5 4 3 2 1

CHAPTER ONE

Jan Blake looked around the east parlor. Nearly every table was full. Guests were laughing, chatting, and drinking tea from delicate china teacups. Soft classical music played in the background. Bright summer sunlight streamed in through the open window, and a light breeze fluttered the curtain gently. Archie Bentham, one of the tearoom's two employees, came through the door from the kitchen, balancing on one arm a giant silver tray piled with bone china teapots and layers of finger sandwiches.

Jan sighed happily. It was her cousin Elaine Cook's and her second summer season running Tea for Two, and so far, it was going along perfectly. The tearoom had been busy every day since Memorial Day, and Jan truly loved keeping the kitchen stocked with pastries and interacting with the regulars and visitors alike. Running this tearoom with Elaine was a dream come true.

Jan looked around once more and saw that everything was in order, so she crossed the hallway and poked her head into the west parlor. Elaine was chatting with a pair of elderly sisters as she cleared their table. The other tables of guests all seemed to be doing well. Maureen Oakley was sitting with her daughter Shannon by the door to the dining room. Jan waved, and Maureen waved back. Jan spotted another table of regulars over by the window, and she made her way to where Rue Maxwell and Macy Atherton were seated.

"Hello, hello," Jan said, smiling as she approached the table. Both Rue and Macy looked up.

"Hi, Jan." Rue set down her Royal Albert Old Country Roses teacup and a tiny splash of Irish breakfast tea spilled out on to her saucer. Rue had perfectly styled hair and was dressed in a tailored jacket and skirt, even on this midsummer day. "It's a beautiful day, isn't it?"

Jan had to smile. Rue was bubbly and outgoing, and it was always a pleasure to see her here.

"Hello," Macy said, a hint of a smile spreading across her face. She was crumbling a blueberry scone with her fingers.

"How is everything today?" Jan asked. Rue and Macy were two of their most loyal customers, though Macy most often found something to complain about.

"The scones are a bit dry," Macy said. "But the tea is good."

"I could get you some extra jam or clotted cream," Jan volunteered. She'd made those scones this morning, with just picked blueberries, and she knew they were fresh, moist, and soft.

Macy shook her head. "Too many calories."

Jan pasted a smile on her face. She knew to expect this sort of thing from Macy, and it honestly didn't bother her, because she had come to enjoy Macy's company. Jan turned to Rue.

"How are those sandwiches? I got the watercress at the farmer's market on Saturday. I love shopping there at this time of year. There is so much beautiful produce in season."

"I love it too." Rue nodded. "And the sandwiches are wonderful. Is that dill mixed in with the cream cheese?"

"It is." Jan nodded. "So how are things going for you both?"

"Oh well, you know. We were just talking about the thief that's been terrorizing the town," Macy said, giving Jan a significant look.

It took Jan a moment to process what she'd just said. "Thief?"

Macy nodded. "It was all over the paper this morning. Didn't you see it?"

Jan had read the *Penzance Courier* this morning, but hadn't seen anything about a thief terrorizing the town.

"It was a small piece in the local section," Rue clarified, giving Jan a smile. "Both Macy and I have guests who've been robbed."

"Robbed?" Jan felt her eyes widen. "What do you mean?"

"Someone came into one of my cabins and robbed one of my guests. Just took her wallet right out of her purse." Macy was shaking her head. Her scone was crumbling into smaller and smaller pieces.

"When was this?" Jan asked. How had she not heard about this?

"Saturday," Macy said. "She was at the pool with her kids, and when she came back, the door of her cabin was open and her wallet was gone. Can you imagine?"

Jan couldn't imagine. What a terrible thing to happen to a guest. That poor woman must be so upset, and scared, and—

3

"Just think of the bad reviews I'm going to get now." Macy sighed. "Who wants to stay at a place that's unsafe? It will probably take months to recover."

Jan wasn't quite sure how to respond to that. "And after all that trouble last year too," Jan finally said. A few months back, one of Macy's cabins had been accidentally set on fire.

"Yes, it does seem like someone has it out for me." She picked up a piece of her scone and popped in it her mouth. "At least Rue's guest wasn't robbed at her inn," she said after she'd swallowed her bite.

"You had a guest robbed too?" Jan asked. Rue and her husband, Ned, ran Northwoods Bed-and-Breakfast, an old, rambling farmhouse that they'd converted into a charming, cozy inn.

Rue took a sip of her tea and set the cup down gently. "It's so terrible. It was a lovely couple who had just checked in Friday evening. I feel so bad for them."

Sometimes Jan had trouble understanding Rue and Macy's friendship. Aside from the fact that they both ran places to stay in Lancaster, she couldn't see what they had in common. Rue was so sweet and bubbly and always thinking of others, and Macy...well, Macy was an integral part of the Lancaster community, Jan reminded herself.

She turned to Rue. "Where were they robbed?"

"They went out to eat at the Pine Tree Grill," Rue said. "And while they were out on the deck watching the sun set, someone took her wallet right out of her purse."

"Oh my goodness. That's terrible." Jan felt awful. What a thing to happen on the first night of your vacation. "Does Dan Benson have any clues as to who is behind all this?"

Trooper Dan Benson was an officer of the Maine State Police who lived in Lancaster, and he dealt with most of the petty crime that happened around these parts.

"He's been out to see my cabin that was robbed, and Rue was just saying he's been talking to her guest as well, but so far there doesn't seem to be much headway." Macy picked up a finger sandwich and examined it from every angle.

"I certainly hope they find this person soon." Jan hated to think there was someone out there on the lookout for wallets to steal.

"I just hope it doesn't get out beyond the local papers. It would be a shame if tourists stopped coming to town."

Once again, Jan didn't know how to respond, so she turned toward a noise at the far end of the room. She realized it was a woman's voice breaking through the quiet din of the busy tearoom.

"It was just here," she was saying, digging into her purse. Jan didn't recognize the woman. She looked to be in her late thirties or early forties, and she had a long mane of reddish-blonde hair and freckles. She wore the sleeveless shirt and capri pants combination that signaled that she was on vacation. She had a large leather bucket purse and was pawing through it, pulling out one item after another, obviously looking for something.

"You had it when we came in," the woman who sat across from her said. She had the same hair and freckled skin, and Jan was certain they were sisters. "I saw you tuck the business card into it. Did it fall out?"

A few of their other guests had turned and were now watching them.

Jan saw that Elaine had already appeared from the other room and was on her way over to the women, a calm smile on her face, but Jan excused herself and headed toward them as well.

"Is everything all right?" Elaine was asking as Jan approached.

The woman didn't seem to hear her. She pulled a pair of sunglasses and a folding map of Maine out of her purse and peered into the bottom of her bag. "I can't find my wallet," she said. "I know it was here when I came in."

"It *was* here," her sister added.

"But it's not here now," the woman continued, looking up at Jan. Jan didn't want to believe it. She would have given just about anything to be able to rewind this scene a few minutes so that it never happened. But a sinking feeling was already spreading throughout her body.

"Somehow, in the time I've been sitting here, my wallet has disappeared."

CHAPTER TWO

J an couldn't believe it. She didn't want to believe it. Could it
be true? How could this woman's wallet have gone missing
while she was sitting here in the tearoom?

"You're sure it was here when you came in?" Elaine was asking. She looked at Jan, her forehead scrunched up. Jan didn't
know if Elaine had heard about the thefts in town yet, but in
any case, this was not good.

"I'm positive." The woman was now going through every
item from her purse, piling them on the table in front of her.
"I had a business card for this place and I tucked it into my
wallet when I stepped inside."

"I remember her doing that," the other woman said.

"And what happened after that?" Elaine asked. She somehow managed to have a warm, encouraging tone to her voice.

"That dapper British gentleman in the bow tie showed us
to this table," she said. She meant Archie. Jan looked around
and saw him carrying a tray of pastries out of the kitchen
toward a table in the east parlor. He gave them a worried look
as he passed.

"And then we sat here and had tea," her sister continued.

"Where was your purse while you sat here?" Elaine asked. Other customers were starting to notice that something strange was going on, and Jan tried to paste a smile on her face to give the impression that everything was okay. She didn't want to ruin anyone's tea with this madness.

"It was right here." She patted the back of her chair, indicating that the purse had been hung over the back of the chair. The sinking feeling in Jan's stomach worsened. If the purse had been hung like that, the bulk of it would have been on the chair behind the woman, where she wouldn't have been able to see it. And judging by the open bucket style of the purse, it would not have been that hard for someone walking by to see into—or maybe even reach into—the purse.

"Did you get up from your table at any point?" Jan asked. Maybe the woman had the wallet in her hand and had left it in the powder room somehow.

"I did go to the restroom," she said. "And I left my purse here. But Krissy was here. You didn't get up and leave my purse unattended, did you?"

The sister, Krissy, shook her head. "Nope. I sat here the whole time you were in the bathroom." A sheepish look crossed her face. "Though I was looking at my phone most of the time you were gone, so I wasn't actually paying all that much attention. But I think I would have noticed if someone had reached into your purse while you were gone."

The woman nodded, though Jan wasn't so sure. In her experience, when people were looking at their cell phones, they tended to tune out the rest of the world.

"Did you see or hear anything strange while you were sitting here?" Jan couldn't believe she was really asking these questions, as if it was really possible that someone had taken this woman's wallet while she had been a guest at the tearoom.

"No." The woman shook her head. "There was nothing…" But then she stopped, closed her eyes for a moment, and then nodded. "Actually, you know what? There was one thing that was weird."

Jan watched her, waiting for her to go on. She glanced around the room, hoping that the conversation would not disrupt their other patrons. A few were glancing their way, but most people seemed to ignore the unfolding drama.

"It was right after you took our order," the woman said, turning to Elaine. Elaine nodded. "You went back to the kitchen, and I turned to my sister and we started talking."

"We haven't seen each other in months," Krissy said. "Tricia has three young kids and this crazy job, so she's impossible to get time with. We came to Lancaster for a few days for a girls' getaway."

"How wonderful that you take the time to catch up with your sister," Elaine said. Jan nodded, noting that the woman's name was Tricia.

"I was showing her pictures of my daughter's tap recital," Tricia was saying. "And someone bumped into my chair. I turned and realized a woman had dropped her sunglasses, and she'd knocked into me when she bent to pick them up."

"Where was this?" Elaine asked.

The woman turned and indicated a space on the carpet just behind her chair. It was almost exactly the same place where her purse would have been hanging.

"I didn't think anything of it at the time," she said. "She said sorry, and she moved on, and I turned back to our conversation. It didn't occur to me that it was anything but an accident. But now that I'm thinking about it, it does seem odd that she just happened to drop her sunglasses right where my purse was."

"And crouching down by your chair and bumping into it would have given her a perfect opportunity to reach into your bag," Krissy added.

Jan was afraid she was right. It did seem very plausible that this woman had "accidentally" dropped sunglasses just behind Tricia's open purse as a ruse to reach in and take out her wallet.

"Did you see her?" Jan asked. "Can you tell us anything about her?"

Tricia thought for a moment. "She had blonde hair. I remember that." She pressed her lips together and looked up. "I think it went down to about here." She used her hand to indicate that her hair went a few inches past her shoulder. "I'm trying to think of anything else memorable about her."

"Was she very thin? Well dressed?" Elaine asked.

"I think so…?" Tricia's voice trailed off a bit. "I'm sorry. I wasn't really paying attention. I didn't realize I would need to."

"Of course," Jan said, trying to be reassuring. As much as she wished Tricia could remember any relevant details about this woman, she had to admit she wasn't sure if she would have been any better.

"I think I know who you mean." Elaine nodded. "I greeted her when she came in. She was blonde, thin, about my height. And she kept her sunglasses on, which struck me as strange at the time."

"Oh, Elaine, that has to be her," Jan said. She could feel her pulse speed up. "Did you get her name?"

Both Tricia and Krissy were watching Elaine intently now.

"No, I'm afraid not." Elaine indicated a table at the front the room. A young couple was seated there now; it was one of the best seats in the whole tearoom, overlooking the front porch and main street. Jan had seated them there when she'd found out they were on their honeymoon. "She was alone, and said she wasn't waiting for anyone. So I sat her over there and brought her a menu. But when I came back to take her order a while later, she was gone."

"When was this?" Jan couldn't believe they'd figured this out so quickly. Elaine had *spoken* with the suspected thief. They knew who it was. It couldn't be that hard to track her down. They'd have Tricia's wallet back before dinner.

"I probably seated her forty-five minutes ago or so," Elaine said. "And it was maybe ten minutes later that I came to take her order and found she'd left." She shrugged.

"That was about the time the woman bumped into me," Tricia said. "It has to be her. Did you see her leave?"

"No, unfortunately," Elaine said. "I'd just assumed she'd changed her mind or not found anything that looked good."

"Now we know the real reason," Krissy said. "Plus, how could anyone not find anything good?" she asked, gesturing down at the layered tea tray they'd emptied of goodies. "This place is awesome."

"Thank you," Elaine said with a smile. "We like to think so." She turned to Jan and nodded. "But it does happen occasionally that customers come in here expecting something different, or find that the full afternoon tea is too pricey, and leave."

"I thought it was quite reasonable," Tricia said.

Elaine nodded again. "We try. But I didn't think all that much of it when I realized she'd left. But thinking about it now, I bet she was the one."

Archie came up next to her and seemed to be assessing the situation. Jan realized that Rue and Macy were watching them. They couldn't possibly hear what they were saying, but they could tell something was going on.

"She came in, looked around, picked a target, staged the theft, and left," Jan said. It all made sense.

And, Jan realized, there was a good chance this blonde woman was the same person who had stolen from the tourists at Pine Tree Grill and the Green Glade Cottages. If they were right, if it had been this blonde woman, hopefully they could track her down quickly and get the wallets returned to those visitors too.

"So it looks like all we need to do is find this blonde woman," Jan said. She was triumphant. She and Elaine had solved a number of mysteries since they'd moved to Lancaster, and this one would be their easiest one yet.

Then she realized both of the sisters were staring at her.

"I was actually thinking I should probably call the police," Tricia said after a moment's pause.

"Of course," Elaine said smoothly, filling in the silence.

"Actually, Jan and Elaine are pretty good at solving mysteries," Archie said. "So you would do well to have them investigate."

"We do like a good mystery," Jan said. "But you're right. You should call the police. Come with me, and we'll get Trooper Benson on the phone."

"Actually, the first thing you should do is cancel your credit cards," Krissy said.

Jan realized that Krissy was exactly right. "Of course," Jan said. "That's what you should do. Why don't you go cancel your cards, and we'll get ahold of the police."

Tricia nodded and stood up, holding her cell phone in her hand. "I'll go outside and do that so I don't disturb everyone."

Jan appreciated her thoughtfulness. Not everyone realized what a distraction it was to talk on a cell phone in a crowded room. Tricia headed for the front door.

"And I'll take care of the bill," Krissy said, reaching into her own purse to take out her wallet.

"Oh no, this is on us." Elaine gestured for her to put her wallet away.

"Are you sure?" She looked uncertain.

"Absolutely. It's the least we can do," Jan added.

"How about I bring you a fresh pot of tea while I go get Trooper Benson on the phone?" Elaine suggested.

"Oh, if I drink any more tea I'll float away," Krissy said. "But I wouldn't say no to some more of those scones."

"Of course. Coming right up." With a swift motion, Elaine scooped up the silver tea server and turned toward the kitchen.

"I'll go call the state trooper," Jan said and turned to follow her cousin.

Dan Benson sighed when he heard why she was calling, no doubt frustrated about another theft. But he promised he'd be right there. Jan went back to serving the rest of their customers, and she tried to act as normal as possible.

Still, even though she tried to hide it, Jan was shaken.

THE REST OF the afternoon was a whirlwind. Elaine tried her best to keep the other customers happy, but her mind kept wandering back to what had happened. When Trooper Benson arrived, she set him and the sisters up in the private dining room to minimize the impact of his presence on the other customers, but there was no disguising the fact that there was a state trooper making an investigation. She heard customers whispering about a missing wallet, and saw many sideways glances when they thought she wasn't looking.

She was actually glad when it was time to close up for the afternoon. She said good-bye to the last customer, and then she cleared their table and carried a load of dishes to the kitchen. Jan and Rose were already there. Rose Young, their employee who both baked and served, was washing delicate teapots in the sink while Jan dried and put them away.

"Why don't you go ahead and take off?" Elaine suggested to Rose, setting her load of dishes down on the counter. She and Jan had completely redone the kitchen when they'd bought the house, and Elaine never tired of the granite countertops, the rich walnut cabinets, and the gleaming double oven and stainless steel fridge. She'd always dreamed of having a kitchen like this one. The dishwasher hummed softly. "We can handle the rest of this."

Archie had already left for the day, and there wasn't much left to clean up. And, if she was being honest, she couldn't wait to talk to Jan about the events of the afternoon, but she preferred to do it privately.

"Would that really be okay?" Rose asked. But she had already turned off the faucet and was slipping her long apron over her head. Rose had been their first employee, and she was loyal and kind, but she was also young. Of course she didn't mind leaving a bit early.

"Of course." Jan finished drying the Blue Willow teapot with the soft dish towel, took one last look, and then set it on the shelf by the back door. "We've got it under control."

"Thank you so much." Rose hung her apron on a hook by the pantry and turned back to Elaine. Her long blonde braid hung halfway down her back. "I was actually kind of hoping to leave a bit early, but after the day you had, I didn't want to ask."

"Oh yeah? Hot date?" Elaine asked, winking. But instead of laughing, as Elaine expected, Rose froze. She didn't seem to know how to respond.

"Oh my goodness, you really do have a date," Jan said.

Elaine saw that it must be true, judging by the way Rose's cheeks were turning a soft shade of pink.

"So what's his name?" Elaine asked, moving to the sink. She plunged her hands into the soapy water and found one more teapot waiting to be scrubbed.

Good for Rose. The young woman had had a tough run. She'd moved back to Lancaster after her mother had had heart trouble, and she had been going through something of a quarter-life crisis since her mother's death, trying to figure out what she wanted to do with her life. She'd seemed to really enjoy helping out in the kitchen of the tearoom—she had been accepted at a pretty prestigious culinary school nearby and took classes in the evenings—and Elaine considered them very lucky to have her as part of the tearoom family. But as far as she knew Rose hadn't dated anyone in the time they'd known her, and she'd never seen her freeze up like this.

Slowly, a soft smile spread across Rose's face. "Brent," she said.

Elaine ran a soft sponge over the porcelain, being careful not to scratch the delicate flowers painted on the side. "And where did you meet this Brent?"

"He's from culinary school." Rose seemed to trying to decide whether to say more.

"So he's got good taste in careers, at any rate," Jan said approvingly. Elaine had to agree. A man who could cook? He sounded like a keeper already.

"Well, he's not really interested in cooking for a career," Rose said. She leaned forward a bit and put her hand on the granite countertop. "He's a software engineer. He's actually taking the class because he has a six-year-old daughter, Emma, and he wants to know how to cook her healthy food. The class isn't part of my regular curriculum and is open to the public. It just so happened that we both signed up."

"Aww…" Elaine couldn't stop herself before the sound escaped. "That's so sweet. He's learning to cook for his daughter?"

Rose nodded. There was a sweet smile on her face. "His wife died of cancer a few years back, and he's been raising his daughter on his own since then. We started talking and kind of bonded because we've both lost someone we loved, and I don't know, we just really hit it off."

"He sounds wonderful," Jan said.

Again Rose hesitated, but then she seemed to make a decision. "I'm really excited. He's really sweet, and smart, and cute to boot."

"He sounds wonderful." Elaine knew that in the early stages of a relationship, everything the other person did seemed wonderful, but this Brent guy really did seem to have a lot going for him.

"Where are you going on your date?"

"He lives in Augusta, and he's taking me to his favorite restaurant," Rose said. "It's French."

"Le Bernadin?" Elaine asked.

"I think so." Rose nodded.

"Ah. You must try the escargot. They are divine."

"Isn't that snails?" Jan asked, scrunching up her nose.

"Trust me, it will be the most wonderful dish you've ever eaten." Elaine's husband had been an army man, and they'd especially enjoyed their time in Belgium, in a region where French language and cuisine was prevalent. She'd grown to love the rich, heavy French cuisine, so full of deep, unexpected flavors. She'd been to Le Bernadin with her special friend—was it fair to call Nathan her boyfriend?—a few weeks ago, and it was like traveling back to Europe again.

"I'll give it a shot," Rose said, but she looked dubious.

"And what are you wearing?" Elaine asked.

"I haven't really decided." Rose pulled her phone out of her pocket and swiped to bring up a photo of herself in a beautiful floral sundress with thin, gauzy fabric held up by narrow straps. "Either this sundress or"—she swiped again, then held up the screen to show a different photo—"this one with blue and white stripes."

"Sundress," Elaine said and the same time that Jan said, "Stripes." The cousins looked at each other and laughed.

"You will look beautiful no matter which dress you wear," Jan said, and Elaine nodded.

"I guess you'll just have to go with whichever one you like best," Elaine added, laughing.

"I don't *know* which I like best." Rose shook her head and tucked the phone back into her pocket.

"Well, you'd better get going then so you can figure it out." Elaine pulled up the stopper in the bottom of the sink and rinsed her hands under warm water.

"Thank you so much," Rose said. "I really appreciate it."

"Of course." Jan waved. "Have a wonderful time."

Rose laughed. "All right. I'll let you know how it goes tomorrow."

"We'll want a full report." Elaine said a prayer that the evening would go as well as Rose hoped as she disappeared out the back door. Elaine couldn't think of anyone more deserving than Rose.

CHAPTER THREE

D idn't your mother ever tell you you'll ruin your eyes like that?"

Jan jumped, and then she looked up to see Elaine step out on to the back porch and flick on the overhead light. She'd been totally absorbed in her mystery novel—which was British and revolved around an amateur chef—and was surprised to suddenly find herself on the back porch of the tearoom instead of in a manor house in the English countryside. Jan smiled and shook her head. "There's still plenty of light."

Elaine held out a glass of lemonade, and Jan reached out and took it gratefully. It was frosty with condensation, and a sprig of rosemary garnished the homemade drink. Elaine then sat down in the wicker chair next to Jan and set her own glass down on the low glass-topped table in front of them.

"Well then, how about this: If you don't look up from that book, you'll miss the most gorgeous sunset of the season so far."

"Now that is a much better argument." Jan placed her bookmark into the pages of her book and closed the cover gently. She looked up and saw that her cousin was right. Beyond the porch, their yard sloped down toward the lake. The sun was gently sinking over the horizon, casting the sky in a chorus of colors, red and pink orange, staining the clouds the softest purple. The surface of Lake Chickadee shimmered, reflecting orange and gold and silver. Their dock was silhouetted against the water, and it looked like something out of a travel magazine. Some children played in the water a ways down along the shore, splashing and shrieking, but otherwise the growing night was peaceful and still.

"It really is stunning," Jan said. Sometimes she couldn't believe she got to live here in Lancaster and run the tearoom with her cousin. More than a year in, it still felt like a dream, especially on nights like this.

"God makes some beautiful things, doesn't He?"

"Indeed." Jan took a sip of her lemonade. It was tart, sweet, and cool. Simply delicious. She took another sip and set it down on the table.

They were silent for a moment, watching the sun slip lower in the sky, vanishing slowly behind the trees. The air felt soft, like silk, and it carried a hint of jasmine and the sweetness of roses. Jan felt the stress of the day melt away.

There was a noise, loud and insistent, and Jan jumped, startled. What in the world...?

It only took her a moment to realize what it was. Elaine pulled the cordless phone out of the pocket of her sweater and studied the number on the screen.

"Where's 516?" Elaine asked. Jan knew she was asking what region the area code represented.

"Long Island," Jan answered. "That's where Van is from."
Had Elaine really brought the phone out here? She knew,
as businesswomen, that it made sense to keep the telephone
handy, but sometimes she didn't want to think like a business-
woman and simply enjoy a quiet evening.

"Should I answer it?" Elaine asked.

"Might as well at this point," Jan said. "Here, I'll take it."

She took the phone Elaine held out and answered the call.
"Hello?"

"Hi there. This is Tricia Dalton, from earlier today? I was
the one who created such a headache for you this afternoon."

Ah. The woman who'd lost her wallet. "You did nothing of
the sort," Jan said, laughing. "How did everything work out?"

"Well, they haven't found it yet. But I wanted to call and
say thank you for being so kind this afternoon. I know it
made things difficult for you, and I am grateful for all you did
to help."

Jan couldn't believe it. After this woman was pickpocketed
in their tearoom, she was calling to thank *them*.

"You're very welcome, of course. I'm just sorry it happened,"
Jan said. "How did it work out with canceling your credit cards?
Were you able to cancel them before they were used?"

"Actually, no, unfortunately. The thief used one of them
before I called. She made a small purchase at a convenience
store, less than five dollars, and then she went to town at the
SuperShop in Waterville. She spent nearly five hundred dollars
there. The credit card company is being great, though, and
they say I won't be liable for the charges."

"Well, that's a relief." Jan thought for a moment. It was a shame the cards had been used, but at least now the police would be able to track where the thief went after she stole the cards. "You told Trooper Benson about the charges, right?"

"Yeah, I did, and he said he would look into it, so I guess all I can really do is wait and hope he catches the thief."

Yes, Jan thought. That was probably all any of them could do. But that didn't sit well with her. Jan didn't *want* to just sit around and wait for the police to solve this thing. This wasn't just some random theft—the thief had come into their home and targeted one of their customers. This was personal.

But Jan didn't know how to say all that, so she simply answered, "Yes, let's hope they catch the thief soon."

She hung up and looked over at Elaine, who had heard enough of the call to follow what was going on.

"I guess we'll just wait for the police to solve it," Elaine said, echoing what she'd heard Jan say. She sounded earnest, but she didn't look convinced.

"I guess so," Jan said. She picked up her glass and took a sip of the lemonade. The rosemary added such a subtle hint of richness, and the glass felt cool and solid in her hand. They sat in silence for a few moments, watching as the last rays of the sun vanished behind the trees and night settled over Lake Chickadee. It was so peaceful here, Jan thought. So calm. But the events of the day made it feel at the moment like it wasn't the untouchable paradise it normally was.

"Then again, maybe it wouldn't be the worst thing if we did a little investigating on our own, would it?" Elaine asked. "After all, this affects us too."

Jan couldn't hold back a smile. Sometimes she was surprised by how her cousin seemed to know exactly what she was thinking.

"You know, I don't think it would be out of line at all." She set her glass down on the table. "I don't see why we couldn't ask a few questions. Who knows, maybe we'll find something the police missed."

Elaine nodded. "Good then. We'll start investigating first thing in the morning. Whoever this blonde woman is, we'll find her."

Jan felt a surge of excitement. She knew Elaine was right. They would find her.

CHAPTER FOUR

When Elaine came downstairs Tuesday morning, Jan was just pulling a tray of freshly baked muffins out of the oven. The whole downstairs was filled with the sweet smell of baking bread, and her mouth was watering before she even made it into the kitchen. She saw freshly made scones and loaves of lemon bread cooling on the counter.

Elaine pulled the belt of her robe tighter and crossed the floor quickly. "Don't mind if I do." She reached for a muffin, but Jan slapped her hand away.

"These are for the tearoom."

"And I need sustenance to run the tearoom," Elaine said. Besides, it was unfair to fill the whole house with a smell like that and expect her to keep away. She tugged at one of the paper liners and lifted the muffin out of the tray.

"We nearly ran out yesterday." Jan put her hands on her hips and shook her head.

"I'd say that's a good problem to have." Elaine pulled the paper off and waited as a puff of steam rose up gently.

"Just the one. I need the rest."

"Of course. I have to watch my figure after all." Elaine took a bite. It was soft, sweet, moist, and totally delicious. She turned and moved toward the door to the screened porch and saw that Earl Grey, the stray cat they had more or less adopted, was eating from a dish Jan must have recently filled. Beyond that, the lake shimmered in the early morning sunlight. She would never get tired of this view. She watched the sparkles dance on the water for a few minutes, and then she turned and noticed the *Penzance Courier* newspaper on the kitchen table. And she almost choked on her muffin.

"Did you see this?" The headline on the front page read: "Rash of Thefts Threatens Summer Season in Lancaster."

"Oh dear. I'd hoped you'd at least finish your breakfast before you saw that." Jan was pulling the muffins out of the tin by the paper liners and setting them on the wire rack to cool.

"It's quite an inflammatory headline." Elaine skimmed the article, which was written by River White, a reporter they'd had run-ins with a few times in the past, though, to be fair he had also helped them occasionally.

The article listed the theft at Tea for Two as the latest in a string of thefts targeting tourists in Lancaster. That was true, Elaine had to admit, but she hated that the tearoom's name had been included in the article. And then the piece went on to quote one woman, a Dahlia Parks, identified as a visitor from Quebec, saying, "It's hard to relax and enjoy my vacation. I worry that I'm going to be next." River also quoted a Janice Murray from Connecticut as saying, "I thought Lancaster was supposed to be this safe, peaceful place, but I don't know. If this goes on, we may go home sooner than we'd planned."

"This is not good," Elaine said.

Jan had already refilled the muffin pan with new paper liners and was pouring batter for orange cranberry muffins into them.

"It's ridiculous," Jan agreed, using a spoon to scoop the batter into the pan. "But I bet it sells papers, and that's what they care about."

Elaine read back through the article again. "It's a shame that the tearoom is now a part of all this."

"Let's just hope it doesn't affect business." A dollop of batter hit the counter, and Jan used a dishrag to wipe it up.

"Exactly." Elaine set the paper down and turned away. "Which is even more reason we need to solve this thing right away. Are you still up for investigating?"

After their discussion the previous night, Jan had called Tricia back and let her know they would try to find the thief themselves. Tricia had seemed dubious, but said Trooper Benson confirmed that they were amateur sleuths helping with the investigation, so she said it was all right with her. She had told them the name of the convenience store and location of the grocery store where her credit card had been used.

"Of course I'm up for investigating, if we can be back to open the tearoom." Jan set down the bowl and scraped out the rest of the batter. "I'm ready whenever you are."

"Don't you need to finish baking?" Elaine took another bite of the muffin. It was delicious. Jan had added just a hint of lemon zest and a pinch of salt, and it really brought out the flavors.

"I'll be done by the time you're ready to go."

Elaine looked down at her pink flannel robe and her thin cotton nightgown. She ran her hand through her hair, which was full of snaggles and flat on one side. "You don't want to be seen with me like this?"

"I was hoping you'd at least want to put on some shoes," Jan said as she smoothly opened the oven door and slid the tray of muffins inside.

"Fine." Elaine sighed playfully. "Give me twenty minutes, and I'll look like a new woman."

"I'd be happy with thirty minutes and the same woman, just with different clothes."

"Deal." Elaine popped the rest of her muffin in her mouth and brushed the crumbs off her fingertips. "See you in a few."

Half an hour later, she was wearing blue capris, a striped shirt, and a light sweater. She slipped on a pair of flats and grabbed her purse, and together she and Jan went out to the garage and climbed into her Chevy Malibu.

"So do we start by going to the convenience store or the grocery store?" Jan asked as she buckled herself in.

"I say groceries," Elaine said. "Let's start with the big kahuna."

Jan nodded, and a few minutes later, they were threading through the quaint small town of Lancaster, which was still waking up for the day, on the road to Waterville.

"So," Jan said, taking a sip of English breakfast tea from the travel mug she'd brought along, "things seem to be going well with you and Nathan."

Elaine gave her cousin a sidelong glance. That seemed to come out of nowhere, but she knew there had been a logical progression in Jan's head. There always was with Jan. It was just that sometimes it wasn't clear to everyone else what it was. "Yes, they are," she said. "We're taking things slowly."

Elaine's husband, Ben, had only passed away a year and a half or so ago, and she hadn't been ready for anything serious for some time, but when Nathan Culver, an auctioneer Elaine had known back when they were kids, had started hanging around quite a bit, they'd fallen into an easy friendship again. And slowly that friendship had developed into something more. She didn't know where it would go or if she even wanted it to go further than it already had, but she cared about Nathan, and she had to admit that after so many months of tears, it was nice to have someone who cared about her again. But that's not what she wanted to talk about right now.

"I'm more interested in how things are going with you and Bob."

"Oh, they're going really well," Jan said, a smile creeping up her face. "He's such a sweetheart."

Bob Claybrook was a lawyer and an old friend, and he had started pursuing Jan almost as soon as they moved to town. He was a kind and generous man, and Jan was head over heels for him.

"You guys seem to be getting serious," Elaine said.

"I don't know." Jan took another sip. "Maybe." She was quiet for a moment. "Actually, he called while you were upstairs and asked if I wanted to go to a concert in the park with him tomorrow night. He said there's something he wants to ask me."

"What?" Elaine almost stomped on the brakes. "Are you serious?"

When she saw the surprise on Jan's face she realized she was nearly shouting. Okay, she needed to tone it down.

"Yes," Jan said. "What's the big deal?"

"He wants to *ask you something*?" Elaine couldn't tell if the innocent look on Jan's face was an act or it if was for real. Was her cousin really that naïve? "You guys have been talking about the future, right?"

"Yes," Jan said uncertainly. "We have been."

"And did that future involve the possibility of marriage?" Elaine asked.

"Yes." Jan nodded. A slow smile was starting to spread across her face. "Yes, we've talked about it."

"You've met his daughter, Susie, right? He made a point to make sure you guys all went out to dinner last month?"

"That's true."

Elaine could tell that Jan could now see where this was going.

"And he turned down that job in Baltimore to stay here with you, right?"

"I'm not sure he's officially turned it down yet, but yes, I think he is planning to."

Elaine braked for a stoplight, but she felt triumphant. "And tell me, Jan. Have you and your beau recently discussed the topic of wedding rings?"

Elaine knew the answer to that. Just a few weeks ago while they were eating dinner, Jan had recounted a conversation she and Bob had had about how neither one of them felt the need for expensive jewelry at this stage in their lives.

"We did discuss it," Jan said. "His wife had wanted a big flashy diamond, and wanted to keep trading up as the years went by. I said I'd only ever had a tiny chip of a diamond and that had always been fine for me."

"But that wasn't all, was it?"

Jan was smiling broadly now. "No. He said that if he ever got married again, he'd probably just have his mother's diamond reset if his wife was okay with that."

"And you were, right?"

Jan laughed. "I always thought a simple setting in a nice traditional gold band was always the best way to go."

Elaine felt her heart was about to burst with excitement for her cousin.

"That's it, then. He's going to ask you to marry him."

"Oh, Elaine, do you really think...?"

"I do. That's exactly what I think. Jan, I'm so excited for you!"

What would happen to Elaine when Jan married Bob? Would Jan move out, or would Bob move in? She imagined the newlyweds might want a home of their own.

Elaine shook her head. She couldn't worry about that right now. She was too excited for Jan.

"There's no need to be quite so excited," Jan said, but she couldn't wipe the smile off her face. "He hasn't asked me anything yet."

"No, but he will tomorrow night. You'll have to get your hair cut before then! And you'll want to get your nails done."

"Why in the world would I want to get my nails done?" Jan looked down at her short, efficient nails.

"So they'll look good in the picture of the ring," Elaine said. Goodness. Had her cousin never done this before?

"And we'll have to make sure you've got something gorgeous to wear, and…"

"Let's not start worrying about that just yet," Jan said.

Elaine started. Why in the world not? Didn't Jan want to look her best? This would be one of the most important nights of her life!

"Look, I hope you're right," Jan continued. "But I don't want to get too excited just yet. For now, let's focus on the matter at hand, shall we?"

Sometimes Elaine didn't understand her always-practical cousin. But she could accept that Jan didn't want to count her chickens before they hatched. Though really, they were halfway out of the shell already, unless Elaine was sadly mistaken. Still, they were pulling into the parking lot of the grocery store where Tricia's card had been used now, so she nodded. "All right," she said. "For the moment, we'll focus on this stolen credit card."

"Thank you," Jan said, nodding.

"And we'll worry about finding you the perfect outfit for your engagement when we get home."

Jan just shook her head and stepped out of the car.

Elaine had been to SuperShop many times, but she didn't particularly like it. For everyday items, she and Jan both went to Murphy's General Store in Lancaster, and for bigger shopping trips, she preferred the newer, nicer grocery store on the other side of Waterville. This shop was smaller and older and, well, dingier, and though it billed itself as having the cheapest prices in town, Elaine hadn't found any significant savings shopping here. Still, the promise must work, Elaine thought, crossing the busy parking lot.

Elaine stepped on to the rubber mat in front of the glass front door and expected it to swing open, but it didn't budge. She looked over the divider at the door that opened out, and it swung open as a woman came out, trailed by three small children. Jan stood and waited for a second, but still nothing.

"It says it's broken," Jan said from behind her, pointing to a handwritten sign on pink paper that Elaine had somehow missed: Automatic Door Broken, Please Push.

"Ah." Elaine pushed on the glass door, and it swung open. "I knew that."

"Of course you did."

As they stepped inside the store, a blast of cool air hit them, along with the smell of sugary treats. They entered into the bakery section, where cookies and colorful cakes were on display. The tile floor was grubby under too many layers of wax, the corral of abandoned carts was messy, and Elaine knew from experience that at least half the carts had bad wheels or broken handles.

"I guess we should start with the manager?" Jan pointed to the window in the wall above the small produce section. Elaine nodded and followed her cousin past the checkout lanes and beyond the displays of sugary breakfast cereals and towers of canned tomatoes, and stopped at the door. They were right next to the display of Mylar balloons and wilting flowers.

Elaine knocked. A moment later, they heard footsteps coming down the stairs, and then the door opened. A small man in a pinstriped shirt and polished shoes stood in front of them.

"If this is about that coupon in the newspaper, please read the fine print. The limit is two per customer." His dark hair was slicked back with gel, and it moved as one piece as he talked.

"Oh." Elaine was put off balance for a moment, but Jan stepped in.

"Actually we're not here about the coupon," Jan said, and his face visibly relaxed at the news. "We were hoping to talk to someone about a purchase that was made here yesterday."

"Oh?" He shoved his hands into the pockets of his pants.

"That's right." Elaine jumped in. "A friend of ours had her wallet stolen, and one of her credit cards was used to make a purchase here."

"Is that right?" He now eyed her suspiciously.

"We own a business ourselves and we know that no one at the store is responsible for this," Jan said, and he nodded. They had looked into this early on in their tenure at the tea shop, after a customer's card had been declined. Merchants were expected to do what they could to prevent credit card fraud, but there was only so much they could do when someone handed over a credit card. It wasn't like there was a picture to match to the card holder or anything of that sort. The stores weren't liable if someone used a stolen card. "And I'm sure you know that the store will get paid anyway."

"That's right," he said, mollified.

"We were simply hoping to talk to anyone who might have seen the person who used the stolen card to get a description of the thief," Elaine explained.

"Ah." He nodded. "Well, I'm not really sure. Do you know how much the charge was for?"

"Five hundred forty-three dollars," Jan said.

"Ah yes. Naturally."

The both looked at him, waiting for him to explain.

"That's a high total," he continued. Elaine nodded. She couldn't imagine how anyone could spend that much at this store in a single shopping trip. "Somehow it doesn't surprise me that our biggest total of the day would be a fake."

"Do you have any way to check whether purchases, especially large ones such as this one, are aboveboard?" Jan asked.

"Cashiers are required to verify that the signature on the back of the card and on the receipt match," he said. "But aside from that, it's really pretty difficult when someone has possession of an actual credit card."

Elaine nodded. "That's what we've found as well." She was curious to learn more about the methods other merchants used—surely there had to be something stores could do to prevent this sort of thing. They might have to do some more research on this at some other time. But for now, she didn't want to risk alienating this man. She decided to focus on what they came here for.

"Would there be any way to talk to the checker who rang up the sale?"

"Sure. When I looked over the receipts last night I noticed that sale, and I know it was Shirley who rang it up."

He gestured to a woman at the last checkout lane with curly brown hair piled on top of her head in a messy knot. She looked to be in her mid forties, solidly built, with a friendly smile.

"Could we see the receipt?" Jan asked.

"I'm afraid not, unless you're with the police."

"We're not," Jan said.

He nodded and cocked an eyebrow.

"I'm sure they will be in soon to talk to you though," Elaine added. "So if you could share what you know, that would be most helpful."

He seemed to not know what to make of this, but he started across the floor, and they followed a step behind. He waited at the end of the row while Shirley finished ringing up an older man's purchase of a half-dozen frozen meals and a gallon of milk. Elaine noticed the canned smooth-jazz music that played out over the store's speakers. If she had to listen to this all day it would drive her batty. Shirley finally waved good-bye to the older man and turned toward them.

"Shirley, these ladies would like to speak with you about a purchase you rang up yesterday."

"Sure thing." She smiled. She wore heavy eyeliner and dark-red lipstick that seemed out of place at this time of the morning, but she was pretty. "How can I help?"

"A friend of ours had her credit card stolen yesterday, and the card was used here before she could report it," Elaine said. She tried to keep her voice light and a smile on her face so Shirley wouldn't get defensive. Elaine continued, "The total was 543 dollars and some change, and we were hoping you might remember the incident and might be able to tell us any-thing you can about the person who made the purchase."

Elaine felt like she was babbling, but the woman nodded. She flipped a switch by the register and the light in the number sign above her register went out.

"Yeah, I do remember it." She gestured for Jan and Elaine to step in closer, and they moved into the narrow space between her row and the next. The manager still hovered at the end of the checkout lane. "It was one of the biggest totals I've ever seen. And it wasn't someone stocking up on diapers or something like that, this was all real food. It was like she was buying enough food to last through the winter."

"What sort of food did she buy?" Elaine asked.

"Oh, a little bit of everything. Lots of cans of soup, instant mac and cheese, crackers, cereal, bread. Average stuff, really. A lot of meat. I hope she has a very large freezer somewhere."

It sounded to Elaine like someone stocking a bare cupboard.

"You said 'she.'" Jan pointed out. "So it was a woman who made the purchase?"

"Yep." She nodded.

"Do you remember anything about this woman?"

She thought for a moment. "I did take a second look when I saw how high the total was. I remember that she had brownish hair, cut about here." She indicated about two inches below her chin. "It was kind of curly."

Kind of curly shortish brownish hair. That described about half the population around here.

"She had pale skin," she said. "Chipped pink nail polish. And she was heavy."

"Was she short? Tall?" Jan asked.

"About my height."

Elaine judged the cashier to be about five foot four. "Was there anything else thing distinguishing about this woman? Anything that stands out?"

"I'm sorry, that's all I remember."

Elaine looked at Jan, who met her eye. This didn't match the description of the woman in the tearoom at all. Was it possible either Shirley or Tricia had gotten it wrong? But it wasn't likely that you would mix up short, curly brown hair and straight, long blonde hair. Were there two people involved in the theft, then?

Then she had an idea. "What about security cameras?" She looked up and saw a round mirror stuck to the stained asbestos tiles of the ceiling.

"The cameras are on the fritz," the manager said from the end of the checkout counter.

Shirley laughed. "'On the fritz.' That's one way of putting it."

Elaine tilted her head.

"They've been 'on the fritz' for years." She gestured at the orb on the ceiling where the camera should have been. "He just keeps that thing there to make people think they're being recorded, but it hasn't picked up a thing since I could fit into a size six."

Elaine laughed. This woman had sass. She liked that. But it wasn't getting her any closer to finding answers.

"Did anyone help her to her car?" Jan asked.

Elaine had practically forgotten that that used to be a service grocery stores offered.

Shirley snorted. "Not at this store."

Her manager grunted, and she smiled. "Just being truthful, Bruce."

"So no one would have seen the car she got into?" Jan asked.

"Nope. I'm assuming it was a semi, judging by the amount of food she bought, but I can't say."

"And there are no security cameras in the parking lot either?"

Shirley's only response was a snort.

"Did you have any other questions?" The manager was obviously not thrilled with this line of questioning.

Elaine looked at Jan. She couldn't see what more they were going to accomplish here.

"Thank you so much for taking the time to talk with us," Elaine said. She started moving out of the narrow lane toward the manager. "We really appreciate it."

"If you have any other questions, you just let me know," he said, but the smile on his face looked a bit forced.

They promised they would, and they walked back toward the automatic door. It swung outward, and they stepped out into the heat of the sunny day.

"Well, that was enlightening," Jan said.

"In more ways than one," Elaine said, and Jan nodded. "But also confusing. The woman she described using the credit card can't be the same person Tricia saw take her wallet, can it?"

"It sure doesn't sound like it."

"So there must be two people involved here?"

"It would appear that way, but it's hard to say anything for sure at this point."

They climbed back into Elaine's car, and Elaine turned on the engine. "Shall we go to the convenience store next?"

Jan fastened her seat belt, and it clicked into place. "Maybe we'll find more answers there."

CHAPTER FIVE

Elaine turned up the air conditioner and made her way across the rutted parking lot toward the street. It was only a short drive to the convenience store where the stolen credit card had been used. Elaine pulled into a strip mall and drove past a Laundromat, a karate studio, and a Chinese take-out restaurant before parking in front of the convenience store on the corner.

"Shall we?" Jan looked nervous.

"Absolutely. I may have to get myself a Slurpee while we're here."

Jan cringed.

"You can't mock it unless you've tried it."

"No, thank you."

"Are you serious? You've never had a Slurpee?"

"Do you have any idea what's in those things?"

"Oh yeah. Tons of sugar and fake food coloring and flavoring. That's what makes them so delicious. They're like frozen candy." Elaine stepped out of the car and shut the door.

Elaine had lived all around the world and enjoyed cuisine from many different cultures, but sometimes you really couldn't beat good old American ingenuity. On a hot summer day, there was nothing like it.

"I'll stick to tea, thank you."

"Suit yourself."

Elaine followed Jan as she stepped over the cracked sidewalk toward the door of the store. The glass was covered in labels and decals for different drinks and convenience foods that could be purchased there. They stepped inside, and goose bumps raised up on Elaine's arms. Why did stores always keep the AC up so high?

They smiled at the woman behind the counter. She had graying black hair and paper-thin skin that feathered out into wrinkles. There were dark circles under her eyes, and her gaze was far away.

"Hello," Jan said, stepping up the counter. "We're here because a stolen credit card was used here yesterday, and we're trying to find out about the person who used the card."

The small store smelled of hot dogs, and Elaine spotted a handful of sad-looking franks glistening on a rotating display next to the frozen section.

"You want to see the security footage?"

Elaine nodded. Either this woman was very perceptive or this kind of thing happened pretty regularly around here.

"Hold on." She stepped away and vanished behind a door built into the wall behind the counter. A calendar from the previous year flopped against the door as it shut.

Elaine looked up. There was a black camera hung above the space in front of the checkout and one positioned to capture the view of the door. The door frame had a stick-on ruler of sorts that measured the height of everyone who came in. So the security footage would record the height of any potential thief, no doubt.

She wandered down one aisle, looking at the selection of prepackaged cookies and chips. The next aisle held pain relievers and everyday household items, and beyond that was an aisle devoted to drinks—six- and twelve-packs and soda and alcoholic beverages on one side, and a cooler filled with every variety of drink on the other. Elaine stopped in front of the Slurpee machine and grabbed a small cup. There were half a dozen flavors, including some ghastly combinations of soda and fruit flavors, but Elaine stuck with the traditional cherry kind. She filled the cup, fitted on a lid, tucked in a straw, and headed back toward the counter, where Jan waited.

"That stuff will kill you," Jan said, eyeing the cup.

"But what a way to go."

Just then the woman came out of the back room, and the door slammed shut behind her. The calendar banged against the door again.

"Here's the footage from yesterday." She held out a DVD.

Elaine was stunned. Just like that? This woman was handing over the security footage from a whole day? There had to be a catch or some problem. "Thank you. This is...the store's security camera footage?"

"That's what I said, right?"

Well then. "Thank you very much." Elaine took the DVD and tucked it into her purse. This had to be a violation of some kind of store policy, but she wasn't about to argue, and even if she did, this woman didn't seem to care. Elaine pulled out her wallet and paid for her drink, and a few minutes later they were back in the car and headed back toward the tearoom.

"Did she really just hand over the store's security camera footage?" Jan asked as Elaine pulled out on to the main road.

"That's sure what it seemed like. I guess we won't know until we get it home." Elaine braked for a red light and reached for her Slurpee. Ah. Tart and sweet and cold. Perfect.

"It could have just been her way of getting rid of us," Jan said.

"It might well have been. I guess we'll know shortly."

CHAPTER SIX

As soon as they arrived home, Jan went upstairs, got her laptop, and brought it down to the kitchen table. While she inserted the DVD and navigated to the program that would allow them to view the files, Elaine set her Slurpee on the table and took a seat. Then she hit play.

Two grainy images showed up on the screen, one from each of the two cameras Elaine had pointed out in the convenience store. The image at the left showed the door of the store; to the right, the cash register. In both images, the sky was dark. Jan looked at the time stamped in the corner of the image. Five thirty in the morning. A man—a trucker, Jan guessed, based on his rumpled appearance—was getting coffee, but otherwise the store was empty. The same woman they'd spoken to this morning was behind the cash register.

"Tricia's wallet was stolen right about three in the afternoon, right?" Jan asked.

"Somewhere around there." Elaine picked up her Slurpee and took a sip. "The purchase at the grocery store was just before four, and the card was used at the convenience store first, so we have a limited window of time to check out."

Jan used a bar at the bottom to advance the image on the screen. The time in the corner went forward, and more customers came into the store. They were an odd mix of grizzled adults looking for coffee, harried parents grabbing small items, and preteens hitting up the candy display. The little room brightened as the day advanced, but it still seemed somehow dim and depressing to Jan. The cashier changed at noon, and instead of the woman they'd seen today, a young man appeared at the counter.

She slowed down when the clock read three. At a few minutes after three, a woman came into the shop with long blonde hair.

"Freeze it," Elaine said, and Jan did, and they studied the image of the woman.

"Is that the woman from the shop?" Jan asked, squinting at the picture on the screen. She was wearing a tank top and shorts along with flip-flops, and her hair was pulled back into a ponytail.

"I don't know." Elaine narrowed her eyes. "I sure wish I'd paid more attention when I seated her. But from what I remember, that woman was pretty thin." She didn't need to say the rest. This woman carried more than a few extra pounds. But then, the cashier had said that the woman at the grocery store had been heavier. "Besides, this is only 3:05. If the wallet was taken right around three, would she have had time to get to Waterville?"

Waterville was a fifteen-minute drive from Lancaster.

"It depends on how close to three it was taken, I suppose," Elaine said.

Jan nodded. If the wallet had been taken a bit earlier than three, it was possible.

"Let's see what she buys," Jan said. They knew the thief had spent less than five dollars at the convenience store. Jan hit Play, and they watched as the woman lugged two boxes of sugary cereal and a twelve-pack of diet soda, then brought them to the counter.

"Not our girl," Elaine said, and Jan nodded. There was no way that cost less than five dollars. They watched as the woman paid with cash and went out of the store, and then kept the footage rolling.

The next time someone interesting came on to the screen was just before 3:30. A woman came into the store alone, wearing big sunglasses. As she entered the store, she looked up, glancing briefly at each of the security cameras, and then looked away.

"That's her," Elaine said. Jan had no way to know for sure, but she felt hopeful as well. This woman had dark hair, just hitting her shoulders, and she wore a baggy sweatshirt and jeans. It was difficult to tell anything about her face, as most of it was hidden behind her large sunglasses. The measuring strip on the door frame showed her height at just under five feet six inches. Who was this woman?

"Let's see what she does," Jan said, and slowed the footage to normal speed.

They watched as the woman headed straight for the refrigerator case and grabbed a bottle of water. She then went right to the counter and set it down. She also grabbed a pack of gum, almost as an afterthought, and tossed it on the counter as well. The cashier hardly glanced down as he rang up the purchase. The woman reached into a canvas bag slung over her shoulder and pulled out a credit card.

"Pause it," Elaine said. Jan did. "Is there any way to zoom in?" Jan played with the controls a bit, but she couldn't find any way to manipulate the image on her screen.

"I doubt we could zoom in enough to look at the details on the card," Jan said, and Elaine agreed it had been a long shot. She played the video again, and the woman paid for her purchase and scurried out before the cashier could hand her the receipt. The whole encounter had taken less than a minute. They would need to make sure Dan saw this.

"That had to be her," Elaine said. Jan had to agree. This was the right time frame, and the woman's purchase couldn't have totaled more than five dollars. Beyond that, there was something about the way she moved throughout the experience— from the glance at the security cameras to the way she almost didn't seem to care what she bought—that made her movements seem odd. Plus, she matched the description of the woman the cashier described.

"She was testing out the card to see if it had been canceled yet," Jan said.

"And when the purchase went through here, she went to the grocery store and loaded up her cart as quickly as she could."

Jan nodded and backed up the footage. They watched the whole episode through again, and as the seconds ticked by, she felt more and more certain that this was the woman they were looking for.

"So." Jan stopped the footage after their thief went out the door again. She felt triumphant. "It looks like we have identified the woman who used the stolen card."

"Now we just need to find out who she is," Elaine said. "And how she's related to the woman who stole Tricia's wallet."

Jan's stomach sank. Elaine was right. Now all they had to do was find this woman and then find the thief.

And she had no idea how to do any of that.

CHAPTER SEVEN

Elaine and Jan were stacking their breakfast plates in the dishwasher and tidying up when Archie Bentham stepped into the kitchen.

"Hello, ladies," he said in his booming baritone. He was wearing a suit with a vest and bow tie, even in this summer heat. "How are you two this fine day?"

"Hello, Archie." Elaine smiled. Archie was a charmer, which made him a hit with the older women who came into the tearoom, but he really had a way of making everyone he encountered feel special. "We're all right. How are you?"

"Oh, can't complain." He was already pulling serving plates and utensils out of the cabinets to start setting the tables in the parlors. He was such a hard worker, and the customers loved his refined manners, listening ear, and upscale British accent. He was a huge asset to the tearoom, and sometimes Elaine couldn't believe he worked for them. But he honestly seemed to enjoy chatting with the customers and sharing his love for tea with them. "Though I must admit, something has been bothering me."

"What's that?" Elaine closed the dishwasher door and moved to the sink to wash her hands. Jan was slicing cucumbers on a wooden cutting board.

"I couldn't stop thinking about the horrible theft last night," Archie said. "And I know our guest saw a woman drop her sunglasses just beside her purse, so that's the logical suspect, but there was another woman in the tearoom acting strangely. I couldn't help wondering if they were connected somehow."

"What do you mean?" Jan set down the knife.

"There was a woman in the west parlor whom I waited on." He pulled a stack of linen napkins in a lovely sprigged summer print out of a drawer and set them on the counter. "She was about your age, I would guess. She had on big sunglasses, a floppy straw hat, and thick lip liner."

"I think I remember seeing her," Elaine said. She'd remembered that hat. It wasn't unusual for women to wear hats inside the tearoom, but this one was quite large. Almost like she was trying to hide beneath it, she now realized.

"I asked her where she was from, as I do with most of our guests, but she was very curt. She didn't seem to want to talk at all."

"Some people just want to get away from that sort of thing when they come here," Elaine said. Archie was the kind of outgoing person who never met a stranger, and in general Elaine was pretty extroverted, but there were times when she didn't want to talk to anyone.

"True enough. Especially because she sat alone."

Jan nodded. "Maybe she just came in for a break."

"Maybe." Archie counted out bread plates and set them on the counter. "But the strangest part was, she kept using her phone to take pictures."

"Pictures? Of what?" Elaine was used to guests taking selfies, but they didn't see that a lot with the older women who came in alone.

"Of everything. The room, mostly, but also the food. She ordered tea for one, and she took pictures of the sandwiches and the tea tray. The teapots. But, like I said, from what I saw, the space in general."

"That's odd." Elaine tried to think of why that would be. "And you think that she's connected to the wallet theft?"

"I don't know." His bow tie moved as he shook his head. "I just can't help thinking it was strange. Could she and the blonde woman have been working together somehow? I don't know. But I just thought that considering the gravity of what happened yesterday, it might be worth bringing it up."

"Of course it is. Thank you, Archie." Elaine thought for a moment. The blonde woman from the tearoom was not the same woman they'd seen in the security camera footage. Could this woman in the big hat have been the one who used the credit card?

"Do you remember what color hair she had?" Elaine asked.

"It was a little hard to tell, under the hat, but I would venture to say brown, though graying a bit."

It was possible, Elaine decided. Maybe the two women were working together. Maybe one was casing the place while the other pounced. Or maybe the hat woman had been there as a distraction. "I wonder how we could find out more. Did you catch any information about her?"

Archie thought for a moment. "Like I said, she didn't say much. But"—he set down the stack of saucers he'd pulled from the cabinet—"now that I think about it, I believe she did pay with a credit card."

Elaine perked up at that. Was there any chance it was a stolen credit card? Maybe from one of the wallets that had been taken the past few days?

Jan, reading her mind, asked, "The cards from the earlier thefts would have been canceled, right?"

"One would assume," Archie said. "But in any case, the credit card receipt would have a name on it."

"I'll go grab yesterday's receipts," Elaine said. She stepped into the office and dug through the top drawer of the desk. She returned to the kitchen a few minutes later with a stack of receipts in a manila envelope. She pulled the stack out and started flipping through.

"Do you know what time she left?"

"I rang her up while you were talking with the sisters in the east parlor after the theft was discovered. So I'd guess somewhere around 3:30?"

"The timing is suspicious," Jan said, and Elaine had to agree.

"You said she ordered afternoon tea. Did she have anything else?"

"That was it. Just the tea."

Elaine zeroed in on a receipt that fit the bill. She could see that it was one order of afternoon tea, and the bill had been paid at 3:26 p.m. It had been rung up by Archie. "It appears her name is Dorothy Schuman."

"Huh. Never heard of her," Jan said. Elaine hadn't either, but that didn't mean she wasn't going to find out who she was. "Thank you for letting us know about her, Archie."

"Of course. I hope I haven't sent you down a rabbit trail that leads nowhere." He picked up the stack of plates.

"We'll look into anything if it gets us closer to the thief," Elaine said.

"Don't I know it," Archie said, laughing, and he took the plates into the east parlor and began setting tables.

Elaine was tempted to head into the office and start Googling the name Dorothy Shuman immediately, but she needed to help Jan get things ready. She filled a big teakettle and set it on the stove to boil, and then she pulled out the bread and started cutting off crusts. She had a tray full of cucumber and cream cheese finger sandwiches ready to go when the door opened and Rose blew in.

She wore a simple blue dress and sensible ballet flats, and her long tawny hair was pulled back into a braid as usual, but something was different. She looked radiant. Her eyes were shining.

"The date went well, I take it?" Elaine asked, and Rose's cheeks turned pink and she laughed.

"How could you tell?" There was a smile on her face that she couldn't suppress.

"Because you look like a woman in love." Elaine set the last of the sandwiches on the tray and brushed her hands together.

"Tell us everything." Jan was setting fresh-baked pastries on to silver serving trays.

"I don't know what to say. But it was good."

"Start at the beginning." Elaine gestured for her to begin talking.

"Well, I decided to wear the sundress…"

Elaine raised a fist in the air.

"…and as soon as Brent picked me up, he said the color really set off my eyes, which I thought was a good start."

"It was indeed." Jan set a peach tart on to the tray.

"He drove to the restaurant, and we talked the whole way, and we couldn't stop talking once we got there. I've never had that happen before. Usually when you're going out with someone for the first time, there are all kinds of awkward silences and weird moments where you're trying to think of what to say. But not with Brent. It was like we'd known each other forever."

"Wonderful." Elaine thought back to when she'd met her husband, Ben. It had been like that with him as well. She hadn't realized it was possible to fall for someone as hard and as fast as she fell for him.

"And how was the food?"

"It was wonderful. I ordered the escargot, and he thought that was so funny and brave. And it was delicious. I never would have known."

Rose chattered about the rest of the food, and Elaine listened, but she also let her mind wander.

It had been different with Nathan. Their relationship was still pretty new, but it had grown slowly, her feelings changing gradually from friendship to something more. That didn't mean their relationship was any less special, she realized. Just different. Maybe that whole "can't eat, can't sleep, can't do anything but think about him" kind of love was a once-in-a-lifetime thing.

"And then we shared a crème brûlée for dessert, and it was so romantic..."

Then again, Jan was pretty head over heels for Bob. They reconnected when she'd moved to Lancaster, and Jan had fallen for him almost right away. And now, it seemed she was about to marry him. Elaine was thrilled for her cousin, but she couldn't help but wonder how it would change things. Surely Jan would want to move out. Elaine tried to imagine rattling around in this big old house all by herself at night. A wave of sadness washed over her. She and Jan were not just business partners and roommates; they'd come to be great friends. It was just the two of them. When Jan got married, Bob would be the most important person in Jan's life. And rightly so. But it was still hard to imagine. Elaine wondered if she'd feel left out.

"And then when he dropped me off, he took like half an hour to walk me to the door, because neither of us wanted the evening to end."

Elaine tried to focus on the conversation. There was no sense getting worked up about how things were going to change yet. Best to just focus on now and be happy for Jan. Besides, there was no telling what might happen between her and Nathan. Who knew—there might be a wedding in their future someday too.

JAN TOO WAS caught up in the story. "Did he kiss you good night?" she asked Rose.

"Just a peck on the cheek," Rose said, and her blush got pinker.

Jan nodded approvingly as she used tongs to maneuver a strawberry tart around a butter cookie.

"So when are you going to see him again?" Elaine asked.

"I don't know." Rose had pulled an apron off the hook by the door and was slipping it over her head. "Part of me hopes he'll call today."

They waited for her to go on, but she didn't say anything more for a moment.

"But...?" Elaine prompted.

Rose sighed. "And then part of me is afraid he will call."

"How so?" Jan was confused.

"I'm just worried because he seems too perfect. There has to be something wrong with him that I just haven't discovered yet, right?"

"Of course there is," Jan said. "I don't know the guy, but I feel certain he's not perfect. Then again, neither are you."

"Though you're pretty close," Elaine added. Rose smiled.

Bob wasn't perfect, Jan thought, but it was those imperfections that had made her fall for him so fast and so completely. Such as the awkward way he laughed when he thought something was really hilarious, which was completely endearing. And the way he always wanted to help other people, no matter what.

On one of their early dates, they'd come across a woman with a flat tire at the side of the road. It had been pouring rain, but Bob had pulled over and changed the tire for her on the spot. They'd missed their dinner reservations because he'd had to go home and change. It was hard not to be pleased by how caring and selfless he was. But sometimes, as their relationship had gone on, Jan had become frustrated about always waiting in the car while he went off and helped someone else. Jan knew it was awful, but sometimes she wanted to be the center of Bob's attention. But you couldn't really complain about a boyfriend who was too nice to other people, and Jan knew how lucky she was to have him.

"But what if he's got some deep, dark secret or some strange habit or something?" Rose asked.

Elaine shrugged. "And what if he doesn't? You'll never know until you get to know him."

"And if he does, you'll have to decide if it's something you can live with or not," Jan added. She'd decided that Bob was worth it, a thousand times over. Rose would have to make the same decision at some point as well.

"But the worst thing you could do would be to see him as this perfect ideal and not try to get to know the real person," Elaine said. "Of course he won't live up to your ideal in every way. But I bet you'll find some ways he's more wonderful than you even imagined."

Rose nodded.

"You're worried about something else," Jan said.

Rose didn't say anything for another moment. Then, she said, "What if I don't live up to his ideal?"

Jan set down the pastries. Rose was so sweet, so earnest. And so young. Jan wondered if she'd ever had her heart broken. Was this fear—understandable as it was—a result of some painful event in her past? Or was she so inexperienced with men that she really didn't know what to think about a man who liked her for who she was?

"Oh, Rose, you can't worry about that," Jan said. "You can only be yourself. Let him get to know you, and you guys will know whether it's a good fit or not."

"And he'd be crazy not to think you're wonderful," Elaine added. "You're gorgeous, kind, talented, and caring. What's not to love?"

Rose kept her eyes cast downward, but she was smiling.

"In any case, it's far too early to worry about all this stuff," Elaine said. "You've only been on one date."

"One date *so far*," Jan added.

"And if it went as well as you think it did, I'm sure he'll call again soon," Elaine continued.

"Try not to let your fear of what might go wrong get in the way of what is going right," Jan said. "It sounds like you had a wonderful first date. Enjoy that."

Rose nodded. Jan knew it was difficult to do, but falling in love was supposed to be fun.

"He'll call," Elaine said, winking. "Just you wait. I bet he's head over heels. He'll call today."

There was nothing but hope on Rose's face.

THE AFTERNOON WAS a bit slower than the previous day had been, and Jan couldn't help wondering if the newspaper article that morning had anything to do with that. But this was still high season for tourists, and it was late in the workday before she had a break. Her twelve-year-old granddaughter, Avery, had come by, and she loved to bake, so Rose was helping Avery make a fresh batch of shortbread cookies. Jan grabbed a couple of the cookies and she went up to the sitting room and sat down at the desk with her laptop. She pulled up a search engine and typed in the name Dorothy Shuman and hit Return.

A long list of results came up, and Jan began sorting through them. The first was the social media page of a woman in her forties. She had posted a lot of pictures of her junior-high-aged kids on their recent trip to the Caribbean and around the large farm table in their high-end kitchen. She lived in North Carolina. Jan decided this Dorothy had a very nice-looking family and a range she would love, but she was unlikely to be the Dorothy they were looking for.

Jan took a bite of the shortbread cookie. It was warm and buttery and delicious. Jan took one more bite, then she brushed her hands together and turned back to the keyboard.

She returned to the search page and sorted through LinkedIn profiles, 5k finishing times, and a newspaper article about a high school senior who'd won a big science prize. Finally she came to an obituary for a Maurice Shuman of Portland, Maine. Jan pulled up the obituary and saw that Maurice had passed away last year, and that he was survived by his wife, Dorothy, two children, and four grandchildren. The couple had been married for more than forty years.

This had to be the right Dorothy, Jan realized. Portland was an hour drive; close enough that she could reasonably have come to the tea shop. And Archie had said that the woman she'd seen had graying hair, and this woman had to be in her sixties.

Jan popped the last of the shortbread cookie into her mouth, and then she opened up a new browser window and typed in "Dorothy Shuman, Portland, Maine." A white pages listing popped right up. Bingo. Jan was a little disturbed at how easy it was to find someone's contact information, but she was grateful for it as well. She stared at the number, and then she leaned back in the chair. Could she just give Dorothy a call? But what would she say?

Just then, Elaine popped her head into the room.

"Everything all right?"

"Oh yes. Everything is fine. It was slow, so I decided to take a break and search for Dorothy Shuman."

"The surreptitious photo taker?"

"That's the one."

"What'd you find?"

"I've got her phone number right here."

"Really?"

Jan broke the other cookie in half and held out one half to Elaine. Elaine shook her head, and Jan shrugged and ate it herself.

"So why aren't you on the phone?" Elaine stepped further into the room.

"I was trying to figure out what to say," Jan said before swallowing her bite.

"Here. I'll take a crack at it." Elaine held out her hand for the cordless phone that sat on the desk. Jan held it out, and Elaine took the phone and bent over to look at the laptop screen.

"Right here." Jan put her finger just under the number on the screen.

"Got it." Elaine dialed the number and stood as the phone rang. Jan listened as the line rang once, twice, three times. And then someone picked up.

"Hello?" she heard through the phone.

"Hello. Is this the Dorothy Shuman who visited Tea for Two in Lancaster, Maine, yesterday?" Elaine asked.

Jan couldn't hear the response, but she saw Elaine's triumphant look fade a bit.

"I'm sorry to disturb you. Did you enjoy your visit to the tearoom?"

Jan waited. Elaine held the phone close to her ear.

"Oh, I'm very sorry to hear that. Well, this should be very quick. We're calling because something very strange happened in the tearoom yesterday, and we're trying to talk to as many customers as possible who were there."

Thank goodness for Elaine. She was so smooth. And it was pretty much true too. The woman on the other line said something, and Elaine answered, "One of our guests had her wallet stolen. We were hoping you might have noticed if anyone was acting suspiciously."

Again, the woman said something, but Jan couldn't make sense of it on her end. She finished the second cookie and waited.

"We got your name from your credit card receipt. Again, we're really upset about what happened and we're trying to find and speak to as many guests as we can who may have seen something."

The woman on the other end of the line was speaking, and then Elaine finished with, "Okay, well, thank you for your time," and ended the call.

"What'd she say?" Jan asked.

"She wasn't the friendliest person I've ever spoken to." Elaine cradled the phone in her hands. "She seemed more surprised than anything when I told her why we were calling."

"Well, that makes sense. If she hadn't told anyone her name, and then we come calling out of the blue, I'd say she has reason to be surprised."

"Yes, but it wasn't just confusion," Elaine said carefully. "She was...I don't know that I would say *defensive,* but that seems to be the closest word. It was like she was trying to be really careful about what she said."

"That could have just been the surprise call. Again, since she hadn't left her name, she had to have been thrown off by our reaching out."

"It could have been." Elaine turned the phone over. Jan could tell she didn't think so.

"You think there's more to it?"

"I think it's a possibility. She didn't just seem surprised. She seemed unhappy."

"I would be unsettled if I'd just realized how easy it is for someone to find my personal information."

"That wasn't what bothered her, I don't think. She was really insistent that she hadn't seen anything strange, and then she hung up the phone before I could ask her more. That was what was so weird. It was like she didn't want to talk about the tearoom at all."

"Like she was hiding something?"

"Maybe." Elaine sighed. "It was hard to tell."

"Well, I guess we can't eliminate her from the list just yet."

"I suppose not. We'll have to see what more we can find." Elaine set the phone back down on the desk. "In the meantime, Priscilla Gates is here with her sister, and I thought you might want to say hello."

"Oh, that's great. Thank you for letting me know." Priscilla was the head librarian at the Lancaster Public Library and a good friend of Jan's. Jan had known Priscilla had been looking forward to her sister's visit, and Jan was looking forward to meeting her.

Jan closed her laptop and followed Elaine downstairs. She'd see what more she could find out about Dorothy Shuman later. If she was hiding something, they'd get to the bottom of it.

CHAPTER EIGHT

That evening, after they'd cleaned up the dinner dishes, Jan had disappeared into her bedroom to call Bob, and Elaine was making one last sweep through the first floor before heading upstairs to the sitting room, intending to call her daughter, Sasha, who lived in Colorado, and then relax with her book. But as Elaine walked into the west parlor, her eye caught on the painting that rested on the bookshelf. She set the phone and her book down on the coffee table and stepped across the room to take a closer look.

She and Jan had found the painting at a booth at Mainely Bargains and had been drawn to it mostly because it showed a woman, dressed in 1920s or maybe 1930 clothing, drinking tea. Elaine had thought it would look nice in the tearoom's west parlor, and after nearly walking away from it, they ended up getting it for a song. Elaine was glad they had. She loved the scene of simple domesticity. The woman sat at a small bistro table set with a vase of flowers and a newspaper, gazing out the window at what looked like a park in full bloom. It was soothing and beautiful. But when they'd brought it home, they'd both been surprised when Archie recognized the artist's mark in the bottom right corner as the symbol his own father used. It was a mark made up of his initials, an interlocking *HAB,* for Henry Arthur Bentham, and he used it to sign his letters. But Archie didn't recognize the painting, and he had no idea who the woman in the painting was. Was there some connection to Archie's father? If so, who was this woman? And how had the picture ended up at a flea market in Maine?

Elaine moved closer to the picture and looked at it closely. The woman had dark brown hair, and wore a dress with a light-pink pattern. The style made it seem vintage—1920s or 1930s, maybe. The woman sat a table with a steaming cup of tea and a vase of flowers on it. To the left of the woman was a light-blue settee with white antimacassars on the arms, and to the right, you could see an old Aga range and a boxy refrigerator. Jan had loved the vintage details of the kitchen, while Elaine was more intrigued by what lay outside the window. Through the treetops, you could see a few old buildings and a church steeple. The level of detail, as well as the sense of warmth tinged with a hint of melancholy, spoke to the skill of the painter.

She was also intrigued by the connection to Archie. Could his father have painted this picture? Was his symbol somehow added to the painting later? But why? Archie had said that his father wasn't a painter. But something was nagging at Elaine. She smelled a mystery. She gazed at the painting a moment longer, and then she turned and headed into the office.

She sat down in front of the computer and typed in the name Henry Arthur Bentham. She scrolled through pages and pages of results, but none seemed to refer to a man the right age to be Archie's father. And none of them were about a painter.

Elaine stood up and headed back into the west parlor and looked at the painting again. Even if the Internet had never heard of him—which you might expect for a government worker who had been long gone by the time the Internet arrived—there had to be some record of him somewhere. She'd do some more digging.

But in any case, it was too bad the frame was in slightly rough shape. It was solid wood, but it was grimy and cracked along the right edge, and the bottom right corner was coming apart. They should probably have replaced the frame before they hung it, but this was such a lovely frame, and if it was original to the picture, she hated to separate them. Elaine ran her hand around the wooden frame, looking for the hundredth time for any details she might have missed in the painting.

She wondered whether the frame was worth repairing. How important was it anyway? Would anyone even notice? Maybe it would be better to just buy a new one? Well, luckily, she knew someone who knew a lot about antiques. She decided to get some advice.

"Well, hello." The warmth in Nathan's voice when he answered the phone sent her heartbeat soaring. "How are you?"

"I'm doing all right," Elaine said. "How was your day?"

Nathan told her about an auction he was preparing for at work, and he also told her about a pristine antique Ferrari 250 GT that he'd been asked to evaluate. Elaine didn't care much for antique cars, but Nathan had obviously found the car fascinating and important. After he asked her about her day, she finally got around to why she had called.

"You know that painting Jan and I bought? The one with the woman drinking tea?"

"Of course. It's a lovely picture."

"The frame is broken, and I'm trying to figure out whether to get the frame repaired."

"Interestingly, frames are a big deal right now in my world."

Elaine hadn't known picture frames were a big deal in anyone's world, but then it did make sense.

"Most people, including museums and collectors, have typically seen frames as secondary to the art, almost an afterthought. But there's a lot of discussion about how a frame should honor the artist's intention and is an integral piece of the art itself."

"Oh." Elaine thought this made some sense. "So you think it's better to keep it?"

"It depends how badly it's damaged, of course. You don't want to spend more to repair it than the painting is worth, of course. But if it's original to the painting, my vote would be to see if you can get it fixed. The look will be more authentic that way."

Well, they did want authenticity. And most likely repairing it would be cheaper than buying a decent new frame.

"All right, I'll see if Heather Wells can repair it then," Elaine said.

"That's exactly what I was planning to recommend."

Elaine thanked Nathan and ended the call. Heather Wells owned We Restore, an antiques restoring shop in Waterville.

Elaine hoped Heather would be able to repair the frame and maybe even tell them something about the style or the artist.

Elaine gazed at the painting again. If only Heather could tell them who the woman in the painting was, or whether Archie's father had really had something to do with painting it.

She replaced the painting gently. She would love to be able to help Archie understand more about his father, and Elaine would be lying if she said she wasn't dying to know too. She wanted to find out more about this woman and how she might be connected to Archie's father.

But that, she thought, heading upstairs with her tea and her book, was a mystery for another day.

CHAPTER NINE

Wednesday morning, Jan woke up just as the sun was starting to peek over the horizon, and as she measured and mixed flour and milk for the day's scones, she prayed. She prayed for her family, for Elaine and the tearoom, for peace in the world and help for all who were grieving. She prayed for her relationship with Bob, that the Lord would bless it and their future together. And she prayed for the mystery they were working on, for wisdom and insight and guidance. She worked through her concerns with the Lord as she kneaded and shaped the dough. And by the time trays of scones were cooling on the counter, Jan had an idea.

She cleaned up the kitchen and went off to take a shower, and when Elaine came downstairs, she was ready.

"We need to talk to the other people," Jan said.

"And a very good morning to you as well." Elaine pulled the belt of her robe tighter. Even in the height of summer, this old house could be breezy and cool in the early hours of the morning.

"Good morning. The kettle is hot."

Elaine smiled and headed for the cupboard and pulled down a mug. She unwrapped an English breakfast tea bag and poured in the water from the kettle, which steamed and spit. Finally, she turned back to Jan. "Now, what people do we need to talk to?"

"The other women who had their wallets stolen." Jan couldn't believe they hadn't done this already. They needed to find out the details about each of the other thefts and see how they lined up—or didn't—with what had happened at the tearoom.

"The ones at the Pine Tree Grill and Green Glade cottages?"

"Exactly."

Elaine dunked her tea bag a couple times and nodded. "You're right. We need to find out what the victims saw and what other people saw. Maybe the blonde woman or the woman in the video footage was involved in those too, and someone saw them. Or maybe the thief left a clue behind."

"I know." Jan tipped the dregs of her own teacup into the sink. "Can you go talk to them this morning?"

"Sure." Elaine took out the tea bag and tossed it into the trash can. "Just give me a few minutes to caffeine up." She added a splash of milk from the jug in the refrigerator.

"And put on some clothes, preferably." Jan sized up Elaine's robe and slippers.

"You're so picky." Elaine took a sip of tea. "Ah. That's the good stuff."

"I'll meet you back here in fifteen?" Jan asked.

"Half an hour. Beauty like this doesn't come naturally, you know."

Jan laughed. "Half an hour it is. Far be it from me to keep you from looking your best."

"I knew you'd understand." She winked at Jan, and Jan grabbed a small basket. Earl Grey was sitting on the screened porch, and Jan took a moment to toss a handful of food into his dish and run her fingers over the soft fur on the top of his head. He nuzzled her hand and purred, and she stroked his back for a few minutes before finally setting him down in front of his dish.

Jan spent the next half hour pulling weeds and watering the neat little rows of plants in their small backyard garden plot. The water in Chickadee Lake lapped gently against the dock, and the chirps of the finches and starlings echoed in the still morning air. The sun felt good against her back as it warmed the air, and the scent of freshly turned soil and sweet herbs made the task less of a chore and more of a relaxing ritual. When she finally gathered up a handful of home-grown spinach and a basket of blueberries and went inside, she found Elaine sitting at the table finishing a plate of locally raised eggs and a bowl of fresh fruit, paging through the *Penzance Courier*. She must have retrieved it from the front walk while Jan had been out back.

"What's the news?" Jan set her haul on the counter and pulled a colander down from the cabinet.

"The thefts are still front-page news," Elaine said. "And there's more about how tourists are spooked."

"Well, putting it on the front page is hardly going to help with that." Jan scooped the blueberries into the colander and turned on the faucet to rinse them.

"I agree." Elaine pushed her chair back and carried her dishes to the sink. "I guess that's even more incentive to figure out what really happened quickly." She waited until Jan had finished with the blueberries, then rinsed her plate and bowl and set them in the dishwasher. "I'll just brush my teeth and grab my shoes and I'll be ready."

A few minutes later, they climbed into Jan's Camry, and Jan pulled out of the driveway and on to Main Street.

"I'm guessing we should start with Green Glade Cottages?" she asked, and Elaine nodded.

"I think so. We'll be more likely to catch the guests before they head out for the day if we get there early. Then we can go over to the Pine Tree Grill to see if anyone there can tell us anything about what happened the night the wallet disappeared."

It was only a short drive to the Green Glade Cottages, and as they drove past Sylvia's Closet, Elaine waved to Sylvia Flood, who just stepping out the front door of her shop. The road forked at Cottage Road, and they turned right at I Scream, the local ice cream stand, to keep to the road that hugged the lake. It was only a quarter mile or so until they came to the gravel road that led to the cottages. Jan drove slowly down the road to take in the scenery.

It was a peaceful place, with small but charming one- and two-bedroom cottages surrounded by towering pines and firs, perched on the edge of the lake. A lounge with comfortable seating, laundry facilities, and a swimming pool at the center of the property gave residents a place to gather, and there were picnic tables and barbecue grills spread out through the grounds. The property was rustic, and it had that timeless outdoorsy authenticity that people came to Maine for, and Macy Atherton never seemed to have any trouble filling the cabins.

Jan parked in front of the main office. "I guess we should start by talking to Macy."

"Probably." Elaine stepped out of the car and shut the door, and together they walked up the crushed-shell path toward the office. Jan pushed open the wooden door and stepped inside. Macy Atherton looked up from the front desk, which was a high wooden counter in front of a wall of key hooks. The room had buttery yellow walls and high ceilings. On the far side of the room, there was a stone fireplace flanked by two sand-colored club chairs. A loveseat and more chairs created a space for guests to relax.

"Well, hello," Macy said. She looked up from the computer screen she'd been staring at and smiled. "How are you two doing?"

"We're fine," Elaine said. She was surprised to see Macy at the front desk. She usually had a receptionist working there. "And you?"

"Short-staffed. Brett is on vacation this week, of all times. And I'm frustrated by the fact that this thief isn't behind bars yet." She gestured to a folded copy of the *Penzance Courier* that sat on the counter. Macy always set the day's paper there, and guests were free to take and read the newspaper as long as they returned it. "But other than that I'm all right."

"We hear you on that," Jan said. The wooden planks on the floor creaked as they crossed the lobby to stand in front of the desk. "In fact, that's why we're here. We were hoping we could talk to your guest who had her wallet stolen."

"To see if she recalls any details that match up with what happened at the tearoom," Elaine added.

Macy eyed them for a moment, and then she sniffed.

"Trooper Benson has already been here to talk with her."

"Of course he has. And we don't pretend to be as important as the police," Elaine said smoothly. "But since one of the thefts happened at our tearoom, we are very interested in finding the responsible parties as quickly as possible. It shines a bad light on our business to have such a thing happen there, don't you think?"

Macy considered this for a moment, and then she nodded. "It hasn't been great for business. We had to comp the fee of the family just to keep them happy and get them to stay. You know how much one bad online review can hurt. And we've already had one cancellation for next week."

"We're worried about our business as well," Jan said. "Those bombastic articles in the newspaper certainly aren't helping."

"You can say that again." Macy looked up as a man in shorts and flip-flips entered through a side door, crossed the lounge area, and walked toward a soda machine. "Well, I can introduce you to Carrie, but I can't promise she'll want to talk to you. If she says no, I will of course have to ask you to leave the property."

Jan looked at Elaine, who was trying to stifle a laugh. Jan looked away quickly. The soda can dropped into the dispenser with a thud.

"Of course," Elaine said. "Now where would we find Carrie?"

Macy sighed. She called the room, and after a few short words with the person on the other end of the line, she turned and took a keychain out of a desk drawer and gestured for them to follow her.

They crossed the lobby and followed the man in flip-flops out the side door and on to a crushed-shell path that wound under towering aspens. They passed the pool, where a lone man swam laps up and back, and the laundry room, then passed a cabin with weathered siding. The name carved into the wooden sign above the door read Escape. From somewhere off in the distance, there was the sound of a hammer and the shriek of children playing, and underlying that, the motor of a boat somewhere out on the lake, but somehow the overall feeling of this place *was* of serenity. Jan could see why families loved staying here. It was simple and relaxing.

They passed cabins labeled Calm and Peace, then stopped in front of the cabin called Serenity. Jan could hear children's voices inside. Macy knocked gently on the door. A moment later, a boy in a blue swimsuit who looked about ten years old opened the door.

"Mom!" he shouted. "That lady is here again!" Two younger girls were sitting on the bed and looked up from an iPad. The cabin was small and snug, but the view through the sliding glass door at the back was incredible. Trees sloped gently down to the lake, which sparkled in the morning sunlight. Jan realized the cabins must be staggered so that each had an uninterrupted view of the water. The décor was simple but soothing, done in peaceful colors of tan and muted green.

A moment later, a woman came out of a door Jan assumed must lead to the bathroom. She was tall, with dark hair, and wore a swim cover-up in a logo pattern. Jan didn't recognize the logo, but given the size of it and frequency with which it was repeated, she assumed she was meant to.

"Hi, Macy," Carrie said, fixing her hair in a bun as she stepped into the main part of the room. "Is there any news?"

"I'm afraid not," Macy said. "But this is Jan Blake and Elaine Cook. They own the tearoom over on Main Street, and they fancy themselves amateur sleuths. They'd like to talk to you."

Jan tried not to let that sting. She knew some people around town didn't take them seriously, but considering they'd once solved a mystery here at the cottages—one that the police hadn't managed to solve, no less—she would have thought Macy could have at least pretended to be a bit more supportive.

"I'm Elaine," her cousin said quickly, holding out her hand. "It's true that we've solved a number of mysteries in the past year, but we also have a personal stake in this. One of our customers had her wallet stolen while she was in our tearoom, and we are anxious to find out who is responsible. We were hoping to talk to you to see if there's anything you remember that corresponds with what happened at our place."

Carrie thought for a moment. Jan noticed that the woman wore sandals with a gold metal design that showed off her perfect pedicure. What was the point of gold metal sandals, Jan wondered. Weren't sandals meant to be casual attire?

"I'm Carrie." She held out her hand and each of them shook it. "I'm happy to talk with you if there's any chance it will help. But we were just on our way over to the pool, and I'm afraid these kids are going to start climbing the walls if we wait much longer. Do you mind coming with us and talking there?"

"That would be perfectly fine," Jan said. "I have three kids. They're grown now, but I remember how it is."

The woman gave her a knowing smile, and then said, "All right everyone, grab your towels." The two girls obediently set down the iPad and took the matching striped beach towels that sat next to them, while the boy started zooming around the room, looking for his. "It's on the dresser, Zack."

He found the towel, a blue version of his sisters', and then followed them toward the door. Carrie slung a tote bag embroidered with a set of initials over her shoulder and slipped on a pair of big sunglasses. Jan noticed the gold logo on the side of the frames was the same as the logo on her cover-up. Jan hoped whatever company it was was paying her to advertise their brand. As soon as they all stepped outside, the boy started running down the path toward the pool.

"Walk!" his mother yelled, and he slowed his steps. So much for serenity, Jan thought.

"I'm going to head back to the office. Holler if you need me," Macy said, and they all nodded. She headed off down a fork in the path, a shortcut to the office, Jan assumed, while Carrie and the kids headed toward the gate that led to the pool.

"Are you enjoying your stay here?" Elaine asked. Their feet crunched against the shells on the path.

"Aside from the wallet thing, very much," Carrie said. "My husband has been going to the golf course every morning, so he's happy as a clam, and the kids are happy just to splash around in the pool all day."

Jan noticed Carrie hadn't mentioned anything she was doing to enjoy herself. Such was life as a mom, Jan thought. She also remembered this part of motherhood, how making sure everyone else in the family was happy came before your own enjoyment. She hoped Carrie would get a chance to do something just for herself while they were here.

"Where are you visiting from?" Elaine asked.

"New Jersey," she answered. "Just outside of Princeton. Are you from this area originally?"

Elaine explained that they had both grown up nearby and had moved back to Lancaster to open the tearoom together. When they arrived at the gate, Zack had already gone inside, but Carrie held the gate open for the girls and for Jan and Elaine, and then headed toward the row of loungers against one side of the fence. She tossed her bag and towel on one, while the girls set their towels on the next chair. Zack had already dumped his things and was racing to the edge of the pool. A moment later, he did a cannonball, and water splashed up all around him. The man swimming laps stopped, shook his head, and muttered something.

"Sorry!" Carrie called, holding up a hand in apology.

"Oh, it's not his private pool," Elaine said. "If he gets upset about kids enjoying themselves, that's his problem."

Carrie laughed and smiled gratefully at Elaine. Jan understood the sentiment, but she also understood how frustrating it might be to have your peaceful, leisurely swim interrupted by boisterous children.

"Want to take a seat?" Carrie gestured to the lounger beside her. Jan and Elaine sat down on the mesh chair facing Carrie, while Carrie leaned against the inclined back of the chair facing the pool. The girls slipped into the pool quietly. "So what do you want to know?"

"Can you tell us what happened the day your wallet was taken?" Jan saw that the area around the pool was shaded by several tall spruce, and it was nice and cool, with plenty of shade.

"Sure thing. It was Sunday afternoon. We were…"

"When did you check in?" Elaine broke in. Carrie didn't seem fazed.

"We'd checked in Saturday, and were having a great time. This is such a cute little town. My sister came here last summer with her family and loved it, so we decided to try it. We've been meaning to get over to the tearoom."

Jan looked over at the pool, where the young Zack was now seeing whether he could splash his sisters from the far side of the pool. She wasn't sure Zack would find much to enjoy about the tearoom.

"So anyway, on Sunday afternoon, we all came over to the pool, and I left my purse in the cabin. I didn't need it, and it never occurred to me that it would be unsafe."

"This town feels so safe," Jan said. "Lancaster is the kind of town where you don't have to, normally."

"That's how it seemed to me." She kept her eyes on the water. The girls were doing handstands in the shallow end of the pool and didn't seem bothered by the splashing, though the man doing laps had gotten out and was wrapping himself in a blue beach towel. "It never occurred to me that I should lock the door or put my purse out of sight."

"Where was it?" Elaine asked.

"It was sitting on the dresser. In full view from the sliding glass door."

"Ah." Jan understood now. "So you think someone looked in the glass door and saw it sitting out, noticed you weren't there, and came in and took the wallet?"

Jan looked down at Carrie's purse, which now sat at her feet. It was made of a nice, supple leather, and had a different silver logo on the clasp. Jan recognized this one, and knew it was a costly brand. It no doubt made her an easy target, advertising its owner's wealth.

"Yep. I'm afraid so." Carrie shook her head. "I take it with me wherever I go now."

"When did you notice the wallet was gone?" Elaine asked.

"After we got back from the pool, we got ready to go out to dinner, and I wanted to check the name of the restaurant. Some French place in Waterville Roger wanted to try."

Jan cast a look at Elaine, who smiled.

"I had a business card for it and I'd tucked that into my wallet. I dug around in the purse and didn't see it, so I emptied everything out, and it was just gone. That's when I noticed the glass door was cracked open, and I was sure we'd left it closed."

"So you think that's the way the thief came in?" Elaine asked.

"Or out." Carrie shrugged. "But in any case, I'm sure that's how they saw the purse and realized it was an easy target."

Jan thought for a minute. Zack was now doing running dives into the deep end. The rules clearly stated that no diving was allowed, but Carrie didn't seem concerned, and Jan stifled her urge to point out the list of rules. Parents had to pick their battles, she knew.

"Did you notice anything else amiss?" she asked.

"No, nothing," Carrie said. "The police dusted for finger-prints on the door, but so far they haven't turned up anything."

"Did you cancel your credit cards?" Elaine asked.

"Right away. Roger knew that was the first thing I needed to do, so I called the different companies as soon as we realized it was gone."

"Do you know if anyone attempted to use the cards before you canceled them?" Jan asked. It had taken less than an hour for the thief to use Tricia's credit card; had she been similarly quick with Carrie?

"If they did try, I haven't heard about it," Carrie said. "But there was a substantial amount of cash in the wallet too."

Jan wasn't sure how much "substantial" was, but she couldn't think of a polite way to ask. She decided the logos said it all.

Jan tried to imagine the scene. The family was out; the bag was in plain sight; someone—maybe their blonde thief? Maybe the brown-haired woman?—had come inside, taken the wal-let, and gone back out before anyone noticed. It didn't sound like a well-thought-out-and-executed plan. More like a crime of opportunity. But who would be causally walking past the cabin in the first place?

"Have the other guests been questioned?" Jan asked.

"Not that I know of." Droplets of water splashed out of the pool and landed on the edge of the lounge chairs. Carrie ges-tured at Zack to stop splashing, and he obeyed. "I wanted them to be, of course, but the owner was wary of making the other guests feel like they were being accused of something. Which I get, I guess. But if it had been their wallets, I bet they would want everyone around to be questioned."

No doubt, Jan agreed. But she could also see Macy's side of it. The opinions of your customers were so important when you were running a small business.

"So you don't know if anyone saw anything that day?"

"I've asked the other people I've run into, unofficially of course, and the people in the cabins on both sides of us say they didn't see anything or anyone odd." She cringed as another cannonball sprayed them all. She turned toward the water and shouted, "Zack, no more!" Then she turned back to them. "But that just supports my theory."

"Your theory?" Jan echoed. She used her hand to brush away water droplets that had landed on her leg.

"Yep. I think it was the maintenance guy."

"Shane?" Elaine looked as surprised as Jan felt. Macy's son, Shane, and his wife, Zale, ran the cottages with Macy. Surely he wouldn't rob his own business.

"No, not him." Carrie pulled her sunglasses off and used the edge of her shirt to wipe them off. "That college kid who's been working on the cabin at the back."

Jan and Elaine looked at each other. "Who?" Jan asked. Macy hadn't mentioned she had a college kid doing maintenance around here. Then again, why would she?

"This guy is named Mark. He's been re-siding the cabin at the far side of the property. I met him because Zack broke a piece of the frame off the window by yanking on it too hard, and they sent him over. Apparently he's good at carpentry."

"Was he able to fix it?" Elaine asked.

"Oh, sure. It turns out he really is great at it. But he was also in our room, and my purse was sitting out the whole time. I even took my wallet out to give the kids money for the snack machines while he was there, so he could have seen that my wallet was inside and that there was cash in it."

It was possible, Jan thought. But it wasn't exactly proof that he was guilty. They needed to know more about this Mark kid.

"Have you talked to him since your wallet went missing?" Elaine asked.

"No. I didn't know how to politely ask him to return the wallet he stole. But I did tell Macy I thought it was him, and I also mentioned him to the police."

"How did Macy respond?"

"She denied it, of course. What else would she do? You can't admit someone you hired is stealing from your guests."

True enough, but Jan wasn't sure even Macy would turn a blind eye to this. It looked bad that someone had been robbed at her property, no matter who was behind it.

"And did the police question him?"

"I suppose." She set her sunglasses back on her face. "Though he's still here, so I can't see as how they did a very thorough job."

Or else they'd found no evidence that he was behind it, Jan thought. She was dubious, but she was fairly certain there were already two people involved in the thefts, and she supposed it was possible he was involved as well. Another splash, followed by droplets of water all over their feet, legs, and the chairs.

"Zack! One more time and you're in time-out!" Carrie yelled.

Jan took this as their cue to go. "Thank you for talking with us," she said as she stood. Elaine, brushing water off her cheek with her hand, followed her lead. "And please let us know if you think of anything else that might help." She pulled a business card for the tearoom out of her wallet and handed it to her.

"Of course." Carrie adjusted the sunglasses on her face. "If you can help get to the bottom of this, I'll be eternally grateful."

Jan and Elaine walked back toward the gate and out on to the crushed-shell path again.

"So what do you think?" Elaine asked as soon as they were safely out of earshot.

"I think it seems a bit unlikely that this maintenance guy was involved, since he doesn't match the description of either woman we know is involved. But we should look into him nonetheless."

"That's exactly what I was going to say."

No more words were necessary. They both turned and headed back toward the office. When they walked in, Shane Atherton was behind the counter, and Macy was nowhere in sight.

"Hello, Shane," Elaine said, smiling as she walked toward the counter.

He looked up from the computer screen. "Hi, Mrs. Cook, Mrs. Blake." He was a large man, solidly built. He wore a T-shirt that said Lancaster Turkey Trot 2014.

"We were talking with your mother a few minutes ago," Elaine said. "Is she around? We have a few more things we'd like to ask her."

"She went back to the house for lunch, I'm afraid. But she told me you two were here asking questions about the wallet that went missing the other day."

"We were just talking with Carrie," Jan said, trying once again to not let her pride get in the way of finding out what they needed. "And she mentioned that you have a new maintenance guy working around here."

"Oh yeah. Mark. Yeah, she really thinks he did it, for some reason."

Jan tried to figure out how to ask this nicely. "Do you know why she might suspect that?"

He shrugged. "He came in to repair the window at their place, and she thinks he scoped it out while he was there. But he wouldn'ta been there if she hadn't yanked so hard the thing broke in the first place."

He seemed to be saying that Mark couldn't have stolen the wallet because Carrie broke the window. Jan nodded as if this made perfect sense.

"Do you think there's any way he might have been responsible?" Elaine asked, leaning her elbows on the counter conspiratorially.

"Nah." He clicked the mouse, and the computer opened a webpage. Jan leaned forward a bit and saw that it was the Web site for a local amateur stock car racetrack. "Mark's a good kid. Besides, the cops already talked to him, and they didn't find any reason to think he was behind it."

Again, Jan wasn't sure whether he'd been cleared or whether Trooper Benson simply hadn't gathered enough evidence to pin it on him yet. They'd have to talk to Dan to find out for sure.

"What exactly does he do around here?" Jan asked.

"He's helping out with some repairs. His family owns a construction company in Waterville, and he's on summer break, so he's picking up some work around town. He's been patching holes in the siding on some of the cabins, and re-siding one that got damaged in that big storm in February."

Jan nodded. Mainers were used to epic snowfalls, but this storm had been a doozie. It had dropped nearly three feet of snow, and extremely strong winds had taken off many roofs and felled hundreds of trees in the area.

"Have you worked with him before?" Jan asked.

"Nah. He was recommended by Mel over at Pine Tree Grill. He did some work for them, I think."

Pine Tree Grill? Jan looked toward Elaine, who met her eye and nodded, almost imperceptibly. Well, now this was getting interesting. What were the chances that this maintenance guy would have done work at the two places that had been hit up before the tearoom?

"Would it be all right if we talked to Mark?" Elaine asked.

"It's fine with me. But I think he was planning to take an early lunch. He had some kind of meeting he had to go to at noon, I think." He gestured toward the door. "But go on back and see if he's there if you want. The cabin is at the back of the property, out by the road. Just follow that path all the way to the end." He pointed to the path that branched off from the main path at the far side of the pool.

"Thank you," Elaine said, and gave him her brightest smile. "We really appreciate your help."

They heard shrieks and splashing coming from the pool area, followed by a stern reprimand from Carrie. Jan gave Elaine a knowing glance and they followed the path as it wound past cabins and under the towering trees.

A few minutes later, they came to the cabin, half-covered in wooden shingles. The new shingles were a bright reddish brown, but Jan knew they would weather to a soft gray just like on the rest of the cabins. A toolbox lay open and a circular saw was plugged into a socket on the outside of the wall of the cabin, but there was no Mark in sight. Either he'd headed out for his appointment, as Shane had warned, or he'd somehow found out they were coming to question him. Would a professional workman go off to his lunch break with his toolbox open and his saw still plugged in? Jan didn't think it was too likely, but then again, how would he have known that they were on their way to question him? Would Shane have called ahead to warn him? But why? She stopped herself. Now she was just being paranoid.

"I guess we missed him," Elaine said, looking around.

"But it looks like he might be back soon." Jan gestured at the tools. "Should we wait?"

"Maybe for a few minutes," Elaine said. They wandered around the cabin, examining it from every angle. It looked just like the other cabins, and now that Jan thought about it, several of the others had had patches where new shingles has been stuck to replace some that must have rotted. Had Mark done that work as well?

"I don't know how soon he'll be coming back," Elaine said a few minutes later. Jan reluctantly nodded.

"Maybe it would be better if we came back some other time."

Agreeing, they turned and headed back toward the crushed-shell path, past the pool, and then to the car. Jan opened the driver's side door and sat down. The air inside the car was baking, and it wasn't even noon yet. She turned on the engine, but it took a few minutes for the air conditioner to begin to pump out cool air. A quick phone call confirmed that Rose and Archie could handle running the tearoom for a while longer and they'd decided that their next stop should be the Northwoods Bed-and-Breakfast, where Rue had said the person who'd been robbed at the Pine Tree Grill was staying. After that, they would try to talk to Mel Stadler to see what he could tell them about this Mark character and also to see what else they could learn about the theft itself. Jan had a good feeling about this plan. She was sure that they would find the answers they were looking for before nightfall.

CHAPTER TEN

Plan in hand, Jan drove the few blocks to the Northwoods Bed-and-Breakfast, and Elaine tried to think through the suspects they had so far. There was that blonde woman whom they believed took Tricia's wallet from the tearoom. There was also the brown-haired woman they'd seen on the security-footage video, who was possibly the same woman from the grocery store. There was Dorothy Schuman, in Portland, who had been in the tearoom at the time of the theft and whose strange manner on the phone made Elaine more suspicious than she had been before. And now there was Mark, the maintenance worker who had done jobs for two of the three places thefts had taken place. Were any of them connected? How were they working together? Elaine couldn't make sense of it.

It was only a few minutes before they were pulling up in front of the old rambling farmhouse that had been converted into a welcoming bed-and-breakfast by Rue and Ned Maxwell. The charming inn was surrounded by a large yard with towering oaks and maples, and Rue had put in a thriving flower and vegetable garden. As they approached, they saw that the minigolf area Ned had put in the expansive backyard was full today.

They parked in the small lot and walked toward the front door. A stone path led through the grass to the wraparound porch, where iron chairs and a swing looked out over the property. Jan rang the doorbell, and a moment later, Rue Maxwell appeared.

"Hello, hello," she said. "Come on in. You're here to talk about the wallet that was stolen?"

"Macy called you?" Elaine asked. Rue nodded. She should have guessed. They stepped inside the entryway, and Jan took in the wide pine floorboards, the high molded ceiling, and the ornately carved handrail that ran up the wide stairs.

"She sure did. Come in, come in." She gestured for them to step inside, and they entered a graceful room with a marble fireplace mantel, a large cherry armoire, and several couches and wingback chairs covered in a lovely floral fabric. A piano in the corner and a chandelier above lent a sense of historical grace. Books and magazines were scattered in neat piles throughout the room, and a vase of fresh peonies sat on a low coffee table.

Elaine sat down and sank into the soft pillows of the couch. Jan perched on the edge of a chair.

"Can I get you something to drink?" Rue gestured to a sideboard in the hallway, where there was a pot of coffee and hot water next to a basket of tea bags, as well as a pitcher of water.

Elaine was never one to turn down tea. "Do you have Earl Grey?" she asked.

"Of course. What kind of hostess would I be if I didn't have Earl Grey?" Rue moved over to the table. "Jan?"

"I'd love to have Earl Grey as well," Jan said.

"Coming right up." While she set the tea bags into the mugs and added water, she chattered away. "Of course, this isn't anything like the tea you all serve. Loose tea tastes a thousand times better than these little bags, and I don't think the quality of the tea itself is as good either. Plus, there's just something about being served tea in a pretty pot. But none of that is practical here, so we simply let our guests help themselves."

Rue came around the couch and set both cups and saucers on the coffee table, on top of a photo book about Maine lighthouses. A moment later she returned with a small jug of milk and a bowl of sugar.

"We drink tea from bags all the time at home," Jan said. "If we went through the full ritual every time we wanted a cup of tea, we'd never get anything else done."

Rue sat down on the couch across from Elaine and looked from one cousin to the other.

"This is lovely. Thank you so much." Elaine reached forward and added cream and sugar to her tea, then sat back. Jan followed her lead. Elaine took a sip. Rue was right, it wasn't as good as the tea they served, even just at home, but it was still very satisfying.

"So. What did Macy tell you?" Jan asked.

"Oh, just that you'd showed up asking questions. Which makes sense. I think it's great. I know that Trooper Benson has been by to talk to our guest Lauren, but you two have at least as good a track record as he does, and it's personal to you."

Elaine nodded. "Is she around? Your guest, I mean?"

"Oh no, I'm afraid not. She and her husband went out for the day."

Elaine wondered why exactly Rue had invited them to stay and have tea if they couldn't even talk to the person they came to see. But she supposed Rue was just being friendly.

"Do you know when she might be back?" Elaine asked. "We'd really love to talk to her to hear what she remembers of the night in question."

"I'm not really sure," Rue said. "But I can definitely tell Lauren you came by and ask her to call you."

"Can you tell us anything about what she's like?" Jan asked.

Rue hesitated a moment, blowing the steam from her cup of tea. "Well, they're a nice couple," she said. "A bit particular, but they seem like good people."

"How so?" Rue's good friend Macy was quite particular too. Lots of people were.

"Oh, you know." Rue waved her hand dismissively. "Lauren and her husband live in some high-rise tower in New York, and I get the impression they're not used to old houses."

"So they've been complaining?" Jan asked.

"Let me guess. About the floors creaking?" Elaine and Jan had plenty of experience with old houses and knew there could be lots of things to complain about.

"And the pipes banging?" Jan added.

Rue nodded, a guilty smile on her face. "And about the fact that there's no central air conditioning."

"They don't realize old houses weren't built that way?" Elaine asked, shaking her head. Most of the older homes around these parts were situated to pick up the breeze from the lake, but Rue had installed window units in the guest rooms in case they were needed.

"They think the window unit spoils the view. Which is true," Rue said. "They're in the Rose Room, which has such a nice view out into the woods."

Elaine nodded. They'd gotten a tour of the inn when they'd first met Rue, and she remembered that room. It really was lovely—but then, all of the rooms here were charming. It was the kind of place she and Ben had loved to stay in when they traveled. She wondered, for a moment, if she and Nathan would ever travel together, and what sorts of places he would like to stay in. But then she stopped herself. Just because Jan was close to getting married didn't mean she would be.

"We would appreciate your letting her know we're anxious to talk to her," Jan was saying when Elaine snapped back to the present.

"Of course. Now. Tell me what you've learned so far. I'm dying to know. Did you figure out who that blonde woman was?"

Suddenly Elaine understood why they were here. Rue wanted to know what was going on. And Elaine understood that—this string of thefts affected everyone in Lancaster, really, and of course Rue had been there during the theft at their place, so it no doubt felt personal—but she wanted to be careful to not spread gossip.

"We're still investigating," she said carefully.

"Aside from the woman our guests noticed at the tearoom, we're not really sure of anything," Jan added.

"But surely you have some suspects," Rue said, nodding.

Elaine hesitated. "We're still trying to make sense of things." She hoped being evasive would get Rue to take the hint.

"Ah. Playing your cards close to the vest, I see."

"Something like that." Elaine tried to look cheerful. "So tell me how Melissa is doing."

"Oh, she's just wonderful," Rue said, her face brightening. Elaine had had a suspicion that mentioning Rue's daughter would distract her, and was pleased to see that she'd been correct. "She's just finishing up her master's degree in geology. Now, why in the world anyone would want to study rocks is beyond me, but she's happy with it, and she has some good job prospects on the horizon, so what can I say?"

"It sounds like she's really doing well," Jan said. "Last time we talked, you mentioned she was dating a young man that you weren't so fond of. How are things on that front?"

Rue talked for a while about her daughter's love life, and by the time she'd asked Elaine for an update on Sasha and Jared, the subject of the suspect list was forgotten. They chatted for a while, enjoying a nice visit, and then finally Elaine pushed herself up.

"We must be keeping you from your duties," Elaine said. "Thank you so much for taking the time to talk with us."

"Of course. And please do keep me posted on what you find out about this wallet thief."

They promised they would, and stepped outside.

"So what do you think?" Elaine asked as they walked toward the car.

"I think Rue is very sweet and it was nice to chat with her. But it doesn't get us any closer to finding out what happened."

"I agree." Elaine sat down and buckled herself in. "So. To the Pine Tree Grill then?"

"Onward." Jan put the car in gear and pulled slowly out of the parking lot. The Pine Tree Grill was just two doors down from Tea for Two, so Jan decided to park at home, and then they walked the short distance to the popular restaurant. They waved to Bristol Payson as they passed the Bookworm. Beyond the hedges that lined the fence, Bristol was bringing a tray of lemonade out to groups of guests seated on the outdoor furniture on the bookstore's front lawn. Bristol did everything she could to make her customers want to stick around, and all summer the yard was filled with people— tourists and locals alike—who came to relax with a book and sit in the sun. It sounded pretty great to Elaine right now, but they kept going, and she and Jan turned at the entrance to the Pine Tree Grill.

The restaurant was housed in a quaint log building. A parking lot was on one side of the building, and some picnic tables sat in the yard, where customers could wait for a table on particularly busy nights. Beyond the building, Elaine could see the lake sparkling in the sun.

Jan held open the door, and Elaine followed her inside. After the glorious sunshine outside, it took a minute for their eyes to adjust to the cool, dark interior, but soon Elaine could make out the worn plank floors, the round tables covered in cheerful checked tablecloths, the large stone fireplace that brightened things up on cold winter nights, and the walls, covered in local Maine paraphernalia. Elaine loved the vintage posters advertising their fair state; there was one of a lobster, one of Owl's Head lighthouse, perched over a craggy cliff, and one of a couple skiing down a steep slope, all done in charming blocky prints. There were also tubes and taps used for gathering maple syrup, as well as old-fashioned syrup jugs and all sorts of old wooden skis, snowshoes, and lobster pots. The back wall had large sliding glass doors that led out to the deck overlooking the lake. The place had a comfortable, casual vibe, and it was popular with visitors and locals.

"Hi there." Elaine turned to see Bianca Stadler in front of them. She wore a loose, drapey dress and her signature cowboy boots, as well as the charm bracelet she never took off. "You guys here for lunch?" Bianca had a wide grin on her face. She was friendly to everyone, but she was always especially glad to see friends from the community come in.

"Actually, I'm afraid not," Elaine said, but even as she said it, she took in the aroma of french fries that hung in the air here, and her stomach grumbled. Goodness, they smelled wonderful. "We were hoping to talk to you and Mel for a minute." She glanced at Jan. She wasn't sure how much to say.

Jan nodded. "I don't know if you've heard, but one of our customers had her wallet stolen while she was at the tearoom the other day, and so we're looking into the string of thefts, hoping to help her get her wallet back."

"Of course. We're happy to talk to you. Come on back here." They followed as she threaded through the tables and then gestured for them to take a seat at one of the tables by the sliding glass doors. "I'll go get Mel and be right back."

Elaine saw that several young people wearing black aprons delivered the house-made hamburgers, fried freshly caught fish, and coleslaw this place was famous for. She noticed Jan looking out over the lake, and saw boats crisscrossing the surface of the water. She could just make out Russell Edmonds's mail boat and a handful of sailing boats closer to Tuttle's Marina.

"Hi there, Jan, Elaine."

They both stood as Bianca's brother Mel greeted them, and after he'd shaken their hands, he sat down. Mel was not quite as gregarious and outgoing as his sister, but together, they were a big part of the reason this place was so beloved.

"I brought us a snack," Bianca said, smiling at Elaine as she set a basket of french fries on the table. A stack of small plates was in her other hand, and she set it down gently.

"I hear you're looking into the wallet thief. Good." Mel passed out the plates, sliding them across the table. "I know we all want this thing wrapped up, and Trooper Benson isn't having much luck. I know you guys will find answers."

"We don't pretend we'll be as good as the police at figuring this out, but we feel like we have to try," Jan said.

"Oh, don't be so humble. You're just as good as the police at this kind of thing." Bianca used her fingers to grab a bunch of fries and set them on her plate. "And you know it too. So what can we tell you?"

Elaine felt her cheeks flush. It was kind of Bianca to say that. She followed Bianca's lead and took a handful of french fries and set them gently on her plate.

"Well, first, we were hoping you could tell about what happened here on Saturday night. That's when the first wallet was stolen, right?"

"That's right," Mel said. "We have the dubious honor of being the first business to be targeted." He smiled and popped a fry into his mouth.

"It was crowded here Saturday night," Bianca said. Elaine and Jan both nodded. It was always busy in here on weekends, especially in high tourist season. "Everything seemed to be normal though. We had plenty of staff and everything was going smoothly until we learned that one of our customers couldn't find her wallet."

Jan had grabbed a handful of the fries and set them on her plate, and was now reaching for the ketchup bottle that sat in the wire basket at the edge of the table.

"What time was this?" Elaine asked before taking a bite of one of the fries. It was perfectly crunchy on the outside, soft on the inside, with just the right sprinkling of salt. It was delicious.

"Around 8:30," Mel said. He reached for the mustard bottle from the wire basket and squeezed a small puddle on to his plate. "The dinner crowd was starting to wane, but a lot of people had gone out to the deck to watch the sun set. It was a beautiful night—a few clouds, but mostly clear, and the sunset was spectacular." He set the mustard back down and then reached for the salt and pepper shakers and sprinkled some of each on top. Elaine watched, incredulous, as Mel dipped a french fry into the concoction and took a bite. She had never seen anyone eat fries like that.

Bianca seemed unfazed. "It was nice. And a good chunk of the customers went out to watch. But anyway, once the show was over, people started to move back inside."

Elaine turned and looked at the deck. It was wooden and quite large, with an area dedicated to tables, as well as a section where diners could gather to stand and look out over the lake. There was a part of the railing that was a different color wood from the main part of the deck; Elaine assumed this was where Mark had repaired the deck, if what Shane Atherton had told them was true. She would ask about Mark in a little while.

"Did people leave their things behind when they went out to the deck?" Jan asked.

"Exactly." Bianca nodded. "And that must have been when the thief struck. We never even thought to tell them to bring their purses with them. Everyone just leaves things sitting out in Lancaster."

"Do you have any idea how many people were inside the restaurant during the sunset?" Elaine took another french fry.

"Unfortunately, no," Mel said, shaking his head. One of his front teeth was crooked, but it only added to his disarming sweetness. "And we can't really remember. I'm sorry, I know that's not helpful. But it was just a typical Saturday night for us; we didn't think we'd need to be paying special attention." He dipped another fry into the mustard mixture, popped it into his mouth, and kept talking. "And during the dinner rush, especially on a summer weekend, we're lucky to remember to collect money from our customers. It's just kind of a mad dash around here."

"In other words, we didn't notice anything out of the ordinary," Bianca said. Her bracelet tinkled as she reached for a fry.

"You must know who your waitstaff was that night, right?" Elaine asked. She tried to phrase this carefully. "Maybe we could talk them, just to see if they saw anything odd." Or to see if anyone acted strangely when they brought it up.

"You're more than welcome to talk to our staff," Mel said. "Mike, that blond guy"—he pointed at a young man with spiky hair just coming out of the kitchen—"was working Saturday night. And Ami, with the brown hair, was working as well. But I've already talked to all of them, as has Dan Benson, and no one saw anything out of the ordinary. Besides, we trust our staff. I highly doubt any of them had anything to do with stealing from our customers."

Elaine reached for two more fries and popped them in her mouth. She thought for a moment, trying to picture the scene. If Mel and Bianca were right, and their staff had nothing to do with it—a claim that she didn't see how they could possibly back up, but she decided to take it at face value for now—then it would have had to have been a customer inside the restaurant who took the wallet.

"What about customers?" Jan asked.

Bianca shrugged. "No one has come forward with any information. And goodness knows we don't know the names of everyone who ate here that night. I know Pastor Mike and Sarah came in, but I highly doubt one of them took the wallet. And most of the customers were people we'd never seen before."

Elaine understood. In the dead of winter, most of the people who came through their doors were locals, but in the high season, they got all kinds of people they'd never seen before—and they were grateful for it. That's how they made it through the quiet times, after all. But it didn't help with the investigation right now.

"How did the customer realize her wallet was gone?" Jan asked.

"I guess when she went to pay." Bianca shrugged. "The first we heard of it was when Ami over there"—she pointed at the brown-haired waitress—"came to let us know that there was a problem at one of her tables."

"Was the customer upset?"

"Naturally," Mel said. "She was . . . well, truthfully, she caused a bit of a scene. She—well, she was upset."

Elaine suspected he wanted to say more but was too kind.

"Did she blame you all?" Elaine asked.

Bianca laughed. "Us, our mother, and everyone we've ever met. She's a piece of work, that woman. But again, you can understand why she'd be upset."

"You said she's a piece of work," Jan probed. "How so?"

Bianca pursed her lips, and Mel reached out and took another french fry, no doubt to avoid having to answer. A beat passed, and then Bianca said, kindly, "Sometimes folks from big cities, who are used to a certain level of restaurant, have a hard time understanding how things are done here in Lancaster."

It sounded as if they'd experienced the same sort of problems and complaints Rue had alluded to.

"Had she seen anything that seemed odd to her that evening?" Elaine asked.

"Other than the fact that we don't serve her *favorite* caviar, no," Bianca said, with a wink. "Though she was so busy blaming everyone for what happened that it was hard to get much of anything from her."

"Bianca." Mel gave his sister a knowing look. Bianca had the grace to look ashamed.

"I'm sorry. That was unkind. Of course she was upset after what happened."

Elaine held back a smile. She got the sense Bianca would have said more if her brother wasn't around. But she also got the sense that she had learned all she needed to about the woman's attitude.

"So you don't remember anything odd?" Jan tried again. Elaine understood the tactic—sometimes people hesitated about mentioning some minor detail, thinking it wasn't important, and it ended up unraveling the whole mystery. But Mel just shook his head.

"We've been through the evening a hundred times between us," Mel said. "And we can't think of anything out of the ordinary. I'm so sorry."

Elaine could see that they were indeed sorry, but she and Jan weren't going to get much else out of them. She understood—they hadn't noticed much about the theft that had happened right under their noses at the tearoom. If you weren't paying attention, it was easy to miss important things. She was grateful when Jan shifted topics.

"We were talking to Shane Atherton, and he mentioned that you'd recommended the guy who's doing some work on their property. Mark somebody?"

"Yeah, Mark Hamilton. He helped us rebuild parts of the deck out there. Those storms this winter were brutal. Anyway, Mark is a good kid, and he does good work. I know his dad from Boy Scouts when we were kids. He runs a construction company in Waterville now, and he's got three sons who all work with him. Mark is at Colby, and he does odd jobs to pick up extra money in the summer."

"So you've known Mark awhile then?"

"Oh yeah. I was there at his christening. Good family. Good kid."

Elaine wondered whether Mel's personal feelings about the Hamilton family—and his innate kindness—were blinding him to the possibility that Mark may have had something to do with the thefts.

"When did he rebuild that deck for you?" Jan asked.

"Oh, mid-May. After we were sure there would be no more snow coming." He laughed, except that they all knew it wasn't a joke. Snow in May was rare, but not unheard of in these parts. But that was more than a month ago.

"And he was not here on Saturday night, was he?" Elaine asked.

"What? No." Bianca shook her head. "Wait, do you think he could have had something to do with this?"

"Not necessarily," Jan said quickly. "It's just that his name has come up, and we're looking into all possibilities."

"No way. Mark's a good kid," Mel said. "I can vouch for him. I've known him his whole life. He wouldn't do something like that. Besides, he wasn't here on Saturday, so how could he be involved?"

It was a fair question, Elaine had to admit. But just because he wasn't here didn't mean he couldn't be involved. He could have scoped out the place while he was here working on the deck, and then passed along information about the business—the layout, the clientele, the fact that no one paid much attention to their bags—to the blonde woman, or to the brown-haired woman. Either one of them could have been here Saturday night, waiting for the right opportunity.

But she could see that they weren't going to get any further by asking about Mark. Right or wrong, Mel didn't believe he was involved. Elaine was inclined to believe him, but would still be doing some more research on Mark when they got home to see if anything came up.

"Thank you so much for taking the time to talk with us," Elaine said, standing up. "We really appreciate it, but we've kept you from your work long enough."

Bianca grabbed one more french fry and stood too.

"Would it be possible to have a quick word with the staff members who were around on Saturday?" Jan asked.

"Of course. Come on over." Mel gestured for them to follow him. They thanked Bianca again, and then followed Mel to talk to Mike, the spiky-haired waiter they had pointed out before.

Twenty minutes later, they trudged back toward Tea for Two. Just as Mel had said, none of the waitstaff they'd talked to remembered seeing anything out of the ordinary Saturday night. They had gotten the phone numbers of a few others who had also been around, but Elaine didn't feel hopeful.

"So. Is our next step trying to get ahold of Mark?" Jan asked as they walked back past the people reading in the front yard of the Bookworm. The hydrangeas that graced the yard were in full bloom, and they were stunning.

"No, our next step is eating a salad to balance out those French fries," Elaine said, laughing.

"Right. Salad first. And then hopefully we'll have a little time to see what we can turn up about this Mark character."

CHAPTER ELEVEN

Jan had put away the lunch dishes and was helping Archie put fresh table settings out in the west parlor. Today had been slower than usual—at the moment they had only one table filled, by a mother and her grown daughter who were just passing through town and had found the tearoom by chance.

"I'm sure they'll come," Archie said, setting a precisely creased napkin down next to a gilt-edged plate.

"Who?" Jan looked up and realized she'd been nudging a spoon into place with her finger longer than was reasonable.

"The customers. This place will be full soon enough, and then you'll miss the peace." He gestured toward the window. "I'm sure it's just the weather that's keeping people home."

Jan smiled. Clouds were rolling in over the lake, and storms were possible later on, but usually that meant more traffic in here. In the summer, good weather kept people outside; storms brought them in. But she couldn't dwell on it, and she wouldn't say what they were both thinking: the newspaper articles about the theft were causing people to avoid the tearoom. Was their reputation tarnished now?

"I'm sure you're right," she said, hoping she sounded more positive than she felt.

But after she finished setting the tables, she decided to head upstairs and call the remaining servers from the Pine Tree Grill to see if they had noticed anything odd. If they could solve this quickly, maybe business would pick back up. An hour later, she had spoken with two and left a message for one more, and was not getting any closer to understanding what had happened that night. Both servers were friendly, but neither recalled anything that had seemed odd the night the wallet was taken.

Jan had just decided to shift gears and start to see what she could find out about Mark Hamilton when Elaine appeared in the doorway of the sitting room.

"Are you ready?" Elaine asked, her face bright.

"Ready for what?"

Elaine held up a clear plastic bag of nail polish bottles. "To get ready for your date tonight."

"Oh. Right." Jan hadn't forgotten, of course. Not by a long shot. It was just that their engagement seemed like such an inevitability that she almost forgot sometimes that they hadn't already decided to get married. "But Bob isn't picking me up for hours. There's still plenty of time."

"Not if you want to look good in your post-engagement photos." She walked into the room and set the bag of nail polish down on the coffee table.

Jan could see that a bottle of nail polish remover and a bag of cotton balls was also inside. Jan could still hear the classical music they played in the tearoom, as well as some voices and the occasional sound of a spoon banging on china, but things must still be slow if there was time for them to both be up here worrying about her nails. "Post-engagement photos? That's a thing?"

"It is, and even if they weren't, of course you'd want to look your best for Bob anyway."

Jan eyed the bag of polish, looking over the deep burgundies, bright cheerful reds, rich corals, and soft pinks. Elaine didn't wear a lot of makeup, but she must have every shade of nail polish they made. "And painting my fingernails some garish shade is going to accomplish that?"

"We won't do anything garish, silly." Elaine gestured for her to come, so reluctantly Jan got up from in front of her computer and sat down next to Elaine on the couch. "I was thinking a quiet, understated pink."

"Does it really take four hours for my nails to dry?"

"Of course not. But we still have to blow out your hair and do your makeup."

"Blow out my hair?" That sounded painful.

"Just trust me." Elaine held out her hands, gesturing for Jan to come closer. "Let me see those nails." She started reaching into her bag.

"Clear," Jan said.

"Clear?"

"I'll only wear clear nail polish."

Jan almost laughed to see how disappointed Elaine was.

"It's clear or nothing."

Elaine thought for a moment, pursing her lips together, but eventually she nodded. "Okay. We'll just shape the nails a bit first, and trim the cuticles."

Jan couldn't imagine why all of this was necessary—he was marrying her for who she was, right?—but she knew that it made Elaine happy, and of course Jan did want to look nice for the big night.

"All right," she said. "Let's see how this goes."

CHAPTER TWELVE

A few hours later, Jan was wearing her favorite loose linen dress. Elaine had smoothed her hair and applied a light amount of makeup, and Jan had to admit that she liked the effect. It was a lot of work—too much work to do every day—but she couldn't complain about the results.

Bob picked her up at seven, just as planned.

"Well, you look nice," he said when she answered the front door. In spite of herself, Jan felt her cheeks flush. There was a strange look on his face, just for a split second, and then it passed so quickly Jan couldn't even be sure it had really been there.

"You're not looking so bad yourself." Bob always managed to look dapper, and tonight he wore creased khaki pants and a checked shirt under a light sweater vest. As a lawyer, he'd gotten into the habit of dressing nicely. His dark hair was edged with gray, and he carried himself well.

"Shall we?" Bob held out his arm, and Jan took it and stepped out the door.

"Good-bye," Jan called, looking back at Elaine, who was hovering awkwardly and flashed her a ridiculous thumbs-up just before she stepped out.

"I hope the weather holds," Bob said, eyeing the sky. Clouds had been gathering all afternoon, and now they hung thick and heavy and dark. Jan hoped the rain would hold off as well—this was an outdoor concert, and there were no plans for an indoor location. But the air was warm and maybe it was in Jan's head, but to her it also felt thick with anticipation.

As Bob drove to Waterville, she told him about their investigation, and also about a phone call she'd had with her daughter Tara. Suddenly Jan realized she was rambling a bit to fill the silence. She must be nervous. Would he get down on one knee? Would he have a speech prepared, or was that something people only did in movies?

When they reached the park in Waterville, Bob retrieved a picnic basket and soft wool blanket from the trunk, and he carried them as they walked across the lawn and settled down on a patch of grass with a good view of the gazebo where the band would be performing. If the skies opened up, at least the musicians and their instruments would be protected. Bob and Jan spread out the blanket and sat down, and he started unpacking chicken sandwiches and crackers and dips and plates of fruit.

"My goodness. You made a feast," Jan said, and he grinned and handed her a plate. A real plate too—not some cheap paper thing. He then unpacked a bottle of sparkling water and poured it into glasses. All around them, couples and young families were settling down, spreading blankets and stretching out on the grass.

"It's a special night," Bob said, and Jan felt her heart flip. She waited for him to say more, but he just winked at her and took a bite of his sandwich. As they ate, Bob told her about the first time he'd heard this jazz trio perform at a benefit for a new wing of the hospital in Waterville, and he'd followed them since. As he spoke, thunder rumbled somewhere off in the distance.

"It's always nice to find something you like enough to follow," Jan said, and Bob nodded, then paused.

"Actually, that's a good segue," Bob started. He took a sip of his sparkling water and set the glass down on the picnic blanket. "There's something I've been wanting to talk to you about."

"Yes?" Jan's heartbeat sped up. This was it. He was going to—

But just then, a woman stepped up to the microphone and shouted, "Hello, Waterville!"

Bob stopped, looked at Jan, and then back at the stage. The woman kept talking, introducing the band and giving a short overview of their history. Then, before Bob could say more, the band started playing. He gave her a smile and shrugged.

"We'll talk after the show," he mouthed, and settled back, bracing his arms against the ground.

Jan relaxed beside him, her shoulder touching his gently as the music filled the park. He felt solid and strong, and the warmth from his skin felt nice.

The band was good—they were very good. And she'd always loved music, though if she was honest, jazz had never been her thing. But she tried to really listen to the music, to let it seep into her and transport her, and she ended up quite enjoying it, though she didn't exactly lose herself in the music.

"Did you enjoy the show?"

Jan looked up to see that Bob was looking at her, a crooked smile on his face. She realized that the music had stopped and the musicians were taking a bow. Around them, people were clapping and cheering. How had she zoned out so badly she'd missed the ending of the show?

"Sorry. I was thinking about the mystery," she said with a guilty smile. Thunder rumbled, closer this time, and she noticed that the wind was blowing the leaves so hard the backs were exposed.

Bob laughed. "That's why I love you, Jan. Your mind never stops turning."

Jan's mind was reeling. Had he just said…? But surely he didn't mean…

But already, he was saying something else. Jan vaguely noticed that people around them were starting to get up and pack up their things.

"In fact, that's part of why I wanted to talk to you about something." He took a deep breath. The poor guy looked nervous. Jan smiled to encourage him. Surely he wouldn't have used the *L* word unless he…

"I've really enjoyed getting to know you this past year, and we've gotten very close. I…"

A flash of light, and then another loud crack of thunder, closer this time. The hair on Jan's arms stood and her skin tingled. People were rushing now, scurrying to get their things packed up. Jan tried to block them out so she could focus on what he was saying.

"I wanted to tell you how much you…"

Just then, the sky opened up. Large, fat drops of rain fell all around them. The cloudburst sent everyone around them scurrying and released a wet, woody smell. Bob sprang up and started gathering their things, whatever he was about to say forgotten in the rush to get to the car. Jan tossed their picnic things in the basket and then held her sweater over her head, futilely trying to protect the hairdo Elaine had worked so hard on, as they ran back to the car.

Bob fumbled with the keys, and by the time he'd gotten the car doors open and the picnic basket into the backseat, they were soaked, and the rain was already lessening. Jan was laughing. This would be quite a story to tell later on, about how Bob's proposal was interrupted by a rain shower.

"So anyway," Jan said as he turned on the lights, "you were saying?"

Bob just laughed. "Well, maybe that's a conversation best picked up some other time. Sitting soaked in the car is not exactly how I envisioned that conversation going."

Jan felt a pang of disappointment, but it passed quickly. He had wanted it to be special. That was a good sign.

"I'll just have to get you to agree to go out with me another time," he said.

Jan smiled. The moment, she knew, had passed, but it would come again. There would be another opportunity. She couldn't wait.

When Bob dropped off Jan, wet, bedraggled, and ringless, Elaine was disappointed, but she made them both cups of herbal tea and they sat out on the porch and watched the summer squall drop sheets of rain over the surface of Chickadee Lake. They discussed the evening, and Elaine concluded that Bob had indeed intended to ask Jan to marry him, and that he no doubt would again soon.

It was peaceful out on the porch, and Jan asked Elaine about how things were going with Nathan, and Elaine said they were going well, but moving slowly. They also discussed Rose and her new love interest, and by the time the last bit of light had left the sky, Jan was feeling relaxed and contented and just sleepy enough to head upstairs to bed.

Just as they were stepping inside, the phone rang. Jan walked quickly to the kitchen and set the cups on the counter before reaching for the phone.

"Hello?" It was a local number, but one she didn't recognize.

"Hi, Jan? This is Anita Picard."

"Oh, hi, Anita."

Elaine had followed her into the kitchen and was rinsing the teacups under the faucet. She raised an eyebrow and watched Jan, waiting to find out why Anita was calling.

Anita was a fixture in town, a rail-thin woman with salt-and-pepper hair and a penchant for wearing sandals in all but the worst weather. She was on the board of selectmen, and she and her husband owned I Scream, the ice cream stand perched on a piece of land at the corner of Main Street and Cottage Road. Jan and Elaine were well on their way to sampling every flavor they sold at the popular spot.

"I'm sorry to bother you so late. But I heard you were looking into the thefts that have happened around town."

"That's right," Jan said. "One of the thefts happened here at the tearoom, so we've been trying to figure out on our end who was behind it."

Elaine was scrubbing the delicate teacup with the sponge, but she was still watching Jan, trying to make sense of the phone call.

"Well, I have another one for you to add to your list."

"What?" Jan's heart sank.

"This evening a woman's purse was stolen while she was eating at the ice cream stand."

"Oh no. What happened?"

"The woman had bought ice cream for her and her kids, and she left her purse at the picnic table while she took the kids to look at the koi pond."

Part of the appeal of the ice cream stand was that at the edge of the property Anita and Charlie kept a couple of hutches with rabbits, as well as a koi pond that also had turtles and a burbling waterfall. The animals were a great attraction for young children, and no doubt contributed to the popularity of the already popular stand.

"And when she came back the wallet was gone?"

"Not just the wallet, the whole purse."

"Oh dear." Jan's heart went out to this woman. But her mind was also spinning. So far the thief, or thieves, had simply taken the wallets from the purses. Why this change? "And no one saw anything?"

"I'm afraid not. No one even noticed until it was too late."

"Oh dear."

"Anyway, I thought you might want to know."

"Of course, thank you for calling." Jan glanced at Elaine, who seemed to have picked up enough of what was going on to make sense of it. *We'll come tomorrow,* Elaine was mouthing. "Would it be all right if we came by the ice cream stand tomorrow and try to talk to the people who were there?"

"Of course," Anita said. "I was hoping you'd be willing. I called Trooper Benson, but of course more people working on this are better, and you guys are so good at solving this kind of thing..."

"We'll be over first thing in the morning."

CHAPTER THIRTEEN

Elaine was just finishing up breakfast—Jan had woken early and eaten before Elaine had gotten up—and now she was reading the newspaper, trying not to get too upset. There was another article about the string of thefts, focusing on the new one at I Scream, but the tearoom was mentioned again as a site of one of the thefts. Elaine really hoped this wouldn't cause business to be even slower today.

Heavy footsteps sounded on the porch, followed by the sound of the doorbell.

Jan looked up from her baking, brushed her hands on her apron, and said, "I'll get it."

"Thank you," Elaine said. She reread the article about the theft at I Scream. The paper didn't include any details that they hadn't gotten directly from Anita last night—a woman had left her purse unattended and had it stolen—yet Elaine still read every word, looking for clues or patterns that might point to the identity of the thief. A few months back, Elaine had read a mystery novel set in the American West where the sleuth had discovered the identity of the crook because his crimes always happened just after he got off work at the local bank. But aside from the fact that their own thief only took wallets or purses and seemed to hit up places frequented by tourists, Elaine couldn't figure out any pattern that might lead to the identity of the thief.

Elaine looked up when Jan walked into the room followed by Dan Benson.

"Oh. Hello." Elaine put down her toast and wiped her face with a napkin. She was grateful she'd gotten dressed before she'd come downstairs this morning. She also felt a thrill of hope. Surely he'd come to tell them that he'd found the thief. Though a small part of her wished they'd been able to find the culprit themselves, mostly she was just glad things would go back to normal around here.

"Hi, Elaine. I'm sorry to disturb your breakfast." He held his blue police hat in his hands. Trooper Dan Benson was tall, with sandy hair and blue eyes. He was a kind man, and he and his family went to church with Elaine and Jan at Lancaster Community Church, but when he was on duty he was all business.

"That's quite all right. Would you like some tea?"

"No, thank you. This won't take long."

Jan moved around to the far side of the counter. She'd been in the middle of shaping maple croissants, and she now resumed that task.

Elaine waited for him to say something, but the longer he waited, the less certain she felt. Was she imagining things, or was he avoiding her eye?

"Did you figure out who was behind the thefts?" Jan asked.

"I haven't made any arrests yet," he said.

"But you will? You know who it was?" Elaine asked hopefully.

"I'm afraid I can't really comment on an open investigation," he said. The way he was twirling his hat around in his hands confirmed Elaine's suspicions. He wasn't coming to tell them he'd solved the case after all. So why was he here?

"However, I've been told that you two have been trying to solve this thing yourselves."

Elaine wasn't sure how to respond. Jan seemed as uncertain as she was.

"We have been asking questions," Elaine said tentatively. "After all, one of our guests was targeted, and we really want to see this thing wrapped up."

Dan nodded. "I can understand that. But it seems that, at least in one case, someone has mistaken you for police."

"What do you mean?" Jan narrowed her eyes.

"When I went to talk to a clerk at a convenience store in Waterville yesterday, she refused to speak with me because she said she'd already turned over the security video to the police."

"She said what?" Elaine couldn't believe it.

"And when I asked her to describe the police in question, her description matched the two of you to a T."

"She thought we were the police?" Jan looked almost as tickled as Elaine felt. "That's hilarious."

"We never told her we were the police," Elaine said, smothering a laugh. How could anyone have mistaken them for the cops? "We just asked questions, but I swear we never did anything to suggest we were there in any official capacity."

"Well, she thought you were." Dan didn't seem to think it was nearly as funny as they did. "And she didn't want to turn the video over to me because of it."

Elaine felt a tiny bit proud that they'd made it to the footage before the actual police had. Surely that meant they were on the right path.

"Did she give it to you in the end?" Elaine asked. "We could get you a copy of the video."

He gave her a wry smile. "Nope. She refused, even after I flashed my badge. She told me to talk to the women police." He shook his head. "That's why I'm here. I was hoping you could make me a copy."

Elaine laughed. "We can do that." Jan nodded and went off to burn a copy of the DVD. She returned a few minutes later and handed it over to the state trooper.

"Thank you. And going forward, please try to make sure everyone knows you are not the police."

"I promise not to flash my badge any more than necessary," Elaine said. At the look he shot her, she held up her hands. "Just kidding."

He gave her a sardonic smile and shook his head.

"Thank you for your time." He turned and headed back toward the hallway. "I'll let you get back to your morning now."

Elaine resisted the urge to ask whether they would see him over at I Scream. Jan walked him to the door, and by the time she got back, Elaine had cleaned up her dishes and was headed upstairs to brush her teeth.

The plan was to go over to I Scream that morning, but the stand didn't open until eleven, so they agreed they'd head over a bit before then. For now, Elaine spent some time on her devotions, and then she went downstairs and started setting tables in the west parlor. Her gaze kept drifting over to the painting. It really was beautiful, and she had been meaning to call Heather Wells about restoring it, but she'd been so preoccupied that she hadn't gotten around to it. Well, now was as good a time as any, Elaine realized. She picked up the painting and headed to the office, where the local phone book rested on a shelf behind her desk.

Elaine flipped to the page where Heather's art restoration business We Restore was listed and dialed the number. It rang a few times, and then a voice Elaine recognized as belonging to Heather Wells answered the phone.

"We Restore, how may I help you?"

"Hi, Heather. This is Elaine Cook over at Tea for Two."

"Elaine. Good to hear from you. How are things in Lancaster?" Elaine heard genuine warmth in her voice. Elaine and Jan had used Heather's expert skills a few times since they'd moved to town, including in restoring an antique teapot they'd bought at a tag sale that turned out to be quite valuable.

"They're just great. Are you enjoying the summer?"

"So far so good. What can I help you with?" Heather asked. "Do you have something fun for me?"

"I hope so," Elaine said, looking down at the yellowed surface of the painting. Even though it could probably use a good cleaning by an expert, the artist's fine brushstrokes were smooth and even, and his skill was evident. "We found a painting at a flea market, and it has something of an interesting story." She quickly filled Heather in on how Archie had recognized his father's mark on the painting, and how they were trying to find out more about it.

"It is a beautiful painting, but the frame is cracked. We'd love to have that restored. I was wondering if you could give me an estimate on how much something like that normally costs."

"Hmm." Heather hesitated. "Well, I can't really give you a great estimate over the phone, I'm afraid. It really depends on a number of factors, including how much damage has been done and what materials have been used. If you bring the painting in so I could take a look, I could give you a more realistic estimate."

"Sure thing," Elaine said. "I'll bring it over in the next day or so."

"Great. I look forward to taking a look."

"Wonderful. I'll see you then."

Elaine ended the call and sat back in her desk chair. It felt good to have to have taken that step. Now she could turn her attention to the wallet thieves. But she wasn't even sure where to start. It was driving Elaine crazy. She felt like the more people they talked to, the further they were from getting answers.

Well, hopefully talking to Anita Picard would help today. The purse had been taken from a crowded hotspot in town in the peak after-dinner hours. Surely someone there had seen something.

A little while later, Jan's croissants were out of the oven and they were on their way to I Scream. The rain last night had taken the moisture out of the air, and the sky was a glorious cerulean blue. The leaves on the trees were a sparkling, gorgeous green. Sometimes Elaine couldn't believe she got to live here.

As they approached the ice cream stand, they found Anita's husband, Charlie Picard, outside hosing down the tables and chairs. The stand didn't open for another twenty minutes, but Anita had said they'd be here early getting things set up. The stand consisted of a small white clapboard building decorated with buoys and lobster traps, and a half dozen picnic tables painted in red, white, and blue, as well as a handful of Adirondack chairs set around the lawn. On one edge of the grassy lot was the koi pond Anita had referenced last night, as well as a set of hutches Charlie had built to house the long-haired rabbits they kept there. Elaine had been told that their daughter Shannon had been very involved with 4-H and raised rabbits when she was younger, and now that she was grown and out of the house Charlie still raised them himself.

"Hello, Charlie," Elaine said as they approached.

Charlie turned off the spray nozzle and looked up. "Hello," he said, setting down the hose. "Getting a jump on the crowds, I see."

Elaine laughed. "I do love your chocolate brownie sundaes, but I'm afraid it's a bit early for me."

"It's never too early for ice cream." Charlie grinned. He was a tall man, and the belly that hung over his belt buckle testified to his personal love of his product. Elaine knew that he'd been raised on a dairy farm in the Midwest and had learned to make ice cream from his grandmother as a boy. He still made most of the stand's ice cream himself, using fresh local ingredients wherever possible, and he was the creative mind behind some of the more interesting flavor combinations they some-times sold. Elaine had quite liked the basil peach she'd tried last summer, but it hadn't gone over as well with the tourist crowds.

"We were hoping to talk with Anita," Jan added, and Charlie nodded.

"She's inside. Go on over. You're here about the purse that was stolen last night, right?"

"Yes," Elaine said. "Anita called us last night, since she'd heard we're looking into the thefts that have been happening around town."

"Well, I hope you find whoever did this," Charlie said. "It's terrible that it keeps happening right here in Lancaster. I feel just awful that one of our customers was a victim."

"Were you around last night when it happened?" Jan asked.

"Nah. I was at home," Charlie said, "watching the ball game on TV. I sure wish I'd been here though. I can't help but think I might have seen or done something to prevent it."

"Maybe you could have," Elaine said kindly. "Though Jan and I were both there when the wallet was stolen from one of our customers, and neither of us saw anything."

"I suppose you're right," Charlie said. "Well, in any case, Anita will be able to tell you more. And I think Jenny, who handled the whole thing, will be in soon, and she can give you more details."

"Thank you so much," Elaine said, and she and Jan walked across the crushed-shell yard toward the small white hut. A long list of ever-changing flavors was tacked to the front of the building. Most of the ice cream was made in-house, and they always had new and interesting flavors. She saw that this week's special was lemon mousse shortbread.

They approached the window and through the glass saw Anita Picard setting up the cash register.

"Hey there. I'll be right out." Anita was in her early fifties, and she was slight and tan and fit. She ran daily, working off the calories she surely must have consumed being around ice cream all the time.

A moment later, Anita joined them on the brick pathway that lined the front of the stand.

"Thank you for coming," Anita said. "This whole thing is just so horrible."

"Of course," Elaine said.

"We want to put an end to this as much as you do," Jan said. "So where was the purse?"

Anita pointed to a red picnic table in the far corner. "The woman was sitting at that table, and her kids had finished their cones and were looking at the koi pond, so she left her purse behind and followed them over there." Anita traced a line from the picnic table to the koi pond with her finger.

"Do you know how long she left it unattended?"

"I'm honestly not sure." Anita shook her head. "You know, I wish I knew how to answer more of your questions, but I'm afraid I wasn't here. We're here a lot, but I had a meeting of the selectmen and Charlie wanted to watch the game. Jenny O'Connor was the manager on duty last night. She's the one who responded when she saw what was going on, and she's the one who called the police."

"Jenny O'Connor?" Elaine repeated the name, but it didn't sound familiar to her. She knew a number of people in town, but certainly not everyone.

"She's a college kid. Goes to Colby. She's been working here the past three summers, and she's great. Totally responsible and with it. She's our man on the ground when we're not here. Or, you know, our woman on the ground."

Elaine thought back to the times she'd been here. It seemed that most of the workers were young, probably in college or even younger. "Do you have a lot of college students who work here?"

"Oh, sure. Actually, most of our kids come from the high school over in Penzance, but we have some college kids too. That's who you get when the job pays minimum wage plus all the ice cream you can eat." She smiled sheepishly. "As much as we love it, ice cream isn't exactly a high-margin industry."

"We hear you on that," Jan said, and Elaine nodded. Tea wasn't much better. Good thing none of them were in it to get rich.

"How well do you know the kids who work here?" Elaine asked carefully.

"Well, I wouldn't say I know most of them exceptionally well, but I do require letters of recommendation when they apply to the job, and we only hire the ones who have a stellar reputation."

Elaine nodded, and Anita continued. "If you're trying to ask if any of them could have been responsible for the theft, I suppose it is possible, but it seems pretty unlikely to me. Katie and Katelyn were scooping, and Kylie was running the register, so the three of them were inside the shack the whole time. The only one who would have left the shack was Jenny, who was drifting in and out of the yard, keeping an eye on things and cleaning up messes. But you're more than welcome to talk to them."

Elaine noted how so far every single business owner they'd approached had said it hadn't been possible that their employees had been responsible for the thefts. She and Jan were no exception. They would vouch for Rose and Archie. Was it true that all the employees at these places really were exemplary individuals? Or was there something that made them all want to believe that it had to have been someone from the outside who was responsible?

"Thank you," Jan said. "We'd like to talk with them. But for now, can you tell us how the customer noticed her purse was missing, and what happened afterward?"

"I'll tell you what I can. Again, I ..." She looked up as a compact car pulled into the small parking lot. "Ah. Actually, here's Jenny now. She'll be able to do a much better job of answering your questions."

Jan and Elaine watched as a tall young woman with long blonde hair stepped out of the driver's seat of the car. She wore a T-shirt with the I Scream logo on the pocket over short white shorts and sneakers, and she carried a small leather purse over her arm and wore large-framed sunglasses. She had a sunny, all-American look. Elaine glanced at Jan, who had met her eye. So she'd noticed the long blonde hair and sunglasses too. Could this be the woman who'd stolen the wallet from Tricia in the tearoom?

"Jenny!" Anita called. The girl looked over at Anita and waved. She started walking toward her. When she got closer, Anita turned to Elaine and Jan. "These are my friends Jan and Elaine. They're trying to find out more about the thefts that have been happening around town, and they'd like to talk to you about what happened here last night."

Elaine watched her reaction carefully, but if Jenny was frightened or made wary by Anita's words, she hid it very well. She took her sunglasses off and folded them, and Elaine noticed her nails were painted a pale shade of baby pink. A wide smile spread across her face.

"I'm Jenny. Nice to meet you." She held out her hand and shook hands with both Jan and Elaine. "I'm happy to talk to you. What do you want to know?"

She was poised and had something you might call presence. She seemed in control of her movements and her words. Most people would no doubt find it pleasant, but in this situation, Elaine wasn't sure controlled was what she hoped for. Control didn't have to mean the opposite of honest, but it sometimes came across that way.

"Can you walk us through what happened?"

"Sure thing." She set her purse down on the closest picnic table, painted in blue and white stripes, which was already mostly dry. "I had just helped a father carry out an order of six sundaes to his family, who were waiting at the stars-and-stripes table over there." She pointed to a table painted like the American flag. "Then I noticed a commotion over at the red table in the corner."

"What was happening?"

"A woman was on her hands and knees, looking under the table, shouting that her purse was missing."

"What did you do?" Jan asked.

"I went over to help her," Jenny said. "She showed me right where she left it, and she said that she'd left it behind when she went to the pond. I asked the people who were nearby. It was pretty full, so I figured someone had to have seen something."

"And had they?" Elaine asked.

"Just one person. An older lady was here with her daughter and grandkids, and she said she'd seen a woman with brown hair walk by and eye it and then look around. She thought at first that it was someone looking for the purse's owner, but something seemed odd about it. But she says she didn't actually see her take it, so I don't know how much that matters."

Elaine shot Jan a look. Could it be the same brown-haired woman they'd seen in the security camera video?

"Did she describe the purse?"

"She said it wasn't anything special. Just a canvas tote with blue trim she was using because it looked beachy."

"Were there any identifying marks on it?" Jan asked.

"Not that she mentioned to me. But I wasn't listening when she talked to the policeman who came, so I'm not sure what she told him. Maybe there was something valuable inside the purse, but I don't know."

Elaine studied the girl. Was she being coy? Did she really not realize how valuable a wallet, stuffed full of credit cards and personal information, could be? Or was she hiding something she did know?

"Do you know how long it was before the woman discovered her purse missing that this brown-haired woman looked it over?" Elaine asked.

"I believe it was just a few minutes, but I'm not sure exactly."

"Did she say anything else about the woman she'd seen?" Jan asked.

Jenny thought for a second before answering. "I don't think so." She shook her head. "I'm sorry, that's what I remember. I do know that she stuck around to talk to the police."

"And you called the police?" Elaine saw that the sun was just barely breaking through the trees, casting soft patterns against the painted wood.

"I did. I used my cell phone." She unzipped her purse and pulled out her phone and scrolled through the calls to show them a call placed to Trooper Benson at 6:30 the previous evening. Elaine felt a little sad and a little proud that she recognized the number. "He came right away, and he talked to both women and asked around to see if anyone saw something. No one else had, so he took his report and promised to be in touch."

"Have you heard from him?"

She shook her head.

"We haven't heard anything here," Anita said. "Jenny called me right after she called the police, and I left the meeting and got here when Trooper Benson was interviewing them. Both women were very cooperative, but I'm not sure there was much useful information."

"It would be helpful to be able to talk to the women," Jan said. "Did you happen to get contact information?"

"That would have been really smart. I realized that afterward. But in the moment, I wasn't really thinking straight. I knew Trooper Benson had gotten their info, and I was just thinking about trying to keep everything running here."

"I should have thought of it myself," Anita said. "But I didn't get their numbers either. Do you think Dan Benson might be willing to share that information?"

"Maybe," Elaine said. The state trooper didn't mind if the cousins sleuthed alongside him, but he wasn't often willing to share information he'd learned. He'd said something about police protocol. "But in any case, we'll see what we can dig up on our own."

"Thank you. I'm grateful for any help you can provide," Anita said.

"I am as well," Jenny said. "Please don't hesitate to let me know if I can help."

"Thank you so much." Elaine stood up. "We'll do everything we can to find this thief."

A few minutes later, Anita had dispatched Jenny to get things ready inside the shack and was walking Jan and Elaine to the road. Elaine wanted to get a read on Jenny.

"How well do you know her?" she asked, nodding to the blonde girl now barely visible through the window at the front of the building.

"Well, like I said, she's been working here for three summers," Anita said. "That's longer than most kids stick around, so I'd say I know her a bit better than most of our employees. She's going to be a senior at Colby this year."

"How is she, as an employee?"

"Great, mostly."

Elaine waited for her to go on, but she seemed to be hesitating about something.

"What do you mean, *mostly*?" Elaine asked gently.

For a moment, Anita didn't answer, but then she seemed to make a decision. "It's just small things. Obviously none of them enough to make me not trust her. I mean, last night, she did exactly the right thing, and I'm not sure any of the younger kids who were here would have known what to do."

"But?"

"Well, the till has been short a couple times when she's been in charge. It happens sometimes, and it's not off by a lot, a ten here, a twenty here, but it's happened enough that it's made me wonder."

"Wonder whether she's pocketing the money?" Jan said.

Anita nodded. "It's probably nothing though. Just an accident, I'm sure." It sounded to Elaine like Anita was almost trying to convince herself.

"Given that, is there a reason she's been here longer than most others? Why do you think she sticks around?"

"Because of the awesome boss, obviously." Anita grinned. "But really, I don't know for sure. But I know that she lives at home, even during the school year, and I get the sense things at home aren't great. I think her mother is sick, based on things she's told me. It sounds to me like she might have multiple sclerosis, though she's never said that directly. I think the flexibility I give her is really helpful. Plus, she makes a bit more than the other kids because she's a manager, so that might be part of it." The sound of the crushed shells crunching under their feet was the only noise for a moment. "Well, and I think it helps that her boyfriend is around town a lot this summer."

"Boyfriend?" Elaine didn't know why she was so surprised. Of course a stunning girl like that would have a boyfriend.

"Yeah, this kid Mark. He's some kind of contractor or something. I know he's been doing repairs around town. He's picked her up after work a few times. He seems like a nice enough kid, and she's crazy about him."

Elaine forced herself not to look at Jan. She didn't want Anita to pick up on the fact that she had just connected Jenny directly to a suspect in their investigation. Mark now had some connection to every place that had been hit up except the tearoom. But the tearoom had been robbed by a woman with long blonde hair, just like Jenny. Were they working together?

They soon said good-bye to Anita and started walking back toward the house.

"What do you think?" Elaine asked as soon as they were out of earshot.

"I don't know about Jenny. She seems great, but something doesn't add up. The till being short. Problems at home. The fact that she matches the description of the thief at our place exactly. Her connection to Mark."

"Right. But would she really steal a purse at her own job?" Elaine asked.

"What better way to throw suspicion off yourself than to be the one who swoops in and saves the day?"

"What about the brown-haired woman the witness saw?"

"She didn't actually see the purse being taken. She just thought the woman seemed strange. But it could have been nothing."

"True." Elaine wasn't sure what to believe. She wanted to think Jenny was innocent, but it was hard to say. One thing was certain though. They needed to talk to Mark, and soon.

"In that case," she said, smiling at Jan, "do we head to Green Glade Cottages next to see if Mark is around?"

"Exactly."

They reversed direction and started walking back down Cottage Road. With every step, Elaine felt like they were getting closer to finding answers.

CHAPTER FOURTEEN

Macy Atherton was sucking on a piece of hard candy, reading a paperback novel, when Jan and Elaine stepped into the lobby of Green Glade Cottages.

"You're back," she said. Jan tried to read her inflection but couldn't figure out if she was pleased or annoyed or what.

"We were hoping we could catch Mark Hamilton," Jan said. "Is he around?"

Macy laid her book facedown on the counter, and Jan could see it was a mystery that had been on the best-seller list the past few weeks. She stared at them for a minute. Jan wasn't sure what to do, and she hitched her purse up on her shoulder to avoid standing there blankly.

"He's out working on the cabin back by the fence," Macy finally said. "Now, I don't want people to think I just let anyone on to the property to harass my employees, and I know Mark didn't have anything to do with stealing that wallet. But I know that you won't leave me alone until you talk to him, so you two go on back. But behave, please."

Out of the corner of her eye, Jan saw Elaine stifling a laugh.

"We promise to behave," Jan said, and Macy waved toward the side door with her hand, grunted a good-bye, and picked up her book again.

Jan followed Elaine out the side door and on to the path that wound through the trees. Dappled sunlight filtered down, and birds were singing in the trees above them. They heard splashing coming from the pool area, but they took a turn at the fork in the path that led toward the back of the property. After a few minutes, they found the half-sided cabin, and with it a young man Jan assumed must be Mark. He was holding a strip of wood with one hand and using a nail gun with the other. He looked up, smiled when he saw them, and set the nail gun down. He pushed up the safety goggles he was wearing and waited.

He was a good-looking young man, Jan decided. Fit and of medium height, with dirty-blond hair and a strong jawline, he had a deep tan and blue eyes that stood out even from this distance.

"Hello. I'm Elaine," her cousin said, holding out her hand. "And this is my cousin Jan."

Jan stepped forward and Mark shook each of their hands in turn. He had a firm grip, and his smile was friendly. He seemed more confused than concerned.

"We run Tea for Two, the tearoom over on Main Street."

"Oh yeah. I've seen that. In that big white Victorian, right? That's a beautiful house. Queen Anne is my favorite architectural style."

Jan was flummoxed. She didn't know many—any—college-age boys who knew what the Queen Anne style was, let alone had a favorite style.

attention to her, but then I noticed that she was looking in the sliding glass door of that cabin." He pointed toward a cabin a ways down the hill. "Peace, I think it's called."

"What did she look like?" Jan asked.

"I wasn't really paying that much attention. But I think she was average height, with brownish hair." He shrugged. "Like I said, I figured she was a guest, and that was her cabin. It was only after the fact that I thought there might be something strange about it."

Could it be the same woman who'd been spotted at the ice cream stand, and on the video? It was hard to say. There were a lot of women with brown hair in the world.

"It didn't occur to me until just now that that might have had something to do with all this."

Was this true? Jan couldn't read him. It seemed a bit too convenient to her that, as soon as he'd realized they suspected him, he'd remembered this woman.

"What did she do after she looked in the door?"

He shrugged. "I'm not really sure. Again, I didn't think anything of it at the time. I wasn't paying too much attention. I went back to my work, and the next time I looked up, she was gone."

She hadn't gone into the cabin he'd pointed to; or if she had, she hadn't taken anything. No thefts had been reported there. But Jan was uneasy. Something about his story didn't add up. Why had he only remembered about her after they'd shifted to questioning him?

"Look, I'm sorry, but I have to get back to work." He gestured toward the cabin. "I wish I could help, but I honestly can't think of anything else that might be useful."

Jan wanted to stay and prod him further, but she could see that they weren't going to get any more answers here, so she thanked him, and then she and Elaine turned and headed back toward the road.

"I want to believe him," Elaine said as they stepped back on to the shoulder of Cottage Road.

"I do too." Jan had to admit he came across as likeable and trustworthy. But wouldn't you try to project that image if you were covering up a crime? Was it possible to fake likability? Jan wasn't sure. "Did you think that was weird that he only thought about that brown-haired woman peering into the cabin after he realized why we were talking to him?"

"I'm not sure," Elaine said. "I mean, yes, I guess. But I don't know. I'm getting more and more confused. And I feel like we're not getting anywhere."

Jan nodded. They needed something new to work with. Some break in the case, or some new clue to emerge. They had talked to just about everyone they could think of and weren't getting any closer to finding answers.

"We could try to talk to the woman whose wallet was stolen at the Pine Tree Grill again," Elaine suggested.

Jan nodded. At this point, that was probably one of the few avenues they had left to try. They walked the short distance to the Northwoods Bed-and-Breakfast again, and Rue Maxwell smiled when she found them on the porch.

"Come in, come in." She gestured for them to step into the parlor again. "You're here again to talk to Lauren, right? She never called you?" She didn't even wait for them to answer before continuing, "You're in luck. She is upstairs. I'll just pop up and see if she has a second to talk with you. Make yourselves at home. Help yourselves to coffee or tea or whatever."

Jan moved to sit down while Elaine wandered over to the beverage table. "Want some water?"

Jan nodded, and Elaine poured out two cups of water from a cut-glass pitcher. Then they sat together on the couch and waited for a few minutes. Jan heard some mumbled voice upstairs, and then, a few minutes later, footsteps on the stairs.

"Jan, Elaine, this is Lauren. Lauren, this Jan Blake and Elaine Cook. They own that lovely tearoom down the road."

Lauren nodded coolly, looking them up and down. She wrinkled her brow and stood where she was. She had long, thick brown hair and a deep tan, and she wore a fashionable long dress and sandals, with lots of gold jewelry. She had a quilted leather purse slung over one shoulder.

"These are the women I told you about, the local sleuths. They're looking into the thefts around town, and they'd like to ask you to a few questions."

Rue indicated that she should sit down across from the cousins, but she stayed where she was.

"I already spoke with the police," she said. She didn't say it out loud, but her look indicated disdain.

"Oh, Jan and Elaine are better than the police." Rue patted the back of an upholstered chair.

"We're not better than...," Jan started, but Elaine interrupted.

"We have managed to solve several mysteries before Trooper Benson could put the pieces together," Elaine said, nodding. "And we're anxious to find the thief or thieves in this case, because one of our customers was also robbed."

The woman didn't move, but she nodded. Still, she looked skeptical. On some level, Jan understood. She was a grandmother with glasses and a few extra pounds around the middle, and Elaine was thinner and taller but still didn't exactly fit the part of a sleuth. But it still burned—they had a stellar track record, and it stung to be underestimated.

"We've already spoken to Mel and Bianca over at the Pine Tree Grill, but we were wondering if you could think of anything that seemed odd or anyone who looked out of place."

"No." She shook her head. "I'm sure it must have been one of those college kids they have working there, and the rest of them must be in on it, since no one saw anything. It's amazing—a room full of people, and none of them saw a thing." The tone of her voice indicated her suspicion.

Jan thought it was strange how both Lauren and Carrie blamed the employees of the places they were robbed. Then she had a scary thought—did Tricia blame them?

"Why don't you tell us what you do remember?" Elaine suggested, her voice warm and even.

Lauren sighed, glanced up at the top of the stairs, and then quickly recounted a version of events that matched Mel and Bianca's almost exactly, except in this case, it was clear she thought someone who worked there was responsible.

Jan realized that Lauren didn't want to be talking with them and she realized they might only have another minute or so before she bolted, so Jan decided to shift topics.

"Were any of your credit cards used?"

Lauren's eyes widened, like she was surprised to be asked such a bold question, and she didn't say anything for a minute.

But she let out a breath and reached for the back of the chair in front of her.

"Yes, actually, one was." She reached into the purse and pulled out what Jan recognized as the latest version of the hottest cell phone. "It took me a while to realize that the wallet was really gone, and I didn't get a chance to cancel my cards until we got back here and looked up the numbers for my different credit card companies." She swiped her finger across her screen and typed in a code to unlock the phone. "By that time, one card had already been used, at a gas station in Waterville."

She held up the phone, and both Jan and Elaine leaned forward to get a better look at the picture she was showing them. It was a grainy black-and-white image from the security camera of a gas station.

"The police were able to get these images," she said, giving them a wry look. "This is the person who used the card."

"May I?" Jan asked.

Lauren nodded and handed over the phone. Jan took the phone in her hand, and she looked again when she saw who was on the screen.

"Do you know who it is?" Lauren asked.

Jan continued to look down at the screen, and then she held the phone out for Elaine to see. The image was grainy, but it showed a woman filling up the tank of a beat-up car. Elaine sucked in a breath.

"Who is it?" Rue asked, leaning toward them from across the coffee table.

"We don't know," Jan said uncertainly.

"Oh, come on." Lauren's voice had an edge to it.

"We don't know who she is, but we think she's connected to all this," Jan said. The woman was mostly blocked by the car in the shot, but even on the grainy still, it was clear that this woman had long blonde hair. "Well, of course she's connected to this, considering she's using the stolen credit card," Jan added.

"What she means is, this woman matches the description of the woman who took the wallet from our tearoom," Elaine said quickly. Jan looked again. The woman in this photo wore a baseball cap that shaded her face, as well as big sunglasses. The brim of her hat was about level with the top of the top of the gas pump. Jan couldn't tell what kind of car she was driving, just that it was a compact in a light color.

Jan nodded. She matched the description of that woman perfectly—tall, thin, blonde. It must be the same person. And this was clearly *not* the same person—the short, heavy, brown-haired woman—who'd appeared in the security footage from the convenience store. But…she looked yet again. It also looked like it could be Jenny. It was hard to tell, with that hat and the sunglasses. What kind of car had Jenny driven? Jan thought it was also pretty small, and in a light color.

"But we don't know who she is," Jan added.

"Would you mind sending me that picture?" Elaine asked.

Lauren looked like she didn't know what to believe and was even less interested in trying to find out. Then, with a sigh, she agreed, and held out her hand for the phone. Jan returned it reluctantly. Lauren wiped the front of the phone on the skirt of her dress, as if to remove all traces that they had touched it. Elaine told her her cell number so Lauren could send the photo by text.

At the same time, there were footsteps on the stairs. "Well, Walter and I were just about to go out for lunch," Lauren said, tucking the phone back into her purse. "So I'd better be going." She turned on her heel and started back toward the hallway. Jan turned in time to see a tall man with dark hair, wearing khaki shorts and a fitted polo, reach the bottom of the steps.

"Have a nice afternoon," Rue called, and Lauren gave her a dismissive wave and stepped out the door after her husband.

"She must have been in a hurry," Rue said, trying, no doubt, to cover the rudeness of her guest. But Jan didn't care. They'd found out what they needed to—that there was definitely more than one person involved in the wallet thefts. And one of them might or might not be Jenny. After so much fruitless searching, it felt good to finally land on clues of any sort. Plus, there was something else she'd noticed.

Jan and Elaine thanked Rue for her help, and soon they were out the door and making their way back toward the tearoom. They had only been walking for a few minutes when Elaine turned to Jan.

"What are you all smiles about?" she asked.

Jan hadn't realized she'd been smiling, but she didn't stop herself now.

"There was something else I noticed in that photograph," she said.

"Oh?" Elaine cocked her head.

"And I think it's going to make it easy to figure out who that woman in the photograph was."

CHAPTER FIFTEEN

It was another perfect, sunny day. The tearoom windows had been thrown open to let in the beautiful golden light, and a refreshing breeze wafted through the parlor as quiet classical music played over the speakers. The tearoom was slow—only a handful of customers had come through. Archie had been chatting with—and charming—a table of older women, but for the most part, Rose, Elaine, and Jan had been standing around and getting in each other's way. The second time Elaine caught Jan rewashing a teapot with a lavender design that Elaine had already cleaned, she made a suggestion.

"Why don't you go upstairs and start researching?" Elaine suggested.

"What?" Jan ran the sponge gently over the delicate painted design.

"We don't all need to be here, and I can see that you're dying to get upstairs and start looking into that license plate number."

Elaine had felt like such a rookie when Jan had told her what she'd noticed in the photo from the gas station. The license plate. Elaine had been so shocked to see the blonde woman that she hadn't even thought to look for any identifying marks on the car. But Jan had not only noticed that the first three letters of the Maine license plate were visible in the shot, she'd memorized them. They both hoped that they would be able to trace the license plate and hoped that would lead them to the thief. They knew the police had access to systems that could track such things easily, but Jan knew from previous mysteries that you could often find information like this online.

"Go on. We can handle things here," Elaine said.

"Seriously. We've got it under control," Rose said, gently cracking an egg against the side of a bowl. She used the shell to separate the white from the yolk, letting the white drip into the bowl. Then she dropped the yolk into another dish with several others.

"Are you sure?" Jan turned off the faucet and reached for the hand towel.

"I'm positive." Elaine gestured that Jan should hand over the teapot and towel. "I'll dry. You go solve the mystery."

Jan hesitated for about half a second, then nodded. "All right then. Thank you." She turned to Rose, who was gently pouring the egg whites into the bowl of a stand-up mixer. "Be careful not to overbeat," she said to Rose.

"Just to stiff peaks," Rose said, nodding. "I've got this."

Jan looked around uncertainly again, but then took off her apron and hung it on a hook before heading up the stairs.

Elaine finished drying the teapot, admiring the delicate brushstrokes that made up the flower design, and then set it on the shelf gently. If things continued to be slow like this, it was going to be a bad season.

For a minute, the roar of the mixer filled the kitchen, and Elaine found herself thinking back to the photo from the gas station they'd seen earlier. She was now certain that there were multiple people involved in these thefts, but she couldn't figure out if they were working together or if these were unrelated thefts or what. And something else had bothered her since she'd seen that photo this morning. So far, the stolen credit cards had been used to buy groceries and gas. These would be considered by most people to be necessities. There was no way to know what the cash that had been stolen was being spent on, but so far, it didn't seem that the thieves were in this for plasma televisions or expensive clothes. Someone was buying things they needed and couldn't afford to buy. These thefts seemed to be driven more by need than greed. That didn't make it right, of course, but it cast things in a different light.

Elaine realized another thing. So far, all of the victims had been women, and specifically, women who had been visiting town. Was the thief avoiding locals on purpose? If so, did that indicate that it was someone from town who didn't want to steal from her friends? Or was it less thought out than that? Could it just be that tourists, who were here on vacation, were by nature more relaxed and less careful about leaving their belongings out? Elaine thought that was possible, but it was truly hard to say.

Elaine folded the tea towel and threaded it through the handle of the dishwasher. Why, she wondered, were only women being targeted? All four of the victims they knew of had been women—did the thief have something against them? But then, she thought, how would one go about stealing a wallet from a man? Most men she knew kept their wallets in their pockets, while women tended to carry them in their purses. A purse— especially one that wasn't being carefully monitored—would be much easier to swipe a wallet from than a man's pocket. This wasn't some bold, daring pickpocket they were dealing with. This was someone—or someones—who went to places likely to be filled with tourists, and then bided their time, blending in with the crowd, scoping out the situation before finding a target.

The logical conclusion, then, was that *this* was the kind of person they needed to be looking out for. But how...

And suddenly, Elaine had an idea. She considered it thoroughly and nodded. Yes, it seemed to make sense to her. She thought it would work.

"What's that smile for?" Rose asked. Elaine looked up, startled. She hadn't even realized the mixer had shut off.

"I just had an idea for how to catch the thief," Elaine said. She straightened the towel one more time and nodded to the mixing bowl, which was now filled with stiff white peaks of whipped egg whites. "What are you making?"

"Macarons. We learned how to make them at school last night, and I wanted to practice, so Jan said since it was slow it would be fine. I'll serve them with the tea."

"*Ooh.* I love macarons." The delicate French cookies were bite-size bits of creamy filling sandwiched between two soft meringue cookies. She'd fallen in love with them when she'd visited Paris and she sampled them whenever she could. They might not traditionally go with an English tea, but she doubted anyone would complain. "What flavor?"

"Chocolate," Rose said.

"I fully support you using this time to practice macarons." Elaine stepped away from the sink and started to put away other teapots that had been drying on towels on the counter. "Speaking of, how's school?"

"Oh, it's good." Rose was now measuring out almond flour and pouring it into a mixing bowl. "I really like it."

Elaine set a delicate rose-patterned teapot on the shelf and waited a moment more, and then asked, "And Brent? How are things with Brent?"

"He called." Rose was now spooning confectioner's sugar into a bowl. Her cheeks turned a bit pink. "We talked for more than an hour. The thing was, it felt like we could have talked all night."

"Did you see him at your class last night?"

"Yes. But he had his daughter waiting at home with a babysitter, so he couldn't stay and chat. But he did ask me out to a movie on Friday night." She measured out a few teaspoons of cocoa powder and added them to the bowl.

"That's great. What movie?" Elaine picked up the lid of a Royal Albert teapot in Old Country Roses pattern and set it gently on the teapot, which was drying on the counter. This one had been a garage sale find and had a small chip in the handle, so it was worth almost nothing, but it was still one of Elaine's favorites.

"You know, I didn't even ask him what movie," Rose said, laughing. "I was just excited he asked. Is that bad?"

"I'd say that's very good."

Rose was quiet for a moment, mixing the sugar and the almond flour gently in the bowl. Elaine thought she wanted to say more, so she set the teapot gently on the shelf and leaned against the counter, waiting.

Rose used a rubber spatula to scoop the flour mixture into the egg whites and expertly folded it in. Then, at last, she said, "I've never met a guy like Brent."

Elaine nodded again. "That's good."

"Yeah, except I'm afraid of messing things up. I don't know what I'm supposed to do." She flicked her wrist, mixing the batter for a moment. "My parents didn't exactly have the best relationship, so I'm not really sure what one looks like. And I'm afraid I'm doing it all wrong."

Elaine let those words settle in for a moment. She knew that Rose's parents had separated before her mother Aliza had been diagnosed with heart disease, although they had eventually reconciled. She'd passed away not long after Jan and she opened the tearoom, and Rose had come to work for them shortly thereafter. She didn't know what circumstances had led to the separation, but it really didn't matter.

"You're not doing it all wrong," she said gently. "For one thing, your parents had decades together. I know things weren't great there for a while, but I would guess they didn't start out that way. And it doesn't seem that it stayed that way either." She wanted to speak carefully, to not tarnish Rose's memory of her mother or offend her father, Clifton, who lived here in town and served as a selectman. "I don't know any of the details, obviously, but they had faced many hard things. Those could certainly take a toll on a marriage."

She knew that Rose had been born in East Germany just after the Berlin Wall fell and adopted as a very young child. Rose's adoptive father, Clifton, and her late mother, Aliza, had had their difficulties, despite becoming close again near the end of Aliza's life. From what Rose had told them, heartbreak had probably lurked not far beneath the surface of their marriage. That was sure to affect even the strongest relationship.

"They did fight a lot, but they tried to hide it from me. Of course it didn't work."

Elaine took a moment to choose her words carefully. "Sometimes we clash the hardest with those we care about the most." She took a deep breath. "And I can see how that would make it difficult for you to know what a happy relationship looks like. But I hope you won't let fear keep you from trying."

For a moment, Rose concentrated on using the spatula to spoon the batter into a pastry bag. Then she looked up at Elaine.

"But let's say things do go well. How do I know it won't end up like my parents? If we're just going to end up leaving each other, I'm not sure I even want to start."

Elaine sent up a quick prayer for wisdom. She knew she was treading on some difficult territory here, and she didn't feel qualified to advise Rose, but she knew the girl was looking for honest answers, and she wanted to help.

"Truthfully, there's no good answer for you." She twisted the dish towel in her hands. "Some relationships turn out wonderfully. Others fall apart. I suppose most of us wouldn't start relationships if we knew how they were going to turn out half the time. The human race survives because love makes us feel invincible, even in the face of the odds. But that doesn't mean it's not worth finding out."

Rose squeezed the batter down toward the tip of the pastry bag.

"I can't promise that you and Brent will end up getting married and being happy. No one can. But I don't think you really need to worry about that at this stage anyway. Just get to know him. See how he acts in different situations. Watch how he treats you, and how he treats other people. See how he relates to his family. All of these things will help you understand who he really is and whether he's someone you're interested in settling down with."

Rose was nodding.

"For now, just have fun. You've been on one date. Enjoy getting to know him. You'll know if you want to keep seeing him or not."

Rose nodded. "Thank you, Elaine. I appreciate your wisdom."

"Well, I don't know that I'd call it wisdom. More just hard-won experience."

"But you and your husband were happy, right?"

"Oh yes. Very much so. But we had our ups and downs, like any couple. Relationships are difficult, but when they're right they're so worth working at."

Just then the front door of the tearoom opened. Elaine peeked out of the kitchen and saw Pricilla Gates step inside, along with a woman who had to be her sister.

"Back again?" Elaine called. "Welcome, welcome!" She turned back to Rose. "Paying customers," she said under her breath. Rose smiled and gestured that Elaine should go welcome them.

"Thanks for talking," Rose said.

"Anytime. And save some of those macarons for me."

Elaine welcomed Priscilla and her sister Harriet, and they chatted for a few minutes. Harriet was visiting from Boston, where she was a high school teacher, and Elaine enjoyed hearing about what life was like in the big city.

One of her favorite parts of the job was hearing about all the different lives people lived. They chatted for a while, and then another set of tourists came by, and Elaine found out they were girlfriends who'd grown up together and reunited every summer for a few days away. Elaine thought it was a charming tradition, and they loved hearing about the history of the house and how she and Jan had come together to open the tearoom.

A little while later, Elaine returned to the kitchen with empty tea trays, and she found Jan helping Rose layer filling into the cookies.

"Any luck?" She set the tray down by the sink.

"I'm afraid not," Jan said as she used a pastry knife to spread rich, chocolaty frosting on one half of the small round cookie. "I looked in every database and Web site I could find, but it turns out only knowing the first three digits of a license plate number means you're left with hundreds of possibilities. Without more information, I couldn't find any way to narrow things down enough to be useful." Jan picked up another cookie and gently set it on top of the chocolate cream, producing a perfect macaron.

"Another dead end. I'm sorry," Elaine said. And she was. But she was also distracted by the little tray of macarons they'd assembled. It looked just like you'd see in the window of a patisserie in Paris.

"Nice work, Rose," Elaine said.

A blush crept up Rose's cheeks, and instead of answering she smiled and kept assembling the cookies.

"It's all right," Jan said. "It's an angle Dan is no doubt investigating anyway, and he'll probably have access to better tools than I do. But I also did some research into Mark Hamilton while I was upstairs. And Jenny O'Connor."

"Oh yeah? What'd you find?"

"Not a whole lot that's new. Mark is from Waterville, big family, his dad is a contractor. Jenny is from a small town way up north by the border, it turns out. She has a younger sister and a deadbeat dad. No hint of whether her mom is ill or not. The most interesting thing I discovered is that they're both theater majors."

"So they're unemployable," Elaine quipped. "Good thing Mark is good with his hands."

"While that may be true, that's not why I found it interesting." Jan set another perfect little cookie down on the gold-and-white tray.

"Oh?"

"They're actors."

"Ah." Now Elaine saw what Jan was getting at. "So you think they might have been able to get away with not being entirely truthful when they were talking to us?"

"Goodness, Elaine," Jan laughed. "I'm not trying to say all actors are liars. Just that they might have a fair amount of practice at projecting a certain image, or knowing what to say and do."

Elaine watched as Jan assembled another cookie and set it on the tray.

"Elaine?" Jan said.

"Yes?" Elaine looked up and smiled at her cousin.

"Would you like a macaron?"

"How did you guess?"

"You're practically salivating over the tray."

"Please have one," Rose laughed. "We have plenty."

"Don't mind if I do." Elaine picked up a perfect little circle of a sandwich cookie and bit into it. It was sweet and soft, with a tiny bit of crunch, and the flavor was just perfect. Rich and chocolately but light.

"What do you think?" Rose asked, her face hopeful.

"I think I need another one to decide," Elaine said, and helped herself to a second cookie, which she ate in two bites. Then she nodded and said, "I think that if you give these cookies to that fellow of yours, he'll be a goner."

Rose laughed, and Elaine helped herself to another cookie before she headed back out to the west parlor to check on their guests.

ELAINE HAD MANAGED to sneak three more macarons in the next hour, and though she could have eaten a dozen more, she knew she wouldn't be able to fit into her pants if she indulged in every treat that came out of that kitchen. Instead, she decided to take advantage of the slow day at the tearoom and bring that painting in to Heather Wells to see if it could be restored. After checking with Jan, who thought it was a good idea, she wrapped the painting lightly in newspaper and then set it in the trunk of her car.

She pulled up in front of We Restore, took the painting from her trunk, and stepped inside the small shop. There was a small area with a few chairs in front of a handsome, intricately carved mahogany bar that Heather used as a front counter, and behind that was a big open space piled high with tables, armoires, musical instruments, and pictures of all kinds, each in various stages of repair. The space smelled musty, but light streamed in through the front windows. A bell over the door dinged as Elaine walked in, and Heather stood up and walked toward the counter.

"Hi there. Did you bring me the painting?" Heather's graying dark hair was pulled back into a low ponytail, and her tortoiseshell glasses were perched on top of her head. Elaine could see that she'd been working on inserting a screw into what looked like an antique doll cradle.

"I did indeed." Elaine lifted the painting to the counter, and Heather helped her unwrap the newspaper. "See, the frame is cracked here. I was hoping you could patch it somehow."

"Oh, wow."

That was all Heather said for a moment, and she continued to stare down at the painting. Then she looked up at Elaine.

"Where did you say you got this?"

"At Mainely Bargains," Elaine said. Why was she reacting like this? "Is something wrong with it?"

"No, nothing's wrong," Heather said. She reached into a drawer beneath the counter and pulled out a flashlight and a magnifying glass. She focused them both on the lower right corner of the painting, the spot where the symbol Archie had recognized had been painted—the little interlocking *H*, *A*, and *B*.

"What is it?"

Heather didn't answer for a moment. Instead, she turned the painting over gently and looked at the back. Elaine had seen the back and was sure there was nothing interesting there. It was just the backside of the canvas, with a wooden bar that went across the back to hold the frame together. Elaine had been disappointed that it hadn't had a clean brown paper backing like so many of the pictures they got at garage sales. But Heather seemed fascinated by a little label on the bottom edge of the back of the canvas. She gently lifted up one edge of the canvas and examined a nail carefully.

"Did you find something interesting?" Elaine tried again.

"I'm not totally sure, to be honest," Heather said. She turned the painting back over to the front. "But this symbol— it looks a lot like the symbol used by an artist who was big in England back before the war. Harley Benningham."

Elaine tried to take all this in. Archie had said this was his father's symbol. Now Heather was saying this was the symbol of a famous artist.

"Harley Benningham?" Elaine repeated.

"Harley Archibald Benningham, technically. He usually went by his full name." Heather peered down at the picture. "I'm not saying this is an original Benningham, of course. But if it was..." She let out a low whistle.

Elaine was still trying to wrap her mind around this last bit of news. Harley Archibald Benningham. He had the same initials as Archie's father. And that middle name. It couldn't be a coincidence, could it?

"I'm not the final say on this," Heather continued. "But I have studied art history and am fascinated in particular by the prewar stuff, especially the photorealistic style. This symbol looks a lot like Harley's symbol. But his paintings are very rare, and I've never actually seen one in person before. There are only a handful of his known paintings in existence, all in museums."

"Really?" How was this possible? Elaine shook her head. Was it just a coincidence? That symbol would be easy enough to replicate. Maybe someone had added it later to this unrelated painting, trying to pass it off as the work of a famous artist. Except that Archie had been so confident that the symbol was his father's...

Heather was busy examining the back of the painting again, looking at the wood that held it together and running her finger along the frame. "So the answer to your original question is, I think I can repair the frame, but I'm not sure it's worth it," she finally said.

"Why not?" After all that talk about this being by a famous artist, Elaine hadn't been expecting this answer.

"I don't think this frame is original to the painting."

Elaine felt disappointed by the news, but the way Heather said it, it seemed like this was a big deal. Elaine couldn't see why she was so excited.

"See the frame? It's a light wood, maybe pine, but stained to match the darker wood of the stretcher."

"The stretcher?" Elaine knew she sounded ridiculous repeating what Heather said.

"This outer part here is the frame. It protects the front of the painting. The wooden pieces that the canvas is stapled to— the parts that make the rectangle shape—that's the stretcher."

Elaine understood now. The wooden part inside that she never paid attention to was the stretcher.

"It makes me think the frame might have been added later. Pine and other light woods are more commonly found in the United States, and the stain and the type of mitered corners here are more typical of later twentieth-century American work."

"And you think the painting is…older than that?"

"Probably. See these nails?" She lifted up the corner of the canvas again, and Elaine saw that it was nails that held the canvas to the stretcher. "Most people started using staples instead of nails soon after World War II. So chances are, this is older than that. And, unless I miss my guess, it's also British."

"What makes you think that?"

"This sticker on the stretcher, for one," Heather said. She turned the picture back over and pointed to a little white sticker on the lower piece of wood.

"The artist would either have built a wooden frame himself and then used nails to stretch his canvas tight over it, or he might have bought it premade from an art supply store. And this sticker"—Heather leaned in and looked again—"lists a Wallingford's Art Supply and an address on Eastcastle Street. It's been a long time since I did study abroad, but..." She set the painting down and pulled her phone out of her pocket. She typed something quickly and nodded. "Just as I thought. That address is in the Soho area of London, which was popular with artists before the war." She touched the screen again and squinted at it. "The shop doesn't seem to exist anymore—another clue it's old—but the artist could have bought the stretcher there."

Elaine tried to make sense of what Heather was saying. The painting was by a famous artist, one whose name was remarkably like Archie's father's. One whose mark—identical to Archie's father's mark—was on the front of the picture. It was probably from the right time period and region. But that didn't prove anything. "Is there any way to figure out whether this really is one of his paintings?" Elaine asked.

"I don't really know enough to say for certain," Heather said. "Again, I'm not an art expert, and I can't tell you if this symbol is authentic or if it was added on later or what. What I can say is that the frame doesn't seem to be from the right time period, but the stretcher—the thing the painting is actually done on—does. So it's definitely possible."

"Okay." Elaine wasn't sure what to say next.

"Given the potential value of this painting, I think it's best if an art expert takes a look at it before I do anything more. I just restore antiques, not evaluate fine art. I would hate to ruin something like this."

"Oh. Okay."

"It's not that I don't want to, believe me. But I do have the name of some art experts I can give you."

"That would be great."

Elaine headed for the door in a daze. Could what Heather was saying be true? Had Archie's father really been a famous painter?

And, even if he was, why didn't Archie know about it?

As Elaine pushed open the door, Heather said, "All I can say is, if this is an actual Harley Benningham, it was quite a flea market find."

CHAPTER SIXTEEN

Friday morning, Jan was just finishing up the day's pastries when Elaine came downstairs, a small piece of paper in her hand. Jan had heard her moving around upstairs for a while, even after the shower had shut off and the blow drier had stopped, and she had wondered what her cousin was up to. But as soon as Elaine held out the piece of paper, Jan understood.

"You up for a road trip?" Elaine asked. Rose and Archie weren't in yet, but she would call them to say they were headed out.

"Absolutely. Let me just grab my purse."

A few minutes later, they were in Elaine's Malibu, speeding down the highway toward Portland. Elaine had contacted Rose and Archie and they were all set. Jan bit her lip. Her cousin drove a bit faster on the highway than Jan thought was reasonable, but knew nagging her to slow down would only cause hurt feelings. She tried to focus on the search she'd pulled up on her phone instead.

"It looks like Dorothy Shuman lives right in the middle of the Old Port District," Jan said, studying the map of the address Elaine had found this morning.

"Really?" Elaine sounded as surprised as Jan felt. The historic area, with narrow cobblestone streets and brick sidewalks, was one of the oldest in the city, but it had been revitalized in recent years and was now filled with quaint shops and restaurants.

"Maybe in an apartment above one of the shops?" Jan squinted at the map. It was hard to tell from the address Elaine had found online. But though she was confused by the address, she was glad they would be visiting the historic district. Jan could take or leave most of the big city, but she did enjoy visiting the old part of town, where you could really feel history come alive.

"I guess we'll see," Elaine said. It took just over an hour to get to Portland, and for a good chunk of that time, Jan filled Elaine in on the latest on her daughter Tara's budding romance with Jack Weston, the game warden. Jan also told Elaine about her granddaughter Kelly's triumph at swim lessons and Avery's week at summer camp.

Finally, they arrived on the outskirts of town, and they fell silent as Elaine navigated through the city streets. They traveled on a few larger thoroughfares, and then were shuttled off into smaller, narrower streets as they approached the waterfront. Finally, Elaine found a parking lot with a small hourly fee and left the car there, and they went the rest of the way on foot.

The red brick buildings gathered along the narrow cobblestone streets were beautiful, and they passed bookstores and coffee shops and restaurants and charming boutiques. In the distance, they could see Portland Head Light, perched on the cliff high above Casco Bay. It was a beautiful summer morning, with a cloudless sky, and Jan would have loved to browse in the stores and sit at an outdoor café and take in the salty sea air, but this morning they were on a mission. Maybe she'd come back here with Bob sometime. For now, they followed the directions on Elaine's phone toward an address on a small side street. As they rounded the corner, they saw that this was another beautiful old street. A few tourists were wandering down the narrow slate sidewalk, but otherwise the little stretch was quiet.

They stopped in front of the building marked with the address Elaine had written down. Elaine craned her neck and looked up. "I guess she must live in one of those apartments?" she asked, indicating windows on the second and third floors of the buildings.

"I don't think so," Jan said. Elaine turned and looked at her, eyebrows raised, and Jan pointed to the shop on the first floor, just in front of them. Through the big plate-glass window, Jan could see about a dozen tables covered in floral tablecloths, and the walls were covered in a rich flocked wallpaper in a deep burgundy. Shelves around the room displayed antique teapots and dainty china cups, as well as groups of silver tea strainers and antique metal bins of tea. A big fireplace with a stone mantel dominated one wall, and an antique gramophone sat on a small side table, alongside a wooden crate full of records. The lights were off and no one was moving about inside, but the place looked ready for service. It was charming. In fact, it reminded Jan of their own tearoom.

It reminded her just a little bit *too much* of their own tearoom. "Oh my."

Elaine had just noticed the sign on the door, then. Tea and Sympathy, the gold letters on the door announced. Opening Soon, a hand-written sign taped to the door promised.

"She's opening a tearoom," Jan said.

Elaine shaded her eyes and pressed her face to the glass. "It looks cute."

"It looks like she borrowed some ideas from us," Jan said, pointing to the gramophone.

"We're hardly the only people in the world to have a gramophone," Elaine said. Jan couldn't think of any others, but she didn't press the point.

"So that's what she was doing in our tearoom," Jan said. "Scoping out the competition." That explained why she'd been taking pictures—so she could remember what she saw and implement it here.

"Or enjoying the surroundings, to see what she could replicate here."

"I suppose," Jan said reluctantly. If she was being reasonable, there probably was very little threat to their own business to have Dorothy's tea shop here. They were at least an hour apart, and the settings—and the tearooms themselves, Jan had to admit—were different enough that it was unlikely they'd lose customers to Tea and Sympathy.

She realized that she should probably cross Dorothy off her list of suspects. She may have been taking pictures in the tearoom on Monday, but now she could see why.

Before she knew what was going on, Elaine had pulled her phone out of her purse and was placing a call.

"Who are you calling?" Jan asked, but Elaine smiled and mouthed the word *Dorothy*.

"Hello. Is this Dorothy Shuman?" Elaine said into the phone, her voice upbeat.

Jan couldn't make out what Dorothy said in response, but she could hear that the tone of her voice was skeptical.

"This is Elaine Cook, from Tea for Two. We spoke the other day. I was calling because my cousin and I are in front of your new tearoom here on Gold Street, and it's charming. We wondered if you had a second to talk to us about it."

Jan couldn't hear what Dorothy said in response, but not long afterward, Elaine ended the call. "She'll be here in a few minutes," she said.

"I imagine she wasn't happy to get the call?"

"I think she was more surprised than anything." Elaine turned and looked at the other shops on the street. The tearoom was next door to a store that stocked high-end pet supplies, and beyond that was a kitchenwares store. Jan walked over and perused the display of Le Creuset pans on display in the window. She loved the cobalt-blue color. If she had a ton of money, she'd outfit the kitchen entirely in...

"Hello?"

Jan turned and saw a woman about their age walking toward them. She wore a brightly colored blouse over black slacks, and her hair was shoulder length and graying.

"You must be Dorothy," Elaine said, walking toward her.

"You're Elaine?"

Elaine nodded. "And this is my cousin Jan. Thank you for meeting us." Elaine turned and gestured to the store. "This is your tearoom? It's lovely."

"Thank you," Dorothy said, and she had the grace to look a bit chagrined. "Let's step inside, shall we?"

She pulled out her keys and unlocked the door before showing them in. Inside the shop, Jan could see the wide-plank floors that couldn't possibly be original—these buildings had to be several hundred years old—but looked like they should be. They were gorgeous, as was the pressed-tin ceiling.

"This is beautiful," Jan said. She could imagine this space feeling warm and inviting, especially on a cold winter day.

"Thank you," Dorothy said as she flipped on the lights. "We open this weekend."

"Congratulations," Elaine said. From the tone of her voice, Jan could tell she really meant it.

"So look," Dorothy said, "I know I was evasive when you called earlier this week. And, yes, I was at your tearoom to scope it out. But obviously I didn't set all this up in the past few days. I wasn't there to copy your ideas, just to see how my shop compared."

Jan appreciated that she wasn't beating around the bush. She got the impression Dorothy was a direct person.

"You did a wonderful job," Elaine said. "I'm sure you'll do great." She paused, as though she was considering what to say next.

Jan jumped in. "What we don't understand is why you didn't simply tell us that's what you were doing. We would have loved to meet you and been happy to chat about your new tearoom. Why the secrecy?"

Dorothy sighed. "I didn't know how you'd react. I've always dreamed of opening a tearoom. When my husband passed away last year and left me some money, it seemed like the right time. So I've been checking out all the tearooms I could find in central Maine, just to see how they do things."

"You were taking photographs," Elaine said.

"To remember what it looked like. Not to copy your ideas."

Neither cousin said anything for a moment.

"One huge advantage you two have is that real British guy. Where did you get him? I'd love to get a chatty British gentleman for my own shop."

Jan stifled a laugh, imagining a factory where one could select just the right British gentleman to work in your tearoom. "Archie lives in the Lancaster area," Jan said. "He's wonderful, isn't he?"

Dorothy nodded.

"Why didn't you just tell us why you were in the tearoom when we called earlier this week?" Elaine asked.

Dorothy looked puzzled. "You started off by asking if I knew anything about a robbery. It sounded like you thought I'd done it myself. Who in their right mind would admit to anything when you start off like that?"

Jan had to admit she could see Dorothy's point. That *had* been why they were calling, and apparently that had been a bit too clear.

"I'm sorry about that," Elaine said. "That was my fault."

"I know this doesn't help now, but in the future, we're always happy to talk and exchange ideas with other small-business owners. Especially local tearoom owners. We have to stick together."

Dorothy looked dubious, but she nodded.

"Would you be willing to show us around?" Elaine asked.

Dorothy hesitated for a second, and then she nodded.

"Sure," she said. For the next few minutes, she showed them the dining room, explaining how she'd repaired the fireplace and found the wallpaper, and then took them on a tour of the kitchen. She admitted she'd been so taken with the homemade cranberry jam she'd had at Tea for Two that she'd experimented with making her own, and Jan couldn't have been more flattered.

A little while later they left, promising to keep in touch, and they wished Dorothy great success with her grand opening this weekend. Then, they trudged back to the car. As Jan buckled herself in, she had to admit she felt deflated.

"I guess that's one suspect crossed off the list," Elaine said, pulling out of the lot and on to the narrow street. Jan nodded. She knew it should be good news. But as they bumped along the rutted road, she couldn't help but think that they were running out of options.

They chatted for a while about Dorothy and her tearoom, and they both hoped she did well, but then they fell silent, and Jan found her mind drifting to Bob and the failed proposal. He'd called last night and asked if she would be free to go for a ride on a boat he'd planned to rent. Sunday afternoon. Jan was hopeful that this time he'd get out what he wanted to ask her. Of course she'd say yes.

Would he want to renovate the house to give them a bit more privacy? She had met his daughter, Susie, a mother of two who did medical billing from home. Susie was charming and very sweet, and they'd gotten along well. But she hadn't met his son Charles, and was nervous about it. She'd gotten the impression from Susie that Charles could be a bit standoffish. Would she get a chance to meet him before the wedding? She hoped so. She...

Just then her cell phone rang. Jan stopped daydreaming and dug her phone out of her purse. She stared at the phone. It was Rose.

"Hello?"

"Hi, Jan. I'm so sorry to bother you. I'm here at the tearoom getting things set up"—Rose had her own key, as she and Archie both sometimes came and left while they were out—"and you guys got a phone call that I thought you might want to know about sooner rather than later."

"Oh?"

"Yeah. Someone named Carrie called. She said you talked to her a few days ago."

Jan nodded. Carrie was the woman whose wallet had been stolen from her cabin at the Green Glade Cottages.

"She wanted to tell you that her wallet has been found."

CHAPTER SEVENTEEN

Jan played the words back over in her head, making sure she'd heard them right.

"Carrie's wallet was *found*?" She pressed the phone to her ear to better hear Rose's voice.

"That's what she said. She told me she thought you'd want to know."

"Where? When?"

"How?" Elaine added from the driver's seat. Jan was glad her cousin had been able to follow the conversation so she wouldn't have to repeat it.

"I don't know. She didn't say, but she did tell me she'd be around the cottages for a while, so if you wanted to talk to her, go there."

"Thank you, Rose," Jan said. "We appreciate it."

"Anytime."

She hung up, then looked at Elaine. "I guess we're going to Green Glade Cottages."

TEN MINUTES LATER, they pulled into the gravel parking lot of the Green Glade Cottages once again, and Elaine and Jan went into the office. Macy directed them to Carrie's cottage, and they made the short walk in record time.

They heard low voices inside, but before they went in, Elaine walked over to a picnic table situated down from the cabin a little ways.

"What are you doing?" Jan asked. Elaine smiled and gestured for her to wait. Elaine set her purse down on the table and shifted the items inside so a black leather wallet was right on top, just barely visible over the edge of the purse.

"Are you nuts?" Jan asked.

"It's a booby trap," Elaine said. She couldn't hold back a smile. This was a great idea, and she knew it. "If the thief is nearby, hopefully she'll see it and we'll catch her in the act."

"But what if we don't catch her in the act?" Jan said. Elaine's cousin clearly thought she was out of her mind. "What if the thief walks away with your wallet?"

"It's a fake," Elaine said, shrugging. She'd left her real wallet, as well as her cell phone, in the car. Even if the thief walked away with the whole purse, it wouldn't be a big loss, as there was nothing valuable inside.

"Are you sure you want to do this?" Jan asked, shaking her head.

"Of course," Elaine said. "Trust me."

Jan didn't seem to know what to say, and Elaine breezed past her and headed back toward Carrie's cabin. As they approached, Trooper Benson opened the screen door and stepped out.

"Hello, Dan." Elaine gave a too-bright smile.

"Elaine. Jan." He let the screen door fall shut behind him. "Fancy meeting you here." He gave them a wry smile.

"Oh, you guys are here," Carrie called from inside. She must have noticed the tension out here, and Elaine silently thanked her. "Thank you so much for coming."

The state trooper looked from Jan to Elaine and back to Jan, and then he shook his head. "Don't mess anything up, okay?" he said as he walked away, still shaking his head.

"Good to see you too!" Elaine called to his retreating back. Jan laughed, and then they turned toward the door.

"Come on in." Carrie held the screen door open. They stepped inside the small cabin. Through the big sliding glass door, they could see a man with dark hair—presumably Carrie's husband—tossing a football around with the kids outside on the flat area behind the picnic table.

Carrie was wearing the same logo sandals, along with a pair of salmon-colored shorts and a crisp white button-down. "The police just left, but I thought you'd want to know too."

"Thank you for calling us." Elaine looked around the small cabin once again. The beds were unmade and suitcases were open, clothes strewn here and there.

"Forgive the mess. We head home tomorrow, and I just couldn't bring myself to spend the last day of our vacation yelling at the kids to clean up."

"Understandably," Elaine said. Jan had wandered off and was looking at something on the dresser, which was also piled with clothing, as well as Carrie's purse. "So what happened?"

"We were coming back from that mini golf place—you know the one, behind the bed-and-breakfast?"

Elaine nodded. "That's very popular."

"No kidding. It took forever to get through it. Especially with those lunatics." She gestured to the back, where her son and husband were wrestling on the ground while the girls stood by quietly. "Anyway, we were driving back when I got a call from that Benson guy."

"Trooper Benson?"

"Yep. Is he the only police officer in this town or what?"

Elaine wanted to laugh. She supposed from the outside it might seem kind of strange that instead of a full police force, they just had one state trooper in town, but crime was usually so minimal around here that it didn't cause a problem for them to only have one dedicated trooper.

"He is," she said.

"Well, he seems nice enough, but Macy seems to think you guys are better at figuring things out than he is, so I thought I'd let you know."

"We appreciate it," Jan said. "So what did he say?"

"He told me my wallet had turned up. Apparently it was in the trash cans behind that cute little general store down the road."

"Murphy's?"

"That's it. Someone there was taking the trash out for collection and saw it in one of the trash barrels, buried beneath some bags. He got it out and thought it might be one of the stolen wallets, so he called the cops. Sure enough, it was mine."

"Could we see it?" Jan had turned away from the dresser and was watching Carrie.

"Sure." She went to her purse and pulled out a buttery white leather wallet with a gold clasp. Elaine didn't recognize the brand, but she could see that it was costly.

"It got a bit banged up," she said, pointing out a small red mark on the front and a brownish stain on the back. Elaine pulled out her phone and took pictures of the wallet. "But I'm so glad to have it back anyway. Plus, a lot of my stuff is still there."

"May I?" Elaine held out her hand, and Carrie handed it over. Elaine opened the wallet and saw that Carrie's driver's license was there, along with some library cards, store discount cards, and a few photos of her kids.

"All the credit and debit cards are gone, but I canceled those anyway," she said. "And obviously the cash is gone."

Elaine looked through each of the slots. She wasn't sure what she was looking for, but she wasn't finding anything out of the ordinary. When she got to the main pocket, where cash was meant to go, she found a handful of receipts.

"I usually stuff my receipts in there and deal with them later—or forget about them," Carrie laughed.

Elaine nodded. She did the same thing. As hard as she tried to keep her wallet clean, she somehow always ended up stuffing receipts into that pocket. She pulled them out now and started looking through them.

The first was from a high-end grocery store in New Jersey. Elaine squinted at the total. Could that number be right? She couldn't imagine how it was possible to spend that much at a grocery store. But Carrie didn't seem fazed, so she set it at the back of the stack and looked down at the next one. This was from a frozen-yogurt shop, and was for about the price of a nice dinner out.

"This yours?" she asked.

Carrie craned her neck and took a look.

"Yep. Me and the kids. Zack wanted three different toppings." She shrugged as if to say *What can you do?*

Elaine didn't say a word, but set the receipt at the back of the stack. She looked through receipts for a manicure, a shopping trip at one of the stores bearing the logo Carrie loved to flash, a haircut and highlight at a pricey salon, and several Starbucks trips. Then she came across one that didn't seem to fit.

Elaine studied the receipt. It was from a drugstore chain popular in the area, specifically from a store in Waterville. The receipt listed the purchases made in the kind of shorthand that made the words fit on one line. Mayblne Lshblst had to be mascara. Revln Chekster was probably blush. Lipstruck was a new brand of lipstick she'd seen ads for. There were several bottles of nail polish too, and in addition to the makeup there were other necessities like soap, deodorant, and toothpaste, as best she could tell.

"Did you buy a lot of drugstore makeup recently?" Elaine asked. She took a picture of the receipt.

Carrie cocked her head. Elaine had a suspicion her makeup came from one of those fancy stores at the mall. And it didn't seem likely Carrie had recently loaded up on nail polish; not when Elaine had just seen receipts for professionals who took care of such things.

"Does this look familiar?" Elaine asked, holding it out.

Carrie leaned in and took a look. Jan leaned in from the other side, and Elaine moved back so her cousin could see.

"This is not mine," Carrie said. Elaine heard both anger and excitement in her voice.

"Look at the date," Jan said, pointing to the small number at the top of the receipt. Elaine saw what she meant. The receipt was from Monday morning. Carrie's wallet had been stolen Sunday.

"The thief bought this stuff," Carrie said, her eyes lighting up.

"And she paid cash," Jan noted.

"Or he," Elaine insisted.

"The receipt is for nail polish, hair dye, makeup, and feminine products," Jan pointed out. "You really think a man bought those things?"

Elaine had to admit she was probably right.

"Did Trooper Benson say anything about this receipt?" Elaine asked.

Carrie shook her head. "I don't think he noticed it." She looked from Elaine to Jan, a smile spreading across her face.

"So," she said, looking at Jan and Carrie, "who's up for a trip to Waterville?"

CHAPTER EIGHTEEN

Jan and Elaine returned from their jaunt to Waterville a while later. They had driven directly from Carrie's cabin to the drugstore the receipt had come from, but they'd been unsuccessful at convincing the manager to allow them to view the store's security camera footage. He'd insisted they would need to come back with the police to view that, and would not let them ask the employees if anyone remembered the purchase. Sadly, it seemed like this time they really did need the police involved. As they drove back to Lancaster, Jan called Carrie and let her know she should tell Trooper Benson to go to Waterville and check it out.

Jan could tell Elaine was disappointed not only about striking out at the drugstore, but also about her booby trap's failure to draw out the thief. As kooky as the idea was, Jan thought it couldn't hurt, but understood that the thief or thieves wouldn't necessarily have been in the places where the purses had been left. If the trap had any chance of working—and Jan was dubious about that—Elaine would have to leave her purse in many more places to try to lure the thief.

Back in Lancaster, the cousins decided to make one more stop before they headed home. They stopped in at Murphy's General Store and talked to Des Murphy about the wallet that had been found in their trash can. Des called his teenage son Nick over, and he described how he'd found the wallet as he was taking the trash out for garbage pickup. Nick was young, but he was generally forthright and honest, and Jan couldn't think of any reason why he would lie about how the wallet had turned up on their property. The logical conclusion was that someone had stolen the wallet, and once they'd taken the cash, dumped the wallet in a trash bin that wouldn't be traced back to them.

The question was, who? Jan was getting more and more frustrated as answers became more and more elusive.

When they got back to the tearoom, Jan was agitated. But she didn't realize how frustrated she was until she'd accidentally slammed the silverware drawer for the third time and Elaine had sent her outside for a bit. Jan, chagrined, sat on the back porch for a few minutes, running her fingers through Earl Grey's soft fur, looking out over the water. She prayed, asking God to direct her steps and to help them solve this mystery. She prayed for her relationship with Bob, and for Elaine and Nathan. Then, when she was feeling calmer, she closed her eyes and listened to the sounds of the boats on the lake and the children playing down by the beach. She let her mind wander.

She thought about Carrie's wallet, and about Lauren's missing one, and Tricia's memory of the blonde woman. She thought about the video footage of the woman at the convenience store, and about the still she'd seen of the blonde woman at the gas station. Something was playing at the edges of her mind, just below the level of consciousness. What was Jan missing in that photograph? She'd already struck out when she'd tried to track down the car through the license plate.

Still, the idea that she was missing some clue in that picture bothered her, so she headed inside and went up to the sitting room, where she used her laptop to pull up the grainy photo Elaine had forwarded her from the gas station again. She looked at the gas pumps, but couldn't see anything she was missing there. She looked again at the woman in the picture. You really couldn't see much about the woman's body, because it was blocked by the car.

If only she could tell what make the car was. Then she would at least have some clue as to what they were looking for on the road, and it might make it easier to search for registration records. But you couldn't see enough of the back end of the car to read the name posted there. All you could see was one half of the trunk area, part of a tire, and a taillight. Maybe some car expert could figure out what kind of car it was, but—

Wait. Jan knew a car expert. She reached for her phone and called her son, Brian, Avery and Kelly's dad. He managed an auto parts store in Augusta and knew more about cars than anyone else she knew. He might be able to help.

"Hello?" Brian said when he answered his cell phone. "Mom?"

"Hi, Brian. How is everything?"

"It's okay. I'm at work though, so I can't talk long."

"Well, in that case, I'll be quick. I'm trying to identify the make of a car."

"What do you have to go on?"

"Part of a tire, half a trunk, and a taillight."

"Do you have a picture?"

"I do."

"Do you mind e-mailing it to me? I'll take a look tonight."

"Sure thing. Thank you, Brian. Love you."

"Love you too. Talk to you later."

She didn't know whether he would be able to identify the car or if it would help in any case, but it somehow felt like she was on the right track.

CHAPTER NINETEEN

Saturday morning, as Elaine was finishing up her devotions and second cup of Earl Grey on the porch, she heard the phone ring. Jan was upstairs taking a shower, so Elaine headed inside and grabbed it.

"Hello?" she said.

"Hi, Elaine?"

Elaine struggled to recognize the voice. "Yes?"

"This is Darlene Iglesias over at the Sugar Plum."

"Oh, hi, Darlene." Elaine brightened. Darlene owned the Christmas gift shop down the road. Elaine loved going in there, where it felt like Christmas all year round. You could purchase hand-blown glass ornaments, fine letter-pressed cards, and keepsakes of all kinds. The store was charming, and tourists and locals alike enjoyed browsing the changing selection all year. "How are you?"

"Well, I've been better, to be honest," Darlene said. Elaine froze. Darlene wasn't one to complain. She was generally upbeat and positive—a natural trait for someone who spent the whole year selling Christmas ornaments, she supposed.

"I came to the shop this morning, and the place had been ransacked."

"What?"

"Racks overturned, ornaments broken, mangers upended."

"Goodness." Elaine shook her head. "Was anything stolen?"

"Yes. The safe was open, and the cash box was gone."

"Oh no." Elaine's stomach sank. This was getting out of hand. This was no longer just pickpocketing. This was breaking and entering, destruction of property, possibly grand theft. "I'm so sorry to hear that."

"It's terrible, isn't it?" Darlene made a noise at the back of her throat. "Well, obviously I called Dan, and he came and took a report. But as he left, he looked around and made a joke about beating you and Jan to the punch this time. He was laughing, and I didn't really think about it until after he left, but it got me thinking. You two are looking into the missing wallets, right? Priscilla Gates told me yesterday you were."

"That's right."

"I hoped that was the case. And, well, I don't want to presume, but I know how many mysteries you've solved around Lancaster, and was wondering if you might want to come take a look."

"Of course." Elaine knew that Jan would be game. "When is a good time?"

"This morning is good."

Elaine knew Jan would be out of the shower soon. "We'll be over shortly."

JAN HAD COME downstairs thinking about what she would do with her six-year-old twin grandsons who were coming to visit this afternoon. Would she take them down to the beach? Maybe out to the sprinkler park over in Waterville? The boys loved that place, but she tended to end up soaked as well. She was just stepping down the last stair when Elaine came flying in from the porch saying something about a break-in at the Sugar Plum. It had taken Jan a moment to make sense of what her cousin was saying, but when she understood, she agreed that they had to get going right away.

It only took them a few minutes to cross Main Street and make their way down to the Christmas shop. The day was already hot and the air felt wet—it would be a steamy one, Jan thought, and she was glad she'd worn a sleeveless linen top.

Elaine pushed open the door of the Sugar Plum, and Jan followed her inside. The store was housed in a small wooden building, and inside, creaky pine floors and tin ceilings made the space feel historic and beautiful, even crammed to the brim as it was with Christmas ornaments, wreaths, statues, crèches, and trees.

"Hi there," Darlene called from the back of the shop, where the cash register stood next to an artificial tree trimmed with delicate glass ornaments in all sorts of shapes. Her long brown hair, threaded with gray, was piled on top of her head in a loose bun, and she wore a beautifully tailored top and long swishy skirt. She looked cool and refined, as always. "Back here."

Jan followed Elaine past racks of quilted stockings and lacy tree skirts to the back. Jan loved Christmas more than most people, but even she had to admit it felt disorienting to be here surrounded by Christmas decorations on a sweltering summer day. But as they got toward the back of the store, she saw at least two trees that had been toppled, ornaments smashed against the floor, and several tables of nativity displays upended.

"You found it like this this morning?" Jan asked.

"Pretty much. This tree had been knocked over too, but I put it back up and have been trying to salvage what I could." She was removing a broken glass drum from one of the branches.

Jan surveyed the damage. The destroyed ornaments alone had to be worth several hundred dollars, not to mention any damage to the display trees and the nativity scenes. Piles of broken glass sparkled on the floor.

"This is horrible. I'm so sorry," Elaine said.

Jan nodded. It really was terrible.

"The thieves really seem to have stepped it up," Elaine continued.

"Yes, this seems to be a whole different level of crime," Darlene added.

They were right, and Jan wasn't sure what to make of it. "Have you determined how the thief got in?"

"It seems like probably the side door," Darlene said, pointing at it. Jan turned and saw that the door had a window on the top portion, with small panes separated by a wooden frame. One of the small panes was broken. "They must have broken the window and reached in to unlock the door."

Jan saw what she meant. She looked at it a moment longer. Something about it seemed off, though she couldn't figure out what.

"You said the cash box was gone?" Elaine asked.

Darlene picked up an angel ornament, looked it over, and hung it on a branch. "Yes," she said. "We broke down the register yesterday at closing just like always and put the money in the cash box in the safe." She indicated a door that led to a small office behind the counter. Jan wandered over and looked inside. The office held a desk, a laptop, and some bookshelves, as well as a small safe. It looked like a pretty standard small business office. But the door of the safe was open, and Jan crouched down look and saw that it had been cleaned out.

"What else was taken?" Jan asked.

"As far as I can tell, that's it," Darlene said.

Jan looked around. Interesting. The laptop was still there, untouched and in plain sight. Jan felt sure it was a newish model, and a good brand very much in demand. Surely there was a secondary market for things like that. So why hadn't the thief taken that as well?

"Do you have any idea how they got the safe open?" Jan asked. It was a standard dark-gray metal safe with a dial lock. Something snagged at the back of her mind.

"That's the strange part," Darlene said. "I don't know. I guess they must have had some kind of code-cracking device or something."

"Do you keep the code written down anywhere?" Elaine asked.

Darlene shook her head. "No need. The code is Tony's birthday. 11-8-55. Neither one of us is going to forget something like that."

Tony was Darlene's husband, a lawyer who did mostly estates and small tax matters in the area. Jan couldn't believe how many people used birthdays as pass codes. Didn't they realize that was the first thing people guessed? She stepped out of the doorway so Elaine could peek into the small office.

"Who all has keys to the shop?" Jan asked.

Darlene gave her a strange look, and then she said, "Well, there's me and Tony. And Melanie, who comes in two days a week. That's it."

Jan had met Melanie. She was a retired school teacher who adored Christmas so much she simply loved being here. She was sweet, simple, and honest. Jan couldn't imagine her being behind this.

"But I don't think limiting this to people with keys makes sense," Darlene said. "Since whoever came in last night didn't use a key."

Jan nodded. She was right, of course. But something still seemed off about this, and she couldn't figure out what.

"Is it just you and Melanie who work here these days?"

"Yep. Well, and Justin, but he's just here for the summer."

"Justin?" Jan stepped toward the table of nativity scenes and picked one up before setting the wooden stable upright. She put the hard-carved wooden Mary and Joseph in their places.

"He's my nephew. My sister's kid. He's gotten into some trouble at school, so my sister sent him here for the summer. Apparently she thinks we can straighten him out."

Jan smiled. She had no doubt Darlene and Tony would help, actually. Their own two children had both gotten scholarships to good colleges, and were well spoken, hard-working, and polite. They were great parents, and she saw why Darlene's sister thought they might help.

"He's been helping out in the shop a couple days a week. To earn his keep, as my sister says." Darlene laughed. "He's a good kid. Just got in with the wrong crowd. I tried to tell her a lot of kids try drugs and it doesn't mean he's a thief, but she's not taking any chances. So we're trying to help him find the right path this summer."

Jan nodded, taking this all in. She found two sheep and set them in their places.

"But he's not behind this," Darlene continued. "If that's what you're thinking. He was home with me and Tony last night. And he only arrived in Lancaster on Monday, so he couldn't have been behind the wallets that were stolen at Pine Tree Grill and the Green Glade Cottages."

Jan nodded. She didn't know what to say. It was possible, of course, that Justin was behind this, even if he had been home in the evening with his aunt and uncle. And just because he couldn't have physically stolen the first two wallets, it didn't mean he couldn't have been involved, or have been behind the later thefts.

On the other hand, it seemed too easy to assume that the troubled teen was behind the break-in. There was no evidence of that, and it didn't seem fair to even suggest it.

"We know for sure," Elaine said, "that he wasn't behind the wallets and the purse. We know it was a woman, or several women, who took those."

"And if Justin had wanted to break in, he could have just taken my keys from the key ring by the door at the house. He wouldn't have needed to break a window."

Jan nodded. Everything Elaine and Darlene said made sense. But it still didn't add up.

They continued to ask questions about when the break-in occurred and look around for a bit. While Elaine listened, Jan fished two wise men out of the branches of the artificial tree next to the table. By the time they left, she was even more convinced something didn't make sense, though she couldn't put her finger on what it was.

"Our thief has just taken a step up," Elaine said as they were on their way home. "We really need to catch this person right away. If we thought the businesses in Lancaster were in danger before, now they really are."

Jan wasn't so sure. But she didn't know what to say, how to explain why it didn't seem so simple to her, so she just nodded.

CHAPTER TWENTY

That afternoon, Jan's grandsons Max and Riley blew into the tearoom, leaving the door wide open behind them. They pounded down the hallway, rushing to the kitchen, where they knew sweet treats always awaited them. Their mom, Amy, Jan's elder daughter, followed a few steps behind.

"Thank you so much for taking them this afternoon," Amy said. Jan barely heard her, as she had already wrapped both boys in a big hug.

"Of course," Jan said as Max wrangled his way free. "I'm glad to."

Riley also broke free now, and before Jan could say anything, they'd made for the counter. She'd set out freshly baked cookies for each of them.

"I'll just be a couple hours," Amy said, turning back toward the hallway. Jan waved. Amy was headed to an eye doctor appointment and understandably did not want two rambunctious boys in tow, and Jan was used to her rushing out the door. Amy always seemed to be rushing wherever she went, though Jan couldn't figure out why she was always in such a hurry. She was married to the vice president of a bank in Augusta, and she could afford to relax a bit by Jan's estimation. But regardless, she was glad for an opportunity to spend the afternoon with her grandsons, and wished Amy would drop them off more often. She was already out the door. That was a discussion for another day.

"Well, well," Archie said, carrying in a tray of leftover sandwiches. "What do we have here? Teenagers?"

"No!" Riley shouted, just before he shoved a cookie into his mouth.

"We're six!" Max added. He was wearing some sort of cartoon dog on his T-shirt, and Jan made a note to ask what it was later. She couldn't keep up with what characters the kids were into these days.

"I could have sworn you were older than that," Archie said, shaking his head. Both boys dissolved into giggles. "So what are you ruffians up to this afternoon, then?"

"Ice cream!" Max shouted.

"I was thinking maybe we could go down to...," Jan started.

"We want ice cream!" Riley echoed his brother. Riley had always been the more timid of the two, following his brother's lead more often than not.

"Well. That was definitive." Archie smiled. "It seems more sugar is in order."

Jan just laughed. She couldn't deny these little monkeys. If it was ice cream they wanted, ice cream they would have. She had already cleared it with Elaine that she would be in and out this afternoon.

"All right then," she said. "Let's go."

"I'll hold down the fort," Archie said dryly.

"Thank you," Jan said, and instructed the boys to head down the hallway quietly and wait for her on the front porch. They were mildly successful—as successful as any six-year-old boys could be expected to be, she supposed—and she grabbed her purse. Then she poked her head into the west parlor and told Elaine she was heading out and invited her to come along. Elaine said she'd keep tending to the handful of customers, but asked Jan to take along her purse and decoy wallet to set a trap for the thief. Jan felt ridiculous, but she agreed, and a few minutes later Jan went out on to the porch and marched the boys down the stairs and out toward the sidewalk. She had her purse slung over one shoulder, and a spare purse of Elaine's, complete with a decoy wallet, on the other.

As they walked, Jan asked the boys about their lives, and discovered they'd recently been to the zoo. While Riley loved the penguins most, Max had been fascinated by the lions. They also told her about some TV cartoon they were into. It seemed to revolve around ninjas, and it sounded terrible to Jan, but they both showed her several ninja kicks as they walked, and they were so cute trying to look like tough men that she found herself smiling.

Soon they made it to I Scream, and after she dutifully dropped the decoy purse down on a red picnic table, they got in line. It was busy today, and while Jan waited in line, she scanned the area. She had an ulterior motive for being here, of course—and it wasn't just Elaine's ridiculous purse trap. She wanted to observe Jenny, and—yes, there she was, inside the building. She was one of three young girls working inside the hut, and she was smiling and chatting with the customers as she dished up their ice cream. The line moved quickly, and when it was Jan's turn to order, it wasn't Jenny who helped her, though Jan was pretty sure Jenny hadn't done anything to avoid her. Jan ordered and paid for two sundaes with the works—what were grandmas for but spoiling their grandkids? Just before she turned to bring the sundaes to the table, Jenny noticed her and smiled and waved. From what Jan could tell, her actions seemed genuine—but then again, she was an actress, so who could say?

Jan handed the dishes of ice cream to the boys, and they carried them carefully to the red table. Jan had to laugh seeing how hard they concentrated on not spilling their ice cream as they walked. It was the most careful she'd seen them be about anything.

No one had touched the decoy purse, naturally. She had to give Elaine credit for trying, but it was kind of a silly idea. She set the purse aside and chatted with the boys about their swim lessons and the camping trip their dad, Van, had promised to take them on. While they ate, she kept an eye on Jenny. She watched as Jenny came out of the building to help a young mom carry all the ice cream for her brood, and then chat and laugh with customers at another table for a few minutes. Then she pulled a rag from her belt and started wiping down empty tables. Jan watched for a sign that anything was off, that Jenny was hiding something or scoping people out, but she came up short. Jenny just seemed like a perfectly normal person doing her job.

Jan couldn't believe how disappointed she was about this.

After the boys had finished their ice cream, Jan threw away their empty dishes and followed the boys toward the parking lot. She tried to act casual, but as the kids were laughing at the fish, Jan was quietly scanning the cars in the lot. What car had Jenny been driving yesterday? Jan felt sure it was a compact, older and a bit beaten up, in a light color. But there was no car like that in the lot. And there was no car with the letters they'd seen in the gas station footage in the first three positions in the lot.

Jan turned back and watched as Jenny helped a young girl climb up onto the picnic bench, balancing a giant chocolate cone. Had Jenny driven a different car today? Why? Did she know her car had been caught on video? Was she was hiding it until things cooled down? Or was it something more innocuous—maybe she'd simply gotten a ride to work today? Whatever the answer was, she left the ice cream shop feeling frustrated. She was getting nowhere.

CHAPTER TWENTY-ONE

Jan and Elaine returned home for a simple lunch of sandwiches and a crisp green salad after a lovely service at Lancaster Community Church on Sunday morning. Attendance was always thin in the summer months when so many people traveled, but Elaine enjoyed the more laid-back feel of the service. Today the accompanist had been away visiting her daughter in San Francisco, so they sang the hymns a cappella, and the unadorned notes sounded almost magical in that sacred space.

As Jan tossed together the salad ingredients, she told Elaine about a conversation she'd had with Christina Brown, who owned the Heavenly Hill Cottages over on the outskirts of Penzance. She'd had three cabins cancel for the upcoming week, she told Jan. Elaine nodded. Macy had told her she'd also had cancelations for the next week. No one wanted to say what they were all thinking—that the thefts really had started to affect tourism.

Elaine tried not to worry about it, even though she'd tallied the week's receipts last night and they'd also seen a significant drop in income. There was no sense worrying about it. Dan Benson was doing everything he could to find the thieves, and so were Elaine and Jan.

After lunch, Elaine shooed Jan upstairs to get ready for her afternoon date with Bob. They were going for a ride on the lake on a boat on a perfect summer afternoon. What could be more romantic? She was certain Bob was planning to propose, and Jan seemed to think so too, judging by the way she didn't argue about heading upstairs to make herself look nice.

Elaine cleaned up the dishes, and then, when Jan came downstairs, she gave her a once-over. She looked very nice in a loose floral dress and sandals. She'd even slicked on a coat of clear lip gloss. Elaine nodded her approval and shooed her out the door, demanding Jan call and update her with good news.

She retreated to her office, planning to take care of some invoices she hadn't gotten to in the midst of their busy week, and then she would take advantage of the Sabbath to relax on the porch and read for a bit.

Elaine didn't want to think too much about what those invoices might mean for the tearoom's bottom line this month. She sat down in front of her computer, intending to open her billing spreadsheet, but instead she opened up Google. She hadn't really intended to run a search on Darlene's nephew. She knew Jan wondered if he was involved in this somehow, but it didn't make sense. Darlene had said he hadn't even been in town until Monday. How could he have been involved in taking the wallets? But she'd just see what she could find.

She Googled the name Justin Iglesias, and found a number of social media profiles. She found a Marine in Florida, a retired teacher in Idaho, and a handful of teenagers, but none lived in Maine, and none looked to be Darlene's nephew.

But on the second page of results she found an Instagram page registered to a Justin Miller. The account mainly showed pictures of teens drinking and making weird faces into the camera. There were several shots of girls with bright lipstick making that fish face all teens seemed to think was attractive these days. She clicked on the profile link, and she saw a photo of a good-looking teen boy with dark hair and a black T-shirt. It listed him as Justin Miller and his hometown as a suburban area outside of Bangor, but in one of the photos she saw a woman who looked so much like Darlene that Elaine was sure it was his mother. So. Justin Miller was Darlene's nephew.

She scrolled through his photos and found two that he'd posted on Sunday. "Saying good-bye" was the caption beneath one of Justin and a girl with heavy eyeliner. It had been taken in front of a sandy stone building. She zoomed in and saw that there was a sign that said Bangor Public Library on the lawn in front.

Well, then. See? He couldn't have been behind the thefts in Lancaster. The proof was right there. He had been in Bangor on Sunday afternoon.

Of course that didn't mean he hadn't been involved in some bigger scam, in the same way that Mark might be. But it didn't add up to Elaine. So far the credit cards had been used to buy gas and groceries, and the cash to buy makeup and other toiletries. It wasn't the kind of stuff teenage boys bought.

Elaine thought back to the receipt from the drugstore. It had definitely been a woman who'd bought those things, she was sure of it. But as she thought about it, something was there at the back of her mind. Something about that receipt. What was on it again?

Elaine grabbed her phone from her purse and scrolled through the pictures she'd taken of the wallet, and then zoomed in on the one of the receipt.

The items purchased were abbreviated, but most of the items listed were pretty easy to make out. Colgate was tooth-paste. Bic Lady 6-pack was razors. That was how they'd figured out that the thief had purchased mostly toiletries and makeup.

She scanned the list, looking for whatever it was her sub-conscious was telling her she'd missed. There were three purchases from a brand named Rio, a well-known nail polish company. On the receipt, each of the purchases was labeled "Rio" and then a number: Rio color N546. Rio color N716, Rio H23.

Elaine studied those entries now. Something was odd about those purchases. She hadn't looked closely before, but now she realized that one was a different format than the others. Two had the letter *N* followed by three digits, while the last one had an *H* and then two digits. Strange. And…Elaine looked over at the prices listed. The first two purchases had each cost $3.99, while the outlier had cost $11.99.

The third entry was not nail polish, Elaine surmised.

But what was it?

She turned to her computer and typed "Rio H23" into the browser.

She couldn't believe what came up. She stared at the screen a moment trying to take it in. It couldn't be. But…

Just then, the office phone rang. Elaine glanced at it and saw that it was Jan calling. Well, that hadn't taken long. Had Bob even waited until they'd gotten on the boat to propose?

She picked up the phone and answered the call. "Already? My goodness. How did he...?"

"Elaine, you need to get down here right away."

"What?" It was Jan all right, but something was wrong. She wasn't happy; she was upset. "What happened?"

"No time to explain. Just hurry. We're at the marina. Come down here now."

Elaine wasn't sure what to make of it, but she knew she had to go. "I'm on my way."

CHAPTER TWENTY-TWO

Elaine was at the marina a few minutes later, but she could see that something was going on before she'd even rounded the bend of the road. A clump of women stood by the railing on the edge of the water, right by the dock that led out into the water and branched off to the various boat slips. A few people were standing around talking to them, including Jan and Bob, John Tuttle, the owner of the marina, and—was that Jack Weston? Elaine felt her shoulders relax a bit. Jack was the game warden, and held a lot of authority in this town. If he was involved, things were probably under control.

Elaine saw that there were several other people standing around, watching the group at the edge of the dock. Whatever had happened seemed to have involved them somehow.

As Elaine got closer, she could see that there didn't seem to be anything terribly wrong with any of the boats tied up in the slips. None of them seemed to be on fire or sinking or anything like that. Just beyond the marina was the boat launch, a small ramp where anyone could load their boat into the water, but aside from a dinghy being loaded into a trailer, there didn't seem to be anything going on there either.

As she approached the small clump of people talking to Jack, Jan saw her and waved, and then she stepped away from the group and came toward her.

"What's going on?" Elaine asked.

"It was the craziest thing." Jan gestured to the boats tied up at their berths behind them. She was keeping her voice low, and half-listening to what Jack was saying to a group of women as she talked. Elaine noticed that Jack had red scratches on his arm. She wanted to ask about them, but decided to just let Jan continue. "We were just stepping on to the boat when we hear a scream from up here." She meant right about where they were standing, Elaine could see. "Well, Bob and I turn, and before we know what's going on, we see a woman running away, a purse tucked under her arm, and Jack Weston barreling up the dock after her."

Elaine's eye widened. A purse. They'd caught her stealing a purse! So where was she?

"Jack got her, and she tried to fight him off, and in the end, she was able to wrangle herself away somehow. He was able to grab the purse, thank goodness."

"Whose purse? Where was it? Who was she?" Elaine had so many questions she didn't even know where to start. How had the woman gotten away? What did she look like? Did anyone see where she'd gone?

"Come on," Jan said, and gestured for her to join her in the group around the women. "Hi there. I mentioned that my cousin was helping me look into the thefts around town. This is Elaine."

"Hi." Elaine looked around at the small group gathered and saw that in addition to Bob, Jack Weston, and John Tuttle, there were four women who looked to be in their early thirties. Elaine didn't recognize any of them, but they were dressed for an afternoon out—capri pants and espadrilles and big sunglasses. Jan moved next to Bob, who pulled her close and started rubbing her arm absently as he took in all that was going on.

"It was Miriam's purse," Jan said, indicating a woman with curly dark hair.

The woman nodded. "We're in a book club together in Augusta"—she gestured at the other women—"and we came here for an afternoon away from our kids. We started with a visit to look at the boats, and then were going to wander into shops and such." She'd clearly already given the others this part of the story, so Elaine didn't want to ask her to go into too many details and slow things down.

"Well, Janice wanted to take a picture of the four of us in front of the boats." Here she glanced at a woman with frizzed blonde hair and white jeans. "So Shelley and I left our purses on the bench right there." She pointed to a wooden bench overlooking the marina. "And we all lined up right here."

"Did someone offer to take your picture?" Elaine asked.

"I have a selfie-stick," the woman who must have been Janice volunteered.

"But while we were all taking the picture, I saw something moving out of the corner of my eye," a thin woman with long brown hair said. "And when I turned and looked, I saw some woman grabbing Miriam's purse."

"What did you do then?" Jan asked.

"I screamed, and she started running."

"And then out of nowhere, this guy comes barreling after her," Janice said, a hint of a smile on her face. So she'd noticed Jack then. She was just the latest to fall victim to Jack's charms. Tall, strapping, tan, and commanding authority, Jack Weston had caught the eye of many single women in town, but sadly for them he seemed to be interested in Jan's daughter Tara.

"I was over at the office talking to John"—Jack nodded at John Tuttle, a man in his sixties with white hair and blue eyes—"checking to make sure the boat registrations were up to date." Jack indicated a small wooden shed at the edge of the pier, right next to where the dock branched out. "I heard her scream." If Jack had noticed the attention all four of the younger women were paying him, he didn't show it. Maybe he was just so used to deflecting female attention it didn't affect him anymore. "So obviously I came running."

"I came too, but a little slower," John said, a self-deprecating smile on his face.

"And what? You wrestled her to the ground?"

"Not exactly," Jack laughed. "I grabbed the purse handles, and she fought it and tried to push me away, even gave me a real good swipe, claws out and everything." He gestured at the scratches on his muscled arm, which weren't bleeding but were a deep shade of pink. "She gave in when I yanked it away. Well, the force of that threw me for a second, just long enough for her to get away."

"Where did she go?"

"Over to the parking area." He gestured at the row of spaces lined up perpendicular to the edge of the wharf. "I got over there as fast as I could, but that SUV was in the way, so I didn't get a real good look at the car."

"It was a small car," the one with brown hair—Shelley, she must be—volunteered. "And a light color. White, or maybe silver."

"Did you get a look at the license plate?" Jan asked.

"No." The woman laughed nervously. "I was too busy trying to make sense of what had just happened."

"What did she look like?" Elaine asked.

"I couldn't tell," Jack admitted, shaking his head. "I was so focused on catching her, I didn't even really notice."

"Was she tall? Short?"

"I think she was tall," Miriam said. "And her hair was red."

"I don't know. I would have said brown," Janice said. "But she had a hat."

"What kind of hat?"

"A baseball cap, I think," Miriam said. "Maybe black?"

Elaine couldn't believe it. She knew that things moved quickly in the moment, but this was the first time someone had actually made direct contact with one of the thieves, and no one could be sure of the details. She either had brown hair or red hair, might have worn a hat, and could be tall or short. "Bob? Jan? Did either of you see her?"

"I wish," Jan said, leaning back into Bob. "But we weren't quick enough."

"By the time we got over to where we could see around the gatehouse, Jack was already coming back with the purse," Bob added. He shook his head. She could tell he was disappointed. He no doubt wished he'd been able to do more. Elaine knew she should just be grateful Jack had been there to stop her. But she couldn't help wishing someone had caught more than a passing glimpse of the thief.

"Was anything taken from the purse?" Elaine asked.

"No, thankfully, it's all in there," Miriam said.

They continued to chat for a few minutes, and Elaine gathered that they were waiting for the police to arrive and take a statement. While the others continued to recount the event, Elaine looked around. The marina had to have security cameras.

"John, are there any surveillance cameras around here?" Elaine asked.

"Yes, but they only point out that direction," the marina owner said, indicating the boats tied up in the water. "For some reason, none of them point at the wharf or the parking lot."

It was probably worth reviewing the footage anyway, just to make sure the cameras hadn't picked up anything strange. But was there any other way to see what had happened? It was a beautiful sunny day, and there were lots of people around. Surely someone had seen something?

"We asked everyone in the vicinity before you got here," Jan said, reading her mind somehow. "No one saw anything. It really was fast. From the time she grabbed it to the time Jack was back with it couldn't have been more than fifteen seconds."

Elaine tried to picture the whole scenario in her head. There had to be a way to trace her. She looked around. Were there any other cameras around anywhere?

And then it was so obvious she almost laughed right out loud.

"You were taking a picture over here, right?" Elaine indicated the area where they'd said they'd lined up for the photo.

"Yep." The unnamed one nodded.

"Could I see the camera you used?" Elaine asked.

Janice nodded and pulled her phone out of her own purse, which was now tucked under her arm. She typed in a code to unlock the screen and handed it over. Elaine touched the icon for pictures, and an app opened that showed the photos taken on the phone.

The last photo was a blur, no doubt taken just after Shelley had screamed. She used her finger to swipe to the right, and found a nice group shot of the women. They were centered in the frame, and you could see the boats bobbing at the marina behind them, and beyond that, the smooth surface of Lake Chickadee. She swiped right again, and found another picture of the women, a bit off-center this time. But at the edge of the frame, the end of the bench where the purses had been set was just barely visible. On a hunch, she swiped right again, and found a similar image, but even more off-center. This shot was angled so the women were at the far right, and there, in the left of the screen . . .

Elaine gasped. "There she is."

She used two fingers to zoom in on the woman, who was just approaching the bench in this picture. She wore a blue baseball cap with some kind of sunburst on it, and her reddish hair poked out from underneath. She wore big round sunglasses that hid most of her face. She hadn't been caught in the act or anything—they hadn't been that lucky—but Elaine felt certain of it. This was her.

"Let me see." Jack reached out for the phone, and Elaine handed it over. "That's her, all right." He nodded and handed it back to Miriam, who gasped and put her hand over her mouth.

"That's her!" she said. "That's totally the woman who stole my purse!"

She passed the phone around, and the others agreed that this was certainly the woman who had attempted the theft. The others got more and more excited as they realized what they had. But Elaine felt her heart sinking. This wasn't the blonde woman in the still shot from the gas station, nor was it the woman with brown hair the grocery clerk had described and who'd been in the convenience store footage. In this photo it was clear the woman's hair was deep red. And she was fairly tall.

Suddenly Elaine's heart raced. She had a feeling she finally knew what was going on.

CHAPTER TWENTY-THREE

By the time Dan Benson had arrived and talked to each of the women and Jack, as well as taken Bob and Jan's statement, the afternoon was passing quickly, and Bob had floated the idea of postponing their boat ride. Jan was disappointed, but she understood. This wasn't how she'd imagined their engagement beginning either, and she saw why Bob thought it might be better to hold off. They would have the rest of their lives together; a few days didn't make a difference, really.

"I'm sorry your afternoon was ruined," Elaine said as they headed back toward the tearoom.

"It wasn't ruined," Jan insisted, and she was surprised to hear that she sounded like she believed it. "It's fine. We'll take a boat ride another day."

"I know it wasn't the boat ride that you were looking forward to," Elaine insisted, and Jan nodded and shrugged. She was disappointed, but her mind was also swirling with the events of the afternoon. "Well, if it makes you feel any better, I think I figured something out before you called," Elaine said.

"Oh?" Jan was touched that Elaine was trying to make her feel better.

"You know that receipt from the drugstore in Waterville we found in Carrie's wallet?" she asked, looking at Jan. Jan nodded. "We thought she'd bought three bottles of nail polish. But I noticed something was strange and did some research, and I realized that one of the purchases was actually a package of hair color."

"Really?" Jan looked at Elaine.

"Really. And guess what color the dye was?" Elaine smiled. "Red."

"Red?" Jan saw what Elaine was getting at now. That meant . . .

"Well, warm copper, technically. But red. Which means . . ."

"The woman at the marina with red hair could be the blonde."

"Exactly." Elaine looked at her cousin again, and Jan smiled.

"Oh my." Jan ran through what all this meant in her head. If one of their suspects really had dyed her hair red, then they were no longer looking for a blonde and a brunette. And since the hair dye had been bought on Monday, it could have been any time since then that she'd dyed her hair. Which meant . . .

"What do you think about making a quick stop for ice cream?" Elaine asked, a knowing smile on her face.

Jan nodded. "I think that is an excellent idea." Jenny's hair had been blonde the previous day, but they could check and see what color Jenny's hair was now. "Especially because I noticed something in one of the pictures."

Elaine's eyebrows raised.

"The baseball cap the thief was wearing?"

Elaine nodded, waiting for her to go on.

"It had the logo for Colby College on it." She had recognized the sunburst logo of the nearby college immediately.

"Oh, wow."

Jan knew that Elaine understood what that meant. Two of their suspects were students at Colby. One of them was a woman. "Which means we really need to have a chat with Jenny," Jan said.

"Yes we do," Elaine said. "Yes we do indeed."

They walked in silence for a few minutes, passing Oldies But Goodies and Gift Me and their own house. Then Jan spoke.

"Could they all be the same person?" Jan asked. She tried to figure out how that would work. Maybe their suspect dyed her hair regularly, changing it up almost daily so as not to be recognized? Or maybe it was just a temporary dye?

"I was wondering about that too," Elaine said. "And I can maybe see how someone might be changing their hair color. Especially since we now have proof that they bought hair dye. But what I can't make sense of is the differences in height and weight."

Jan nodded. She couldn't figure that out either. The cashier at the grocery store had described a short, heavy woman, and the video footage from the convenience store showed the suspect there not even topping five foot six. But the woman at the gas station had been thin in addition to blonde. Tricia had described the woman as tall as well. Jan couldn't see how anyone could change those fundamental things about herself.

"It doesn't seem possible one person could be behind this all," she said. Elaine nodded, but didn't answer. They walked in silence for a few minutes more.

"What?" Jan asked. She could see Elaine was mulling something over.

A crooked smile appeared on Elaine's face. "I was just thinking how my strategy would have worked."

Jan laughed. "All right, fine. I'll admit it. Your strategy of leaving your purse laying around might have worked today, if you'd happened to be where the thief was at just the right time."

"Thank you."

"That doesn't mean I think it's a great strategy for catching the thief in general, but it might have lured her in this case."

"All I heard you say is that I was right."

Now they both laughed, and they walked in companionable silence, each lost in her thoughts, until they arrived at I Scream a few minutes later. Jan quickly scoped it out. Jan's heart sank when she found Jenny serving ice cream behind the glass partition. Her hair was blonde. Unless she'd somehow dyed her hair back to blonde in the hour and a half since the theft, the woman at the marina wasn't her. But Jan couldn't ignore the connection to the college. They had to talk to her.

"I guess we have to get in line if we want to talk to Jenny," Elaine said, smiling.

"This is a rough gig," Jan answered, and followed her cousin to the back of the line. This place was hopping on a sunny Sunday afternoon, and even with two windows open, the line was several customers deep. But they'd only been waiting for a few minutes before Anita Picard saw them and came up to them.

"Jan, Elaine, how are you?" she asked. "Did you hear? There was another incident today, down at the marina! Can you believe it?"

Jan knew better than to be surprised by how quickly news traveled in this town. "Actually, we were just down there," she said. "That's why we're here now. The suspect in that incident was wearing a baseball cap with a Colby logo. And we were hoping to talk to Jenny."

"To see if she recognizes the woman, since she goes to Colby," Elaine added. It was close enough to the truth—that was part of why they wanted to talk to her—that Jan nodded.

"Of course." Anita seemed awed by how much they knew. Jan could tell she wanted to ask more questions, but instead she simply nodded and said, "Jenny has been here all afternoon. I can vouch for that. But I'll go in and send her on her break."

"Thank you."

Jan tried not to be disappointed that they didn't need to order ice cream after all. They took a seat at one of the tables near the koi pond, and a few minutes later, Jenny came out of the building, looked around, and smiled when she saw them.

"Hi there," she said, approaching. "Anita told me you wanted to talk with me."

He face was open, her smile genuine. Nothing in her manner gave the impression that she had anything to hide. Then again, was she just a good actress? But she had to know that they thought of her as a suspect. Would even a Broadway star be able to look so cheerful and, well, innocent, in this situation? Then again, maybe Jenny didn't seem nervous because she didn't see them as threatening. Talking with two older tearoom owners was hardly the same as being interrogated by the police.

"Thank you for talking with us," Elaine started. "We were hoping you could help us with something."

"Of course." Jenny smiled and looked from Elaine to Jan expectantly.

"I'm not sure if you've heard, but there was another attempted theft today down by the marina," Jan said, watching her carefully.

"Oh no!" Jenny's brow creased, and she shook her head. "I hadn't heard."

Was she telling the truth? It seemed to Jan that she was. And she hadn't been behind the attempted robbery, she was now sure. Between the hair and Anita's assurances that she'd been working, there was no way Jenny could have been the woman down at the waterfront. But that didn't mean she wasn't tied to this somehow.

"A woman tried to swipe a purse, sort of like what happened here," Elaine said. "We have a picture of the woman, and we noticed that she was wearing a Colby hat. You go to Colby, right?"

Jenny nodded, her blonde hair cascading down her shoulders and catching the sun. Elaine pulled out her phone and opened the picture she'd had the women send her.

"We were wondering if you recognized her," Jan said as Elaine held out the phone.

Jenny took the phone and looked down at the screen. She used two fingers to zoom in on the picture. She stared at the enlarged image of the woman for a minute, and then she shook her head.

"I'm sorry," she said as she continued to look down at the screen. "It's really hard to make anything out about her, but she doesn't look familiar."

A small boy was holding out a stick at a small box turtle perched on the rocks at the edge of the koi pond. He reminded Jan of Brian, who'd been fascinated by wildlife of all kinds when he was young.

"Are you sure?" Elaine asked. "I wondered if she might go to college with you."

Jenny let out a breath and shook her head again. "She might very well be a student. But with the hat and the sunglasses, it's really hard to tell anything about her. Based on what I'm seeing here, I don't recognize her."

Jan realized she'd been hoping something about Jenny's reaction would feel off. She had really hoped Jenny would betray in some way that she was hiding something. But all Jan got from her reaction was that Jenny was telling the truth.

"You know what's scary?" Jenny said, moving the picture so she could study the background better. "It's that this kind of thing happens all the time these days."

Jan glanced at Elaine, who met her eye and raised her eyebrow.

"What do you mean?" Jan asked.

"There were a bunch of thefts similar to this one at college last spring. This kind of thing must be happening all the time and we just don't hear about it."

"I don't know that it happens all the time," Elaine said carefully.

"But can you tell us about these thefts at your college?" Jan asked. Colby was in Waterville, just twenty minutes away. Was it possible...?

"It was the craziest thing," Jenny said. She swung her legs around so she was facing the picnic table. "People's wallets kept disappearing from their purses in the library."

"What do you mean?" Jan asked.

She shrugged. "Girls would be studying at the library, and they'd leave all their stuff at their desk while they went out to make a phone call or to send a text. And when they'd come back, their wallets would be missing. It totally freaked me out at the time, and it made me paranoid about leaving my purse unattended anywhere. You never know where this kind of thing will happen."

Did she really believe repeated thefts like this happened all around her, every day? Sure, crime was a part of life, but two similar patterns of thefts in a short span of time in a similar geographic area seemed to be more than just general probability. Or did she really not see the connection?

"How many girls had their wallets stolen?" Jan looked at Elaine, and could see by the way she was leaning toward Jenny that she was as intrigued by the possibilities of this news as they were.

"I don't know. Maybe four or five?"

"Just women?"

"Just wallets taken from purses, I think." Jenny shrugged. "But then, most guys keep their wallets in their pockets, so it would be harder to take wallets from guys."

"Did any of them get their wallets back?"

The boy had now abandoned the stick and was reaching out for the turtle, but his mother stopped him. He stomped away. Jan had to suppress a laugh. Little boys were all the same.

"I'm not sure," Jenny said. "I never heard about if they did."

"Did they ever catch the thief?" Elaine asked.

Jenny shrugged. "If they did, I didn't hear about that either. The school year ended, and I left campus, so I can't be sure."

Jan tried a different tactic. "Do you know if there were any theories about who was behind those thefts?"

"I really don't know. I'm sorry. I don't spend that much time in the library, and I just heard about it through friends. But I know it was happening and it's eerie how similar these thefts here are."

Eerie was one way to phrase it. Jan didn't believe in coincidences. And, unlike Jenny, she didn't believe groups of thefts like this just happened all the time. Someone—or several someones—was behind this, and Jan was beginning to believe it was the same person who had made a target of Colby College women in the spring.

"Thank you for your help," Jan said. She could see that they weren't going to get anything more useful out of Jenny. Once again, Jan thought she was either a very good actress or she genuinely didn't know anything more. At this point, Jan was betting it was the second option. "We'll let you get back to work."

"I wish I could be more help," Jenny said. "Please let me know if there's anything else I can do."

"We will." Jan pushed herself up, and Elaine followed. As soon as they were out of earshot, Jan looked at Elaine.

"So," she said, and Elaine smiled, "I guess we need to look into some thefts at Colby College?"

"You read my mind."

CHAPTER TWENTY-FOUR

That evening, once they'd enjoyed a light dinner, the cousins moved out on to the porch. Elaine had her laptop tucked under her arm as they both settled into the wicker chairs. The sun was hanging low in the sky, catching golden light that sparkled and danced on the surface of the lake. They could see diners on the deck of Pine Tree Grill taking in the view, and neighbors up and down the lakefront settling out on porches to enjoy the night. One boat was still out on the lake, towing a tube with two shrieking children behind it. Their laughter filled the air around the quiet lake.

"Where do you think we should start looking for information about the thefts at Colby?" Jan asked.

Elaine dragged her eyes away from the idyllic lake and opened her laptop. "I think I'll start with Google," Elaine said, and she typed in "Colby College wallet theft."

The first article that came up was from the Colby College newspaper, with the headline "Another Library Theft: Is Anyone Safe?"

"Seems a bit dramatic," Jan noted.

Elaine agreed, but she clicked on the link and started skimming. It was much like Jenny had said. The article was about the fourth theft that had taken place in the Colby library. In each case, students had been in the library studying and had gone outside to use their cell phones—the library got notoriously bad cell signals, apparently—and had left their things on top of their desks.

"You'd think after the first couple thefts, people might have started taking their things with them," Jan said.

"Well, college kids. You know how they're all invincible." But secretly Elaine agreed. It seemed foolish that students had kept leaving their things out in the open. Then again, college students were not always the most rational of creatures.

Something caught Elaine's eye down by the edge of the water, where the grass sloped down toward the dock. Elaine looked again, and then she watched as lightning bugs started to twinkle in the evening air. They were beautiful.

At the end of the article was a link to a previous piece that had appeared in the paper a few days before, about how the campus police were still looking for information about the third such theft. Elaine pulled up the article and skimmed it, then tilted the computer screen so Jan could see it better.

After Jan had read it, she said, "All the thefts happened in the library."

Elaine nodded. That seemed pretty clear.

"Why do you think that is?"

The boat lugging the tubers had slowed and was headed in toward a dock a little ways up the shoreline now. More lights were twinkling on as twilight deepened into evening.

"I don't know," Elaine said. "Maybe that's the only place students leave their bags unattended?" But even as she said it, she doubted that. A college campus felt like a safe haven for students, Elaine knew. The whole place felt like home to them. She bet kids were leaving their stuff unattended lots of places on campus. "Or maybe it's a good place for a thief to hide? With all those stacks of books and weird little nooks and crannies you get in every library, maybe it makes the most sense. The thief would hide out between rows of shelves, looking for bags left out. It wouldn't be that hard to dash out from between the stacks, grab a wallet from an unattended purse, and dash back into the cover of the shelving."

"Maybe," Jan said. "Or maybe there's a more logical explanation." She indicated she wanted the laptop, and Elaine handed it over. Elaine watched as Jan opened a new browser window and typed something quickly. But before Elaine could make it out, Jan was already navigating a search page and clicking on a link. She watched as a page opened.

"Genius," she said. It was the Web site for the Colby College library. There was a place where you could search the library's holdings and an announcement about a special exhibit in the front gallery, and then, on the far right side, toward the bottom of the page, there was a section with photos of the library staff. Elaine watched as Jan scrolled down the pictures and stopped when she came to one. She enlarged the photo. Elaine leaned in to take a closer look.

"What do you think?" Jan asked. "I think this could be the woman from the convenience store security footage still."

Elaine looked at the woman in the picture. She had shoulder-length brown hair and a narrow face. She was wearing a button-down shirt and big glasses.

"I don't know," Elaine said. The hair was right. But you couldn't really see much of anything in that picture at the convenience store. "It could be, I guess."

"I guess it is kind of a leap," Jan said, clicking to make the picture return to normal size. Elaine noted that the name under the picture was Jade Lacombe, and her title was Associate Research Librarian. Elaine nodded, and Jan continued to scroll down the page. There was another woman, Lisa Nordstrom, with the same title, who had shoulder-length graying blonde hair. As far as Elaine was concerned, she was as likely to be a suspect as Jade, but she couldn't really tell. None of the images they'd seen gave them nearly enough information to be able to really tell much about the suspects they were looking for.

"Are there any articles that say the thief was caught?" Elaine asked.

Jan went back to the first search window and systematically looked through all the articles that came up in the school newspaper.

"No. Not that I can tell." Jan clicked back over to the library's Web site and looked again at the profile pictures.

There was nothing to say that the thief worked at the library, she knew. It could just as easily have been a student, or a janitor, or anyone else who could have wandered the floors unnoticed. Or, as in their own case, there might very well be more than one person involved. A theft ring of some kind. Or a copycat thief.

But Elaine had a feeling about this. It was too much of a coincidence to not look into further at the very least.

"Well, I guess we know what our next step is," Jan said.

Elaine felt a smile spread across her face. "I guess we're going to visit Colby."

CHAPTER TWENTY-FIVE

Elaine startled awake. What had woken her?

The moon was casting a beam of light in through Elaine's open window, and the soft breeze ruffled the curtains gently. She listened, lying in bed, waiting. Was it some noise from out on the lake?

Then she heard it again. A scraping noise, and then a thump. And it wasn't on the lake. It was inside the house.

Elaine sprang out of bed and grabbed the closest thing to a weapon she could find, her table lamp. She yanked the cord from the wall and clutched the brass-finish lamp in one hand, and held up her cell phone as a flashlight in the other, and then she headed out of her bedroom. She paused at the top of the stairs. She heard footsteps. Someone was definitely downstairs. She glanced at Jan's door. It was closed, the light off. Elaine briefly thought about waking her, but then decided there was no time to spare. She began heading down the stairs, clutching the banister carefully. The footsteps stopped. Elaine hesitated.

"Who's there?" she called out.

Instead of an answer, there was a burst of activity. Someone flew out of the office and into the kitchen. Elaine yelled, and the figure cursed and ran out the door. She fumbled for the light switch and flipped it on, and the kitchen and hallway were flooded with light. Whoever had been in the office was gone, but Elaine wasn't sure if anyone else was in the house.

"What in the world?" Jan came downstairs in her floral nightgown, rubbing sleep from her eyes.

"Someone was here," Elaine said. "Someone was in the house."

"What?" Jan woke up quickly. "Are they still here?"

"One person ran out. I don't know if there's anyone else."

Jan crouched behind Elaine as they moved together toward the door of the office. No one was inside. Then they moved toward the kitchen and looked behind the island and in the cupboard. Elaine's heartbeat started to slow as they continued to search the rest of the rooms on the ground floor and discovered them empty. She set the lamp down on the counter.

"He must have come in the door to the screened porch," Elaine said. "That's how he went out."

"He?"

Elaine nodded. She wasn't sure why, but she thought it was a man. Could it have been Mark Hamilton? She wasn't sure.

"I locked that kitchen door before bed," Jan said. "I know I did."

Elaine went over to examine the door. It was just a doorknob lock, she realized. Not a deadbolt. Easy to pick. She looked around but didn't see anything else out of place.

"I'll call 911," Jan said, and Elaine nodded. Whoever it was had gone, but the police needed to know about this. What did they want? Had someone been trying to send them a message? Or was it simply another theft in Lancaster? And what kind of world was it when "simply another theft in Lancaster" was something people really said?

Elaine moved carefully toward the door of the office, where the thief had emerged from. At first nothing looked out of place. The desk and chair and bookshelves were exactly where they were supposed to be. The filing cabinet was there. Gingerly, so as not to disturb any fingerprints left behind, she opened the drawers and peeked inside. But they looked fine. Even her laptop was still on the desk where it belonged. Then she noticed something.

The drawer on the desk, the locked one where she kept the money box...there were scratch marks on the wood around the lock. She studied them, not touching them in case there were fingerprints, and then she looked down at the floor and saw an unfolded paper clip.

Someone had used a paper clip to try to pick the lock. Someone had broken in to steal from them. But how could anyone have known where she kept her money box?

Elaine's heart sank. This wasn't some random theft. This was someone who knew what they were doing. This was targeted. She felt violated. She felt afraid. And, inexplicably, she felt confused. Things were escalating from random wallet grabs to targeted breaking and entering. Were the thieves getting bolder? Or was this some new thief, inspired by—or hoping to take advantage of—the thefts to start their own copycat ring?

Either way, they were all in trouble. After tonight, she realized the truth—no one was safe, not even in their own home.

CHAPTER TWENTY-SIX

Jan, bleary-eyed and raw from the frightening night, still had to grin when she saw the front page of the *Penzance Courier* the next morning. "Theft Thwarted by Quick-Thinking Game Warden; Lancaster Grateful for His Fast Actions." It was true enough, but it was the photo that accompanied the article that got Jan laughing. In it, a muscular-looking Jack Weston was front and center, and the four women who'd been taking the picture surrounded him, all making goo-goo eyes at him.

Jan couldn't help herself, and she could use a light conversation after the night she'd just had. She picked up the phone and called her daughter Tara, who lived nearby. Tara was a jewelry designer whose pieces were carried at some local stores.

"Hi, Mom," Tara said.

"Hi, sweetie. I hope I didn't wake you."

"Nah. I was just doing some yoga. How are you?"

"I'm fine. I just wanted to know if you'd seen the paper this morning." She decided not to bring up the events of the night before—no need to worry Tara.

"Nope. Not yet. Why?"

"It looks like you have some competition."

"What?"

"There was another theft yesterday down at the marina. Bob and I were there, but we didn't see it firsthand. But Jack Weston did, and he chased the woman down and rescued the purse. And on the front page of the paper, you'll see four women very much taken with your boyfriend."

"He's not my boyfriend."

"Well, maybe he should be." Jack was quite a catch, after all. It was high time for Tara to settle down.

"Mo-om." Tara sighed. "We've only gone out a couple of times. I like him, but we're just seeing where things go."

"All right." Jan knew you couldn't force things like this. "I just wanted you to know."

"Uh-huh. Thanks, Mom. Now I have to get back to my downward-facing dog."

"That sounds painful."

"Bye, Mom."

Jan hung up and looked down at the picture from the marina for another moment, but her mind kept drifting back to the break-in at their home last night. Arnie Sheffield, the Kennebec County sheriff's deputy, had responded to their 911 call, and he had dutifully taken notes and fingerprints. He had counseled them to change the lock on the porch door, which they'd already decided to do, and promised to be in touch if they found anything. Jan was not optimistic. All she knew was, they needed to step things up and put a stop to this madness now.

Which was why they were headed to Waterville this morning. After she'd done the baking and Elaine had eaten, they got in Elaine's car and made the quick drive to Waterville to visit Colby College. For as long as she'd lived in the town, Jan hadn't spent much time on the college campus, aside from an odd lecture or performance at the theater. She was glad Elaine seemed comfortable navigating the collection of red brick buildings sprinkled around the leafy green lawns.

It was charming, that was for sure. Jan could imagine lazing under the trees on an autumn day with a book and a cup of tea. Jan had attended college briefly, planning to major in engineering, but she'd had to drop out for financial reasons. Usually this didn't bother her; she knew life was all about learning, and she had been constantly reading and learning throughout her life. It was only when she came to places like this that she felt a pang of remorse for what she hadn't had. Still, all three of her kids had had the opportunity to go to college, and Jan was immeasurably proud of that.

It wasn't hard to find the library, it turned out. It was the most striking building on campus, a three-story red brick building with a white portico held up by stately columns and a tall white clock tower on top. It was a gorgeous building, with a green lawn in front of it that sloped down toward a lake.

Elaine parked in a nearby lot, and headed toward the front door like she owned the place. Jan followed a few steps behind. They walked up the big stone steps and in through the front doors. Inside, the air was cool, a nice change from the warm morning. They were standing in a large, airy atrium. Jan looked around at the high ceilings, the polished floors, and the stacks of books just barely visible beyond the imposing front desk. Elaine was already marching right up to the front desk.

"Hi. I'm Elaine Cook." Elaine smiled. A bored-looking girl who couldn't be much out of her teens looked up from what appeared to be a chemistry textbook.

"Hi," the girl said. She was thin and pale and had a bluish-green streak in her strawberry-blonde hair. "Can I help you?"

The library was eerily quiet, Jan thought, but then she remembered that it was summertime, and most of the students would be off campus.

"I'd like to speak with Jade Lacombe," Elaine said.

Wow. She was going for the direct approach then. Jan held her breath.

It took a minute for the girl to respond. Jan tried to read her expression in that time, but she couldn't make out what was going on.

"I'm afraid Jade doesn't work here anymore," the girl finally said. She set her book down and looked up at Elaine.

"Oh," Elaine said, casting her eyes at Jan. "When did that happen?"

The girl shifted in her seat. "A few weeks ago, I guess. I'm not really sure."

Jan couldn't tell if she really wasn't sure or just didn't want to say.

"Can you tell me why she doesn't work here anymore?" Elaine asked.

The girl watched Elaine for a moment, and then she shook her head. "I guess maybe she got a new job somewhere else?"

"Do you happen to know where she got a new job?" Jan asked.

The girl looked up like she hadn't noticed Jan before.

"I'm sorry, I don't really know," she said. She looked around, like she was checking to see if anyone else was around. Then, she said, "Look. All I can tell you is, she stopped working here right toward the end of the semester, and no one really talked about why. She was just gone one day, and they really kept it quiet what happened."

Now this was starting to sound plausible.

"Is there anyone around here who might be able to tell us more about what happened?" Elaine asked. The girl glanced at a door behind her. It looked to Jan like it led to offices, but it was hard to tell.

"Normally I'd tell you to talk to the director, but I'm afraid she's in Italy right now. And my boss isn't in yet. So I'm not really sure what to say."

Jan looked at Elaine.

"We're also interested in finding out more about the thefts that happened here in the library this spring," Jan said. "Can you tell us anything about that?"

"I don't know," the girl said. "What do you want me to tell you?" Then, quickly, she added, "You guys aren't from a newspaper, are you?"

"No." Jan smiled. "Though I'm flattered you think we could be reporters."

The girl shrugged. "We have strict instructions not to talk to reporters about this."

Well, that was interesting. Jan met Elaine's eye again.

"I promise we're not reporters," Elaine said. "But I am curious as to why the school was so insistent about that." Elaine leaned forward to rest her arms on the desk. Elaine seemed to think this was a friendly gesture, but Jan noticed the girl lean back slightly. "Is there anyone else we could talk to about that?"

"Uh..." The girl looked around as if searching for answers. "I'm not sure. I think it's because it looked bad, all those girls getting their wallets taken. Parents and alumni don't like to hear about that kind of thing. This really is a very safe campus."

"How many wallets were taken?"

Just then, a woman wearing a pencil skirt and white blouse breezed in through the front door. "Hi, Hilary," she said, ducking behind the big counter through a door to the side. "Sorry I'm late. Rex's dentist appointment ran long." Without stopping, she went right through the door that led to the offices.

"Look," Hilary said. She glanced at the door that the woman—no doubt her boss, Jan thought—had just vanished behind, and then turned back to them. "All I can say is that there hasn't been a wallet stolen since right before the end of the semester."

"At the same time as Jade stopped working here suddenly."

"Yes. But also the time when students stopped spending time in the library and started packing up to go home for the summer. So it's hard to say why."

"But you can say that the thefts ended right around the time Jade mysteriously stopped working here."

"I didn't say mysteriously," Hilary said. "But quietly, yes. But then again, most of the students went home too, so there's not necessarily a connection."

"Thank you," Elaine said.

"You've been very helpful," Jan added. They turned to go, and neither one said anything until they were back in the car.

"It was her," Elaine said, pulling her seat belt across her lap.

"We don't know that. It could have been a student."

"Could have," Elaine said as she started the car. "But wasn't."

"There's no way to say that for sure," Jan said. "Besides, even if it was her, there's no way to connect her to what's happening in Lancaster."

"There's no way to connect her to it *yet*," Elaine said. She put the car in gear and checked her mirrors. "That's our next step."

CHAPTER TWENTY-SEVEN

J an's granddaughter Avery came flying at them when they got back to the tearoom. Elaine couldn't help the small flutter in her heart when she saw her. Avery was Jan's granddaughter, but she had a special place in Elaine's heart.

"Grandma, guess what? Rose is showing me how to make macarons," Avery announced before they'd even closed the front door. She stood at the end of the hallway, by the kitchen, holding a pastry bag. Avery was only twelve, but she'd taken quite an interest in baking, and she was a frequent visitor to their kitchen.

"That's wonderful," Jan said, and pushed the door shut. "And what a lovely surprise to find you here."

"Oh yeah. Mom called to see if she could drop us off because she had some dentist thing, but you didn't answer," Avery said. "She figured it would be okay."

"Of course." Jan was fishing around in her purse, looking for her cell phone. She was really bad at answering it, Elaine knew.

"I'm delighted you're here." Elaine indicated that Avery should give her a hug, and she did, being careful to hold the pastry bag away from Elaine. When she pulled back, Elaine asked, "Where's your sister?"

"She's playing out on the dock."

"Sounds nice and safe." Elaine wasn't really worried. Avery's sister, Kelly, was naturally athletic and swam like a fish. Even if she somehow ended up falling in the lake, she would be fine.

"Oh yeah, I do have a message from your mom," Jan said, looking down at her phone.

Avery laughed. "I hope you tell her it's okay for us to come over."

She scurried back into the kitchen, and Elaine followed close behind. First, she peeked out the window and saw that Kelly was lying on the dock reading, holding her book over her to block the sun. Then she turned to survey the kitchen. It looked like Rose was making strawberry macarons this time.

"Hi there. Hope you don't mind," Rose said, using her arm to indicate the mess on the counter. She was using a dish towel to scrub at something on the wall under the light switch.

"Of course we don't mind, as long as you share," Elaine said. Jan came up to the counter and dipped her finger into a mixing bowl filled with pink dough.

"Delicious," Jan pronounced. Then she turned to watch Rose while Avery went back to squeezing out tiny disks of dough. "What's that, Rose?"

"Oh, I'm sorry." Rose straightened up and stopped scrubbing. "I put this new nail polish on, and when I went to turn on the light, it left a mark on the wall." She squinted at it and started scrubbing again.

Elaine moved closer and tried to get a look at the spot. "That?" She laughed. Rose's red nail polish had left a tiny pink mark on the wall. She wouldn't have even noticed it. "Don't worry about that. No one will see that."

She turned to Jan, waiting for her to say something similar, but Jan was looking at the mark, a strange look on her face. She wasn't upset, Elaine could see that. It was more like—it was like she'd just put something together.

"Jan?"

She snapped her eyes wide and turned to Elaine.

"Is everything okay?"

"Oh yes," Jan said, and took one last look at the tiny mark on the wall before turning to Elaine. "It's not a problem, Rose. No one will even notice."

There was something she wasn't saying. Elaine would probe later. For now, she turned back to Rose.

"Is it safe to assume the nails mean you have a date coming up?"

Color crept up Rose's fair cheeks. "We're going to dinner. And he asked me to pick him up so I can meet his daughter."

"Wait, wait, wait. Who is this?" Avery had stopped piping the dough on to the cookie sheet and was looking at Rose. "You have a boyfriend?" She sounded almost hurt that she hadn't been informed.

"His name is Brent," Jan volunteered. She had gone over to the sink to wash her hands.

"They met in her cooking class," Elaine added.

"I can't believe you didn't tell me you have a boyfriend." Avery still looked stunned that she'd been left out of this turn of events.

"He's not my boyfriend," Rose said. "At least, I don't think so."

"What do you mean you don't think so?" Avery's eyes were narrowed, skepticism on her face.

"I mean, we haven't really talked about it. I'm not dating anyone else, and as far as I know he isn't either, but we haven't really discussed it."

"Well, why don't you just ask him?" Avery couldn't seem to understand what the holdup was. "You like him, right?"

Rose nodded.

"And he likes you?"

She nodded again.

"Then it sounds like you have nothing to worry about. But just to be sure, why don't you pray about it?" Avery went back to piping dough on to the baking sheet.

Once Avery had said the words, Elaine laughed out loud. She felt like a complete idiot. Of course Avery was right. Elaine couldn't believe she hadn't thought of that.

"Of course," Jan said. Elaine could tell by the way her cheeks turned pink that she was chastened too. Here they were supposed to be the grown-ups, the ones who knew a thing or two about love, and Avery was the one who apparently knew the most.

"Yep." Elaine nodded. "Do that."

"That sounds like good advice to me," Rose said.

"I suspect that after you pray about it for a while, you'll know the best path forward," Elaine said. She looked at Jan.

Jan nodded. "And then tell us what happens. We're all living vicariously through you here."

"No we're not. You're about to get engaged any day now," Elaine said.

"What?" Avery set down the pastry bag. "Are you *serious?*"

Jan looked embarrassed for about half a second, looking down at the counter, but then a wide smile spread across her face. "Yes, but don't tell your mother yet please. I don't want her to get all worked up until it's official."

"What, my mom, get worked up?" Avery laughed. Wow, even at twelve, she understood sarcasm, Elaine thought. "Okay, so tell me everything," Avery continued. "When is the wedding? Where? Most important, do I get to wear a new dress? I saw this blue one at the mall last week but Mom wouldn't buy it for me…"

Avery was off and running, grilling Jan about wedding details, none of which had been decided yet. Still, Elaine was happy that Avery was excited, and she prayed that the rest of Jan's family would be excited for her as well. And she prayed that she would continue to be happy for her cousin, even as it meant big changes were ahead for her as well.

NORMALLY BY THIS point in the day in early summer, the tearoom would be packed, even on a Monday. But today there were only a few guests. Things had been so quiet that they'd sent Archie home, and while Elaine handled the serving, Jan decided to take a few minutes to head upstairs and see if she could find any information online about Jade Lacombe.

She swung by the kitchen for a glass of iced tea and a few macarons to help her think more clearly. Rose was just taking the last batch of shells out of the oven and was placing them on a cooling rack.

"Those look great," Jan said.

"There are some finished ones over there," Rose said, indicating a plate of cookies with cream piped between the layers.

"They look wonderful." Jan wandered over and took down a small plate with a flowered border, and then she set two of the finished cookies on the plate. Then she took one more. "Quality control," she explained.

"Of course." Rose smiled. Jan set the plate down and reached into the cabinet for a glass.

"That's pretty great that you get to meet Brent's daughter," Jan said.

"Yeah." A look Jan couldn't read passed over Rose's face.

"What is it?" Jan pulled out the ice tray and plucked two out. "What was that face?"

"What face?"

"The face that says there's something you're not saying about his daughter."

"Oh." Rose laughed. "My mom always said I would be a terrible poker player."

"That's not necessarily a bad thing." Jan plopped the ice cubes into her glass. "Are you worried about meeting his daughter?"

Rose nodded. "That's part of it. But it's more the fact that he *has* a daughter that's making me a bit nervous."

"How so?" Jan grabbed the pitcher and poured the iced tea. "Are you worried his daughter won't accept you because you're not her mother?"

"No. Not yet anyway. I mean, we're light years away from worrying about that." She scooped the last cookie on to the cooling rack. "I don't know. I like kids. I like them a lot. And I'm sure Emma is great. It's just that…it's not just him, you know? There's more at stake here."

"Yes. There is." Jan leaned back against the counter. "And I can see how that could seem scary or overwhelming."

"I mean, I know it's silly to worry about at this point. I'm not about to become a stepmom or anything. We've just gone out once."

"No, not silly at all. If you're going to get involved with him, it's very relevant. There's always going to be a third person in your relationship, in some ways. He is always going to be thinking about his daughter."

"As he should," Rose said.

Jan knew Emma was young, and that brought its own set of challenges, but concern for your children didn't go away when your kids were grown. Both she and Bob had grown children, and Jan had worried about how they would react when they found out they were dating. Your kids were always your babies, no matter how old they got. "Does it make you hesitate?"

Rose didn't say anything for a moment. Then, carefully, "A bit. Not because of her, exactly. But because things won't be as easy as they would be if he was…well, unencumbered. And because if things do work out—having a child, it's a big responsibility, you know? Like, I don't know if I'm ready for it, I guess."

"It is indeed a big responsibility." Jan tried to choose her words carefully. "And there will be sacrifices you both will have to make."

Rose nodded.

"I suppose you'll have to decide if those sacrifices are worth it," Jan said.

"What do you think?"

"What do I think?" Jan smiled. "I can't really tell you what to think. I don't know enough, and that's a very personal decision for you."

"But you have an opinion."

Jan thought for a minute. "My children were—still are— the greatest joy of my life," Jan said. "If I had to do it all over, I wouldn't change a thing, not if it meant I got my children again." She crossed her arms over her chest. "My guess is that you'll never regret letting Emma into your life, no matter how things work out with Brent. You'll enjoy getting to know her, I'm sure, and I am certain she will bring a depth to your relationship that you wouldn't have otherwise. It will mean some sacrifices, for sure, but I bet you'll find they're more than worth it."

Rose nodded. "Thanks, Jan."

"The one thing I know for sure is that Avery is right. Pray about it. Put God at the center of your relationship, and you'll know what's right, because God's desires will become your desires."

Rose didn't say anything for a few moments, and Jan hovered uncertainly. Should she say here and talk more, or should she go and leave Rose to her thoughts? Eventually, she decided to give the girl some space.

"I'm headed upstairs," she said, picking up her plate and her glass. "Holler if you need me."

Rose smiled and nodded, and Jan went out of the kitchen and headed to the stairs. The windows were open in the sitting room on the second floor, and a nice cross-breeze was keeping the room cool. Jan set down the glass of iced tea she'd brought upstairs with her, grabbed her laptop, and sat down on the comfy couch.

First she checked her e-mail and saw a message from Brian. He was responding to the picture of the back end of the car she had sent.

Mom,

Based on the shape of the taillight I'm ninety percent certain this is an older-model Nissan Sentra. They changed the shape of the back end a few years ago but the taillight remains the same.

Hugs,
Brian

Jan had to laugh. Messages from her son were totally different from messages from her daughters. Tara and Amy were usually chatty in their e-mails, while Brian just got right to the facts and moved on. Oh well. At least now she too was 90 percent sure of the model of the car in that photo. Now all she needed to know was what to do with that.

Next she opened a search engine and typed in the name Jade Lacombe.

The first thing that came up was the page on the Colby library Web site they'd seen earlier. She didn't think there was much useful there, so she searched on. She had a Facebook page, but the privacy settings were set so that only friends could view her posts. Still, Jan looked at the list of her friends on the left side of the page and noticed a Ryan Lacombe. From the profile picture, she could see that he was a young man, and he wore a baseball cap with a logo Jan recognized as belonging to the San Francisco Giants. She clicked on his page and discovered that he was originally from Waterville, Maine, and he was a student at the University of California, Berkeley.

How was he related to Jade? Jan scrolled through his posts and saw pictures of the boy at parties, hiking in the woods under tall evergreens, and eating meals at various restaurants. He was tagged in all the pictures; he hadn't posted them himself, and she got the impression he was not very active on the social media site. Still, she kept scrolling, until she came to a post from about a year ago. This one Ryan had posted himself, Jan could see. *My mom's scans came back clear; she's cancer free!* it read. Jade Lacombe was tagged in the post.

Well. Jan was sad to hear that Jade had suffered through cancer, but thrilled to hear that she'd beaten it. Even if she was a suspect, Jan wouldn't wish cancer on anyone. And now she knew that Ryan was Jade's son, though she wasn't sure how that was helpful. She continued to scroll through the posts, but didn't see much of anything useful. Jan then looked at Ryan's list of friends, and she saw a Mitch Lacombe. It had to be some relative, she decided, so she clicked on his page.

Hmm. It looked like he lived in Sarasota, Florida. And... Whoa. It was immediately clear that Mitch Lacombe loved to post rants. He had posts ranting about the IRS, the government, and the guy in the pickup who cut him off, and about…well, this was interesting. There was a rant about his ex-wife.

> *Just signed the papers. Thank goodness I'm done with that crazy woman. It's official. Could not get out of that marriage fast enough. I guess I should have known she was crazy years ago but that's me, always looking for the best in people. Took a lot of fighting (Jade did not want to let me out of it!) but no alimony. Just a few checks until Ryan is out of college. He is the only good thing to come out of that marriage. Love you, kid!*

Jan read back through the post again. It was heartbreaking to see messages like this. Mitch and Jade had no doubt loved each other at one point. They'd promised to love and cherish each other. And this was the result.

But despite the sadness of this, Jan had learned a bit more. The post was from six months ago. Jade had been divorced recently. And, if this post was to be believed, she was not getting alimony. Depending on what her other bills and resources were, that could potentially cause serious financial hardship. Especially on top of recent cancer treatments. Jan had no way to know what her insurance had been like, but any major disease could drain bank accounts, she knew.

Jade had had a bad stretch, that was for sure. Could that have driven her to steal? There was no way to say.

Jan went back to the main search page but didn't find much else. If only she could talk to Jade somehow…But no matter what search she ran, she couldn't find contact information for her online. Well, no matter. She had to be local if she was involved with the thefts. Jan headed down to the office, grabbed the phone book, brought it upstairs, and flipped to the *L* listings.

Jan found a listing for "Lacombe, M" in Waterville. Her heart sank. She was guessing this phone line was registered to Mitch Lacombe, who lived in Florida now. She realized the phone book was at least a year old. Still, she picked up her phone and dialed the number. She held her breath as the line rang, and then the familiar tones that signaled a number that was no longer in service.

Jan didn't know what else to do. There wasn't anything directly linking Jade to the thefts. Everything was coincidence; it was all circumstantial at this point. But…she didn't know. She just had a feeling that Jade had to be involved in this somehow. How could she get in touch with her?

Jan went back to the main search page and found the initial place they'd seen her, the Colby College Web site. She found the page with the library staff and zeroed in on the picture of Jade. She traced her eyes over the curves of her face, the bones of her cheeks. Was this the woman from the security pictures? From the marina? Jan couldn't tell.

The thefts at the college library had stopped right after Jade had been let go for unknown reasons. That was proof, wasn't it? But how could she know for sure?

Jan read the short bio that ran beneath Jade's picture. It said she lived in Waterville and listed her as a graduate of the University of Maine at Augusta. Too bad she couldn't…

Well, wait a minute.

Usually colleges had alumni networks, didn't they? She opened a new window and typed in University of Maine at Augusta. There was a link to an alumni site there, but when Jan clicked on it, she was taken to a page where she had to log in. But she had an idea.

Tara had gone to the University of Maine at Augusta, and she was pretty involved in alumni events, Jan knew. Jan picked up the phone again and pulled up her daughter's name. Tara worked out of her home, but like most young people these days, she didn't have a home phone line, so Jan called her cell.

"Hi, Mom. Long time no talk," Tara quipped when she answered the call. "What's up?"

Jan was always tempted to answer "apogee" when asked this question, but she resisted the urge. Jan had homeschooled her children and had really enjoyed teaching them about science, and the kids all knew that apogee was the highest point in a satellite's orbit. But she also knew that they generally rolled their eyes at her corny science jokes.

"I need your log-in information for your college alumni account," Jan said.

"Why?"

"I think I'm getting close to figuring out who's been stealing wallets all over Lancaster."

"Of course you are." Tara laughed. Jan could hear some kind of soft music playing in the background. "And my log-in information is going to help?"

"I think so," Jan said.

"If you say so. My username is tblake, and my password is peterblake."

"Not very creative." Jan typed the letters in as she spoke. "You know a hacker could guess that pretty easily." She'd heard horror stories of hackers guessing passwords and cleaning out bank accounts.

"Well, you didn't figure it out, and you're my mom and a sleuth, so I guess I'm not too worried."

"Fair enough." Jan hit Return and waited while the site processed. "I'm in."

"Please don't go sending e-mails as me or anything like that," Tara said.

"Scout's honor." Jan knew her daughter was mostly joking. Mostly. "Thanks."

Jan hung up and clicked on a link that took her to a database of alumni contact information. She typed in the name Jade Lacombe and hit Return, and held her breath.

There she was. Jan clicked on the link for Jade Hastings Lacombe, class of 1991. An e-mail address, phone number, and physical address in Waterville was listed. The note at the bottom of the page said the information had been updated two months ago.

Jan decided to try one more general Internet search, and this time she typed in the words "Jade Hastings Lacombe."

Adding her maiden name brought up a whole new series of hits. The first one Jan clicked on was a blog written by, as far as Jan could tell, someone who reviewed romance novels for a living and went by the name RomanceChica. Most of the posts on the blog were reviews of new books coming out from various publishers. But a few posts were more personal, and the one that had brought her to this page was a post RomanceChica had written about her childhood friend Jade Hastings, who was going through breast cancer. The post featured a picture of the two of them—RomanceChica a big, vibrant woman in a flowered shirt and wild curly hair, and Jade…

Jan gasped. Could it be? She leaned in and looked closer. It was her, all right. But she had…

Jan's pulse sped up, and she could feel that throbbing in her veins that told her this was it. This was the clue that she had been missing.

Quickly, before she could lose her nerve, she dialed the number she'd gotten from the alumni page, held her breath, and hit Call. The phone started to ring. It rang and rang, but no one picked up. No answering machine, no voice mail. It just kept ringing.

Just then, Kelly started yelling from the bottom of the stairs. "Grandma! Come look what I found!"

CHAPTER TWENTY-EIGHT

When Jan heard Kelly calling, she reluctantly ended the call and headed down the stairs. She cringed. She didn't want to hush the girl, but her yelling like that didn't exactly add to the kind of soothing environment they tried to create for their guests. She did her best to hurry. She made her way down the stairs, holding the banister tightly, and found her granddaughter waiting expectantly at the bottom.

"Look at this." Kelly held something blue in her hand.

"What is that?" But as Jan leaned forward, she saw what it was. A debit card. It had the logo of a Maine chain of banks on it. "Where did you find this?"

"It was right by the back door. The one that leads to the porch? I was trying to teach Earl Grey to shake paws, and he wasn't cooperating. He kept wandering off to sniff things, and one of the things he found was this."

Jan took the card gently.

"It was lying there in the grass by the door."

"Wow." Jan could only think of one reason a debit card would be lying in the grass by the back door. Scenes from last night came rushing back to her. The scary run down the stairs. Searching the first floor for any sign of the intruder. Arnie Sheffield concluding that the intruder had picked the lock on the kitchen door, probably with something simple like a credit card. "Great find, Kelly."

Jan looked down at the name on the card. And as she realized what it said, a wave of understanding came over her.

She needed to call Darlene.

As soon as they closed down the tearoom for the day and sent Rose off to get ready for her date, Jan dragged Elaine out to her car. Elaine had planned on calling Nathan, but Jan insisted that she had solved the mystery, and that she would explain on the way, so Elaine followed.

"Do I get to know where we're headed?" Elaine asked as she buckled herself in.

"Sure. To this address. Can you route us there?" Jan asked, handing over the piece of paper with an address on it that Elaine didn't recognize.

Elaine dutifully punched the address into her phone and positioned it so Jan could see it on the dashboard. Jan put the car into gear and pulled out on to Main Street. The late-afternoon sunlight slanted into the windshield, and they both squinted and put down their visors. Jan had the radio tuned to a contemporary Christian music station, but she turned it down as they got going on the main road.

"What's at 1169 Long Road?" Elaine asked. Sometimes Jan got cryptic like this when she got excited, and Elaine knew she didn't mean to, but it could still be maddening trying to make out what she was trying to tell her.

"Jade Lacombe."

"Really?" Elaine had to admit she was impressed. "And you think there's a pretty good chance she's involved?"

"I know she is," Jan said.

"How's that?"

"Get this. Jade Lacombe had cancer."

"That's awful." Why was Jan looking at her so triumphantly?

"She had chemo. Which means…"

"She's had a really rough time?"

"That's not the half of it. The past few years have been brutal for her…"

"Did you research her or stalk her?"

"Look, I just went where the questions took me. But my point is, she *lost her hair* during chemo."

"Okay…" Elaine couldn't see why Jan was so excited about this. Chemo was awful, and she knew that for many people losing your hair was the worst part.

"Elaine, I saw a picture of Jade during that time. She had a blonde wig."

Suddenly, Elaine understood what Jan had been trying to tell her.

"Her hair is naturally brown, but she had a blonde wig?" Elaine knew some people liked to try out different hair colors and hairstyles when they lost their own hair. It wasn't really all that surprising that Jade might have wanted to go blonde, really. But the point was that she had brown hair now, but, presuming she still had the wig, she could easily become blonde. It made sense. But it wasn't conclusive by any means.

"Wigs are not that hard to come by," Elaine said. You could get them at any costume shop. "And besides, we know there is more than one person involved in these thefts. Even if you could explain the changes in hair color, you can't explain the changes in height and weight."

"That's where we've been thinking about this all wrong," Jan said. "Grab my laptop." She had laid it on to the backseat when she'd gotten into the car, and now Elaine reached back and grabbed it. She opened the lid. Three images were pulled up—the still shot from the gas station security camera, which showed the head and shoulders of a tall woman with long blonde hair; a screenshot from the convenience store footage, which showed a heavier brown-haired woman who barely came up to the five feet six inches marker on the strip by the door, and the photo taken by the marina, which showed a lanky woman with brassy red hair.

"Look at the convenience store video first."

Elaine enlarged the first picture, and then she pushed the button at the bottom to let the video run. She watched as the woman entered the shop wearing big sunglasses and looked around the store tentatively, like she wasn't sure what she was looking for, and picked out a bottle of water and approached the counter, where she added a pack of gum. She pulled a wallet from her purse—a white leather wallet; now that they'd seen Carrie's wallet, they knew this was hers—and took out a credit card. There was a moment where she looked directly at the camera, and Elaine paused it there and zoomed in on her face. Was this the woman whose picture they'd seen on the library Web site? She searched and tried to make it out, but the sunglasses obscured so much of her face that she couldn't tell. She started the video again and watched as the woman tucked her purchases into her purse and went toward the door.

"Okay," Elaine said. "But there's no way this is the same woman as one at the gas station." She pulled up the still shot from the gas station.

"Why not?"

"Well, for one thing, the convenience store woman is, well"—Elaine tried to phrase this politely, then realized how ridiculous that was considering they were talking about a thief—"she's a bit…she's got a few extra pounds. Not too many. And I mean, who doesn't these days, really? I know I do. It's just that…"

"But what is it that makes you say that?" Jan asked. "I thought so too. But then, look at her face. It's actually quite thin, when you really look at it."

Elaine looked carefully at the woman's cheeks and realized Jan was right.

"It's that she's wearing a bulky sweatshirt, and a skirt that's not flattering, right?"

Elaine realized she was right. She'd been thinking the woman in this footage was overweight, but when she really looked carefully, it was just the way she was dressed, and probably the angle of the camera, that made her look that way.

"Okay." Elaine looked back at the gas station shot. This one was grainy and black and white, but it was clear that the woman was taller than the roughly five feet six inches woman in the convenience store. She towered over the small car in the shot. This woman had long blonde hair—it was impossible to tell if it was a wig, though Elaine would concede that it was possible—and big sunglasses. Was it the same pair? Elaine couldn't tell. Most of her body was blocked by the car, but the bit of her shoulders you could see made her seem slim—but possibly not any more so than the woman in the other video, she had to now admit. "But how do you get past the fact that she's obviously so much taller than the first woman?"

"How tall is a Nissan Sentra?" Jan asked.

"How do you know this is a Nissan Sentra?"

"Brian helped me figure it out. So how tall is it?"

When had Jan done all this? But if Brian had told her this was a Nissan, Elaine believed it. He did know cars. "I have no idea."

"A new one is 58.9 inches. This is an older model, but without the year I couldn't get an exact measurement. But it's probably in that neighborhood, since cars models don't change all that much. So let's go with 58.9 for now."

"Please tell me there was a reason you looked that up."

"That's four feet, eleven inches, basically," Jan said.

"Okay..." Elaine struggled to see where she was going with this.

"The woman in the convenience store video is about five foot six, so she would be about seven inches taller than the car."

"Ah." Elaine saw now. The woman in this shot was at least a foot taller than the car. "But that only shows that it can't be the same woman. This blonde woman is too tall."

"That's what I thought at first too." Jan accelerated as they went up the ramp to get on to the expressway. "But then, look under the body of the car."

"Huh?" Elaine wondered if Jan was starting to take this conspiracy theory too far, but she dutifully did. All you could see was the woman's head and shoulders.

Wait a minute. All you could see were the woman's head and shoulders. You could see the tires, but her feet were not visible under the car. What in the world...?

"No feet, right?"

"Where are they?"

"She's standing on the curb."

"Really?" Elaine looked closer, but you really couldn't see anything under the car.

"She has to be. I mean, unless she doesn't have feet, but even then, she'd have some sort of prosthetic device, right?"

Elaine saw that she was right. The woman had to be standing on the curb around the gas pump. And curbs like that were usually about...Elaine's heartbeat sped up. They were probably five inches or so. Which would make this woman just about the right height to be the woman in the convenience store video.

"Okay. So it's possible this is the same woman," Elaine admitted. "But what about the third picture?" Elaine pulled up the photo taken at the marina. This woman had reddish hair tucked under her Colby cap, but aside from her hair color, she could have been the same woman. Possibly. Elaine studied the picture, trying to gauge the woman's height, but from this angle it was hard to say.

"Remember that hair dye?" Jan asked. Elaine nodded. She saw where Jan was going. The red hair dye from the receipt in Carrie's wallet.

"Okay. That's circumstantial though. We need more."

"All right, then. Check out her nails."

Elaine knew better than to argue, though the request seemed strange. She used her fingers to enlarge the image of the woman. "She's got nail polish on?"

"She does. And it's red, which is the shade bought on Carrie's receipt."

Elaine could see the connection she was trying to make, but it seemed flimsy to her. "Lots of people wear red nail polish."

"True. But she changed it from the pink color she was wearing earlier in the week after that trip to the store."

"How can you...?" But then Elaine remembered. "The cashier at the grocery store said the woman wore pink nail polish."

"Not only that, there was a pink mark on the wall by where Carrie's purse was, and there was a pink smudge on her wallet as well."

Jan had gotten off the highway and was turning away from the main commercial area of Waterville.

"Huh?" Elaine didn't wear a ton of nail polish, but she wasn't following. "Nail polish doesn't bleed everywhere."

"No, but it can leave scuff marks. Especially the cheaper brands. The kinds you get at drugstores."

Was this true? Elaine guessed she had had this happen before, when she hadn't been patient enough to apply a topcoat. But this was a stretch...

"I made the connection when Rose was trying to clean the smudge her nail polish had left on our wall," Jan said. "And I saw a similar smudge on the wall in Carrie's cabin."

Elaine thought it was possible, but it wasn't enough to prove anything. But taken all together, she could admit there was enough circumstantial evidence to make the case that there was only one thief. And, she also admitted, it was not too much of a stretch to believe it might be Jade.

The GPS led them quickly off the main roads and through a series of winding back roads. Maine got remote quickly once you got out of the central part of town, and they started to pass rusted-out trailers mixed in with modest wood-framed houses and a few more ornate homes. Finally, they turned on to a small dirt road and pulled into the long, rutted driveway of a small wooden house. The once-white paint was now a grayish mushroom color and peeling along the bottom edge, and the gutter was hanging at an angle. But Jan let out a whoop, and Elaine saw why: a beat-up silver Nissan Sentra sat in front of the house. The first three letters of the license plate matched what they'd seen in the gas station video still.

"This is it!" Elaine was as excited as Jan now. This was her. It had to be her. They'd found the thief!

"I think it's her." Jan didn't even try to hold back her satisfied smile. "So what do we do now?" Jan asked.

Elaine didn't hesitate. "We knock on the door."

CHAPTER TWENTY-NINE

Jan held her breath as Elaine rang the doorbell. There was movement inside. The front curtain moved. Then, a moment later, the door opened a crack.

"Hello?" The woman had a deep, raspy voice.

"We'd like to speak with Jade Lacombe please," Elaine said. Jan could only see a sliver of her in the open doorway, but she could see right away that this was her. This was the woman from the pictures. She had brassy red hair that didn't match her brown eyebrows and chipped red nail polish.

"I'm sorry, I'm busy." She closed the door with a thud.

Elaine rang the bell again, but no one answered.

Fifteen frustrating minutes later, they were in the car again and headed back toward home. They had knocked on the door. They had rung the doorbell. Jade hadn't answered.

"Well, I guess we know what our next step is," Elaine said. Jan nodded. On their way back, they stopped by Dan Benson's house, a white bungalow with blue trim a little ways from the center of town. His son's tricycle was resting on the front lawn.

"Oh boy," Dan said when he opened the door. He was laughing. "What can I do for you two?"

Elaine ignored the tone of his voice and strode inside. "We know who the thief is."

Jan thought he looked dubious, but he asked them to sit down in the living room. Jan could see that the television was on in the other room and she could hear his wife and children upstairs. They sat, and Elaine proceeded to lay out the case they had against Jade Lacombe. The skeptical look on his face faded as she spoke, and Jan jumped in to add details as well.

"And when we got there, the car was in the driveway," Elaine finished. "The one from the video. So we know it was her."

He looked from Jan to Elaine and back again and sighed. "I can see you have been working hard," he said, and smiled. "And you know what?"

Jan looked at the framed family photos on the mantel and the rows of books on the shelves.

"I think you're right."

"You do?" Jan asked. Well, that hadn't been all that hard after all.

"I do." He nodded. "That license plate number you recognized? I looked into it too. My buddies over in Augusta ran it through the system for me, and our automotive expert figured out pretty quickly that it was a Nissan Sentra, just like you did." He nodded at Jan. "And it turns out there's only one Nissan Sentra in the state with the numbers from that license plate, and it was registered to Jade Lacombe."

"So if you know it's her, why haven't you arrested her?" Jan asked.

He sighed. "I went out to see Jade Lacombe myself yester-day. But no one answered the door. Someone was inside the house, I am sure of it, but no one answered."

Jan was aghast. "You're the police! She can't just dodge you like that."

He shrugged. "I didn't have a warrant to enter the house, so she can and did."

"Well, why in the world don't you get a warrant?" Elaine asked.

"The same reason I can't take what you've told me and go in, guns blazing, and arrest her. There's no proof."

"You have video of her using the stolen card to gas up her car. How much more proof do you need?" Jan asked.

"It looks like proof to you and me. But any good defense attorney will rip that evidence apart. How can you tell it's Jade using that card? You can't see her face in the video. You can only see part of the license plate number. You can't see what kind of car it is in the video. Sure we can try to explain how we deduced it's a Nissan. But can we do that beyond all reasonable suspi-cion?" He shrugged. "That's what a jury has to do. And there's nothing in the footage that conclusively links the theft to Jade LaCombe. And the same is true of the other pictures and video we have. She changes her disguises enough that it's hard to pin it on on her, at least in a way that will hold up in court."

"So that's what matters? Not stopping her before she steals again, but whether you have enough evidence to win in court?" Jan felt herself growing angry. That was crazy. It couldn't be legal.

He shrugged again, just slightly. "I'm afraid I don't have enough proof yet."

Jan wanted to stand up and scream at him, but instead she sat there and tried to keep her frustration under control.

"So what are we supposed to do, then? Sit here and wait until she strikes again, and hope one of us is there to catch her?"

He didn't have an answer for that, Jan could tell. Well, fine. Then they would figure out a way to prove it was Jade. Jan wasn't sure how yet, but there had to be a way to end this thing once and for all.

"We have to simply catch her red-handed," Elaine said. "And I have an idea. I know how we can catch her."

Trooper Benson raised an eyebrow, but then he sighed and gestured for her to go on. As Elaine spoke, Jan could see that he was skeptical. And Jan had to admit, she was too. It was a ridiculous plan, really. But she could also see that he didn't have any better ideas, because eventually he sighed and said, "All right, we'll give it a shot."

CHAPTER THIRTY

The next morning, Jan and Elaine trekked over to the Sugar Plum. It was stiflingly hot, and Elaine could tell Jan was dreading this conversation as much as she was, but they both knew it had to happen. In some sense, she'd known since Darlene had first called about the break-in at her shop. That theft hadn't fit the pattern; she'd realized that right away. It didn't make sense that someone would go from surreptitiously swiping wallets to pay for necessities to breaking in and trashing her store. And the break-in at their home, as scary as it had been, had also seemed to be an outlier. Someone had come in looking for cash and gone straight for the cashbox, leaving behind the laptop and other valuables. It was a far cry from grabbing a customer's wallet while she'd been gabbing with her sister. In addition, she had been sure it was a man she'd seen running out the back door, and so far everything pointed to the wallet thief being a woman. And once they'd found the debit card they knew for sure. The name on the card was Justin Miller. Darlene's nephew.

Jan pushed open the door of the shop, and Elaine followed her cousin inside. The mess they'd seen a few days ago was gone, and the shop was back to its beautiful and festive self. Bing Crosby was crooning about a white Christmas, which seemed incongruous in this heat, but the shop itself was cool and smelled like cinnamon and balsam. Elaine's eye caught on a lovely candleholder, but she forced herself to focus on the task at hand. Darlene was seated at the counter at the back of the shop and she looked up and smiled when she saw them walking toward her.

"Hello, hello," Darlene said. "How's it going?"

Jan looked like a deer in the headlights, so Elaine spoke up. "It's going all right. We've definitely made some progress on the mystery front." She paused as Darlene's face brightened. "And I have some good news and some bad news," Elaine continued.

"Okay." Darlene nodded. "I'm ready."

"The good news is, we think we know who is stealing all the wallets in Lancaster," Elaine said.

"Well, that is very good news indeed," Darlene said.

Before she could get too excited, Elaine continued. "The bad news is, the break-in at your shop is not related. Or at least, only related in that the perpetrator was hoping the crimes would be conflated." Goodness. Elaine was nervous, for sure, but did she have to use words like *perpetrator* and *conflated*? She didn't even know what she was saying.

"Okay . . ." Darlene looked less pleased now. It was like she could sense what Elaine was about to say. Elaine rushed to put her out of her suspense.

"There was a similar break-in at our house a few nights ago, while we were sleeping," she said. Darlene's face registered shock—she hadn't known that—but Elaine didn't stop to elaborate. "And the next day, we found this right outside our door." She pulled the debit card out of her purse and set it on the counter. They had decided not to turn the card over to the police, at least not until they talked to Darlene. When Darlene saw what it was, her face fell.

"We believe it was used to pick the lock on our back door," Jan said.

Darlene didn't say anything for a minute, but tears welled up in her eyes.

"I'm so sorry," Elaine said.

Darlene shook her head. "I'm the one who should be apologizing to you. If what you're saying is correct, my nephew broke in and tried to rob you in your sleep. That must have given you quite a fright."

Quite a fright was a bit of an understatement, but Elaine would let that go.

"I'm sorry to have to tell you this," Elaine said.

"So the break-in here? When this place was trashed? That was him too?"

"It seems that way," Jan said.

Darlene said something under her breath in Spanish. Elaine picked up the words *mother* and *home*. "I should have guessed. I guess part of me did have suspicions, but I didn't want to believe it."

"Of course. Who wouldn't want to believe the best of their family members?" Elaine asked.

"I was supposed to help straighten him out." She shook her head.

"Well, he hasn't been here long. There is still plenty of time," Jan said.

"On the plus side, he didn't actually steal anything from us. He was just going for our cash box, but he didn't get it open before I made it downstairs, and he didn't take anything else," Elaine said.

"I guess I can be glad for small mercies." Darlene gave a halfhearted smile.

"We reported the break-in when it happened, but we haven't told the police about the debit card," Jan said.

"Thank you," Darlene said. "I appreciate that. That will allow me to march Justin down to Trooper Benson and make him confess in person."

Elaine smiled. That was not going to be a fun conversation, Elaine knew. On the other hand, a brush with law enforcement might be exactly what the boy needed to straighten him out, though she and Jan had already decided not to press charges.

"You said these break-ins are not connected to the wallets that have gone missing?" Darlene asked.

"That's right. We feel confident he had nothing to do with those thefts," Jan said.

Darlene nodded. She found comfort in that, Elaine could tell. But she tilted her head. "Can you tell me who is behind those?"

"Not yet," Elaine said. "But we'll have answers soon."

THEY LEFT THE Sugar Plum, reassured by Darlene's promises to speak to Justin immediately and bring him to the police to confess. It felt good to have that mystery resolved, though they felt bad for both Justin and Darlene. What must be going on in that boy's life that he acted out in this way? Jan knew that these things were complicated, and he was young. Everyone made some bad decisions when they were young. Hopefully this turn of events would set him on a better course.

Instead of heading back to the house, they walked down Main Street past the marina, toward the public beach next to the boat launch. The town had brought in sand by the truckload to create a beautiful little area to swim or splash around in the cool, clear water, and the place was hopping today in this heat. Families were spread out on blankets on the rocky sand, and teenagers were sunning themselves and joking and laughing by the picnic tables. People of all ages were splashing in the shallow water. Jan knew from experience that the water was bracingly cold, but refreshing on a hot day like this one. Jan and Elaine laid their trap, spreading out a blanket on the sand and leaving an open canvas tote right in the middle. Elaine made sure the edge of her decoy wallet was clearly visible as you passed by. Then they settled down at a picnic table twenty yards away.

"This is crazy, you know that, right?" Jan asked. Part of her couldn't believe she was going along with this. But she didn't have any better ideas. And if Trooper Benson had done his part, there was at least a slim chance that this could work— slim being the operative word.

"Just wait. It'll work. You'll see." Elaine adjusted her sunglasses and looked out over the crowd.

Jan scanned the crowd too. Linda Somes and her family were under an umbrella not far from the boat launch, and

Julie Yeaton was in the water splashing around with her two-year-old grandson. No sign of Jade.

Jan still couldn't believe Dan had agreed to go along with this crazy plan Elaine had cooked up. They had decided that he would go to Jade's house and tell her that they were going to door to door warning everyone that there was a thief in the area and were warning women in particular to pay attention to their purses. He would add that places like public beaches were especially likely targets, since people generally left their things unattended at the beach. He was effectively suggesting that she hit up the beach—and Jan certainly hoped she would. The state police in Augusta had agreed to send undercover officers to patrol the beaches, and though Jan couldn't tell who it was, she knew there was one here now. She supposed that was the point—that you couldn't tell. She wasn't sure they needed to be here, since the police were supposed to have it covered, but Elaine had insisted she wanted to be here to catch Jade herself, and Jan wasn't about to miss out on all the fun either. The tearoom was slow; Archie and Rose could handle the few customers that would trickle in.

She saw movement to her left, but when she turned, she saw it was just a little boy chasing his sister across the sand.

"Sunblock?" Elaine asked, pulling a small tube out of the little fabric purse she had draped over her shoulder.

"Please." Jan held out her hand, and Elaine squirted some into it. They both slathered it on, and Jan adjusted the brim of her sunhat, and then they sat and waited. They chatted a bit. Jan told her cousin that Bob had asked if they could reschedule their foiled date for the next evening. They also chatted with Lydia Pierce, who came up and asked them some questions about the thefts for this week's edition of the *Weekly Wave*, but mostly they just sat and watched.

Two hours later, no one had even seemed to notice the purse they'd left out, and they hadn't seen anything suspicious or anyone who resembled Jade. They were just about to pack it in when a man's voice sounded right next to them: "I hear there's a covert investigation going on over here."

Jan jumped at the sound of the man's voice, but she saw Elaine's face light up when she realized it was Nathan.

"Nathan! You scared me!" Elaine swatted at him, but she was laughing and leaning toward him. "What are you doing here?"

Nathan was usually working at the auction house at this time in the afternoon. Today he was wearing a slim-fitting short-sleeved blue shirt and well-cut pants that he'd rolled up before stepping on to the sand. Jan could see his loafers were tucked into a bag he had slung over his shoulder.

"I had to drive out this way to check out a collection of old violins someone discovered in their grandmother's attic, so afterward I thought I would stop by the house and say hello. Archie told me you were here, so I decided to come see how it's going." He reached his bag. "And I decided you might need sustenance." He pulled out two black-and-white cookies that Jan immediately recognized as coming from Murphy's General Store, and he followed with two bottles of Elaine's favorite lemonade.

"God bless you," Elaine said as she took the cookies and passed one to Jan.

"This is perfect. Thank you so much."

"Of course." He gave Elaine a wink. "This crazy plan is your doing, I assume?"

"You'll stop mocking me when it works." Elaine broke off a piece of the chocolate side of the cookie and popped it in her mouth. Elaine seemed really relaxed with Nathan, Jan noticed. Comfortable. They'd known each other since they'd been children, and somehow that familiarity gave them an ease with each other.

"Pull up a piece of bench." Jan scooted over a little so he could take a seat, but he shook his head. "I need to get back. But good luck. I hope you catch the thief."

"*Shh*," Elaine said. "Don't say that too loud. We don't want anyone to know what we're doing."

"Right. Sorry." He winked. "And don't worry, you guys fit right in here, sitting there fully clothed on that bench. No one would ever suspect that you're not just like all these other people who are playing in the water, building sand castles, and sunbathing."

"Oh, you, get lost," Elaine said, shooing him away. She had a huge smile on her face, and he laughed and waved before starting back across the sand.

"I'll call you tonight," Nathan called as he kept walking.

Elaine munched on her cookie and returned to scanning the people on the beach, but Jan was thinking through what Nathan had said. He was probably right, she realized. They were too obvious. Was that why Jade hadn't shown today? Had she recognized them and decided not to risk it? She wasn't sure, but she decided that in any case they needed to blend in more if they had any shot at catching the thief in the act.

Families around them were starting to pick up and head out, and as she sat there, Jan came up with a plan for the next day. Tomorrow, she thought, they would have better luck.

CHAPTER THIRTY-ONE

"Guess what?" Rose came through the door with a big smile on her face.

"What?" Jan set down the hot muffin tin she'd just taken out of the oven. The blueberry peach muffins had filled the whole kitchen with a sweet scent.

Rose hung her purse on the hook by the door and slipped an apron over her head.

"I want to hear this!" Elaine walked in after spending time in the office, where she'd been busy processing that stack of invoices she'd been avoiding. "What happened?"

"Well, I did what we talked about. I prayed about my relationship with Brent. It seemed so obvious once Avery brought it up." Rose washed her hands and then dried them on the towel by the sink.

"Out of the mouths of babes," Elaine said.

"I prayed that God would give me wisdom about this relationship, and that He would bless it, and that He would guard our hearts," Rose said. "That He would protect Emma and help us to always act in her best interests. And most of all, I prayed that He would be in charge of our relationship. This is the first time I've really met someone I feel like I could marry, but I know that that's not enough sometimes. So I prayed that God would direct our steps and that He would be at the center of everything."

"That's wonderful," Jan said. She had prayed the same prayer about her relationship with Bob, and now look where things were headed for them. She hoped God had good things in store for Rose and Brent too.

"That is wonderful." Elaine elbowed Rose. "So what happened?"

"I met Emma," she said. She reached for the muffin tin and started to take the hot muffins out by the papers.

"And?" Jan asked again. "How did it go?"

"Great. I was so nervous, but she is such a sweet kid. So well behaved and so smart. She'd got this beautiful dark hair and his blue eyes. I really liked her. And she seemed to like me."

"That's wonderful," Elaine said. "He must be serious about this relationship."

So Jan thought so too. That was a good sign.

"Well, after dinner, as he was walking me to my car, he told me that he wanted us to date exclusively. He asked if he could call me his girlfriend."

It took Jan a minute to realize that the squealing noise she heard was coming from her. Elaine was clapping and had also let out a little shriek.

"And then he asked if we could pray together, and we prayed that God would be in charge of our relationship and guide us," Rose continued.

"That's so wonderful!" Elaine was saying. Rose nodded.

"I'm really excited. But I'm trying to remember that God is in control. Just because Brent wants to be my boyfriend doesn't guarantee anything about the future. We just need to keep trusting God with that."

"Amen." Jan was so thrilled for Rose. After everything she'd been through, she deserved happiness.

"What's all this?" Archie asked, stepping into the kitchen. "It sounds as though something delightful has happened."

Jan had to laugh at Archie's stiff delivery, and Elaine and Rose quickly filled him in. Jan listened but her mind was also drifting off to her date with Bob tonight. Would he finally ask her to marry him? She sure hoped so. Jan loved him, and she was ready to start planning their life together. But she knew that no matter what happened, God was in control of their relationship and He wanted the best for both of them. As long as He was at the center of their relationship, they were right where they needed to be.

Still, she couldn't help feeling a little thrill when she looked down at her left hand. Tonight, there would be a ring on that fourth finger. She couldn't wait.

A LITTLE WHILE later, Jan finished setting the tables in the parlors, and when she came back to the office she found Elaine and Archie huddled over the computer.

"What's going on?" she asked, poking her head inside.

"Check this out." Elaine turned the screen so Jan could see what they were looking at. It appeared to be a Wikipedia entry for someone named Harley Archibald Benningham.

"Who's that?"

"I don't know a thing about Harley Archibald Benningham." Archie pointed to a grainy black-and-white picture on one side of the screen. It showed a thin, balding man with a dark mustache. He wore a suit and a tie, but he didn't look happy to be in front of the camera. "But that's a picture of my father."

"What?" Jan grabbed on to the door frame.

"When I went to talk to Heather Wells, she recognized the symbol in the corner of the picture as the mark of an artist named Harley Archibald Benningham," Elaine explained. "I realized the initials were the same as Archie's father's name, Henry Arthur Bentham."

"Not to mention your full name is Archibald, right?" Jan looked at Archie, who nodded. "So that connection is pretty clear. It's not such a common name that it's likely to simply be a coincidence."

"Well, obviously I wanted to find out more, so I came in here and did an Internet search for Harley Benningham," Elaine said. "And this is what came up."

"Huh." Jan leaned in and read some of the text.

Benningham had a decidedly realistic style, some suspect in response to the modernist style that was increasing in popularity.... A veteran of the Second World War, most of Benningham's paintings had a melancholy feel... paintings quite rare and highly prized...famously reclusive, avoiding openings and eschewing interviews.

She peered again at the photograph of the man on the screen. "And this is your father?" she asked, looking up at Archie.

"It is."

"And you're sure his real name was Henry Arthur Bentham?"

"Quite sure. All of his government paperwork and military records were in that name."

"Which all leads to one logical conclusion," Elaine said. "Harley Archibald Benningham is not the artist's real name. Your father was a painter before you were born, and he painted under a different name, but he used his own mark on his work."

Archie nodded. "It does seem that that's a possibility." He seemed too stunned to be able to say more.

"But why didn't you ever know any of this?" Jan asked. "He really never mentioned anything about painting?"

Archie shook his head. "My father was just a hard-working government employee when I knew him. Sure, he could draw—when I was a child he would sit with me and we would draw together, and from a very young age I noticed he was good at it. Perhaps exceptionally so. But he was my father, so I practically worshipped him anyway. I would have thought he was an amazing artist if all he knew how to draw were block letters."

Elaine smiled. "I hear you there. I felt the same way about my dad. But we will definitely take the painting to an art expert to have it evaluated," she said. "Heather gave me the name of one."

"That's good. Then maybe we'll get some answers," Jan said.

"But they probably won't be able to tell me the things I'm most curious about," Archie said. "Which are, who is this woman, and why would my father have painted her? And even more puzzling, why didn't he tell me the truth about his past?"

Neither of them seemed to know how to answer.

CHAPTER THIRTY-TWO

Paula and the kids came over after lunch, and both Avery and Kelly were bouncing up and down with excitement. They were thrilled to have been recruited to help with the stake out today, and Elaine was glad to have them along. She realized that what Nathan had said was true. They looked too conspicuous. Even if Jade had been there yesterday, she wouldn't have tried anything with the two of them sticking out like sore thumbs. She hoped that today things would go a little better.

As they all walked to the beach, Avery was full of questions. "So how are we going to catch this thief?"

Elaine explained that she and her sister would be doing nothing to catch the thief; Jan and Elaine would leave out a decoy purse and try to trap her, but the kids were there just to have fun—and to make Jan and Elaine seem like they belonged. Paula nodded at this. She had come along mostly because—like any good mother—she was uncertain about the idea of her children being used in a plot to trap a thief.

But as soon as the kids spread their blanket out on the beach and ran down to the water and the adults had settled into beach chairs under a striped umbrella, Paula seemed to relax, and she started asking Jan about where things stood with Bob.

Elaine took a minute to set up her decoy blanket, but then she settled back down and listened as Jan and Paula discussed what would happen when Jan got engaged. Avery had spilled the beans to Paula the day before.

"We want to make sure you know that we support you and Bob," Paula was saying with a wide smile. "Brian and I just want you to be happy. Brian isn't always good at expressing his feelings, but we both think Bob is wonderful and we hope you two are very happy. Oh, and Avery has already picked out the dress she wants to wear at your wedding. It's blue and sparkly. Hope that's okay."

Jan laughed and told Paula that they would have a simple wedding, maybe in the backyard or at the church, most likely with just family. Elaine was listening, but she was also scanning the crowd, looking for any sign of movement, any sign of a blonde—or brunette, or redhead—coming toward her purse. She noticed Officer Floyd Adams from Waterville over by the trees, trying to blend in. He was wearing swim trunks and flip-flops as well as an old T-shirt, and he was grilling with a few buddies. Not a bad gig, honestly.

Avery and Kelly were playing nicely in the water. Kelly kept diving under the water to do handstands, while Avery was swimming out to the dock at the far end of the swimming area, where a lifeguard kept watch. It was just a typical, quiet weekday afternoon. She and Jan had spent so many afternoons inside this summer that it was nice to just be sitting here enjoying the sunshine. Maybe it wouldn't be so bad if the thefts continued and no one came to the tea shop. Maybe then they could just sit at the beach every day. It would be great until they could no longer afford to pay their bills, Elaine realized.

She sat up and tried to remain vigilant. She needed to make sure she was scanning the beach regularly, looking for anyone—anything—that seemed out of place. But still, the longer she sat there in the warm sun, the more relaxed she felt, and the harder it was to keep her eyes open. She felt herself start to drift off…

"Elaine!"

Elaine sat upright. What—oh, right, she was at the beach and Jan was looking at her with her eyes wide.

"Look!"

Elaine turned toward the direction Jan was pointing, and she gasped. A woman with long blonde hair was wandering around the beach, heading straight for the blanket and purse they'd left out. She was wearing oversize sunglasses and—Elaine sucked in a breath—the same Colby hat she'd worn in the picture on the marina. This was her! This was Jade!

Jan was snapping photos with her phone camera. Hopefully no matter what happened next, this would provide documentation for the police. Elaine watched as Jade approached the empty blanket. She was cool and smooth. She didn't look around to see if anyone was watching. She didn't do anything but act like she owned this purse and blanket. When she got close enough, she reached over, grabbed the bag by the handles, and kept moving. She was so quick, so confident, that if she hadn't been watching specifically for it, Elaine never would have seen it. She *had* been watching and still had almost missed it. And then, Jade just kept walking.

It took Elaine a moment to react. It had worked. Her crazy plan to lure Jade here and trap her had worked! She was so excited she almost couldn't believe it. But then, just as quickly, she realized she had to stop her!

She pushed herself out of the chair. For one brief, terrifying moment, Elaine considered trying to tackle Jade, but everything in her fifty-seven-year-old body told her this was a bad idea. Still, even though Jan was still snapping pictures, which should provide all the proof Dan needed, she couldn't just let Jade walk away like this.

"Help!" she shrieked. "Purse thief!"

Jade was trying to walk like everything was normal. Several people around Elaine turned and looked, trying to figure out what was going on. A few people started to get up. Jade, seeing that people were paying attention, gave up on trying to blend in and started running.

"She stole my purse!" Elaine shrieked again. "Help!"

Elaine realized that Paula had launched herself out of her chair and was now chasing after Jade. Thank goodness for Paula, who ran regularly. And just as quickly, she saw Officer Adams take off across the sand as well. Another man, a burly shirtless guy who'd been building a sand castle with his kids, also got up and moved to block Jade's path. Elaine felt helpless, stuck, useless.

"I got it!" Jan was yelling. "I got a picture of her!"

Jade was now sprinting toward the parking area at the far end of the beach. Elaine held her breath. The burly man was positioning himself to block her path. Officer Adams was rushing at her from the side, his flip-flops kicking up sand with very step. And Paula ran up behind her. Jade dashed to the right, but she wasn't quick enough. The burly man grabbed her by the arm, stopping her progress, and Officer Adams lunged for her and wrapped his arms around her waist. She fought as best she could, but the two men ended up wrestling her to the ground. When she was down, Officer Adams pulled a pair of handcuffs from his swim trunks—how had that worked? Elaine couldn't help wondering—and slapped them around her wrists. Then he hauled her to her feet, and Elaine saw that her sunglasses had fallen off and the blonde wig had been knocked askew, revealing dyed red hair.

It was her. It was really her. And they'd caught her!

Paula reached for the purse, which had fallen to the sand in the scuffle, and held up Elaine's wallet triumphantly. "Got it, Elaine!" she called.

Everyone on the beach was now looking at the group by the entrance to the sand. Elaine knew they'd caused a scene, but it had been worth it.

"You have the right to remain silent," Officer Adams was saying. The beach had become so quiet the sound carried easily across the sand.

Elaine's instinct was to run up and try to get Jade to confess, to explain, but she knew better than to interfere when the police already had her in their custody. She and Jan would follow them to the station and answer any questions they had there.

For now, Elaine took a moment to enjoy the fact that it was over. The thief had been caught, and there was no chance she was getting away this time. Her crazy plan had worked. Then again, she had always known it would.

Still, it felt good to know that things would go back to normal once again. Visitors and residents would feel safe. Business would pick up again. And—most important—they could go back to enjoying summer in this beautiful small town they called home.

CHAPTER THIRTY-THREE

It had been an eventful day, but Jan wasn't thinking about any of that as she and Bob sat on the dock in the backyard. He'd taken her to a lovely dinner at the Hearthside restaurant, and he'd seemed nervous and jittery throughout the whole meal. It was kind of adorable, actually. Was he really concerned about what her answer would be? Or was he simply nervous that they were going to get interrupted once again?

Jan had expected him to drop down on one knee as dessert was being served, but he hadn't, and had suggested they go for a walk. They'd ended up here, looking out over the lake as the sun slipped behind the trees. The sky was a glorious shade of orange, and the lake was still and calm. The boards of the dock felt warm from baking in the sun all day, and after the big meal Jan was feeling relaxed and peaceful. They sat in silence for a few minutes, and Jan used the moments to pray that God would be present in their interactions tonight and in what lay ahead. Finally, Bob seemed ready, and he turned to Jan.

"I've been wanting to talk to you for a while now," Bob said before clearing his throat. "And the time has never seemed right. But thank you for being patient with me, and for being here with me tonight." He turned to her and took both of her hands in his.

Jan nodded. Her heartbeat sped up. This was perfect. She'd been disappointed when he hadn't asked her to marry him at that outdoor concert, and when their boat ride had been interrupted, but she could see now that this moment, with the sun setting over the lake, was perfect. God's timing always was.

"I have come to care about you more than I ever imagined possible," Bob said, and then took a deep breath.

"I feel closer to you than I thought I could," Bob continued. "And I have enjoyed getting to know you more and more each day. I love you."

Jan's heart soared. "I love you too."

"Which brings me to my question." He let go of one of her hands. This was it! He was reaching for a ring! But then all he did was wipe his hand—which had become a bit sweaty, true—on his shorts and take her hand again.

"Jan, you know that a few months ago I was offered a job in Baltimore. A dream job, really. Defending people unfairly accused of crimes. It's something I've always dreamed of doing, but it was never the kind of law I ended up practicing. But now, my old friend from law school runs the practice, and he wants me to be partner."

Huh? What was Bob doing, talking about the job?

"And even though my life is here now, and the people I care about are here now"—he looked directly into Jan's eyes—"I can't seem to find a way to say no."

What was he saying? Was he trying to tell her he was moving to Baltimore after all?

"But I also can't leave you behind. I love you too much to go away from the most important woman in my life."

He coughed, and then he pulled his hand away again and reached into his pocket. This time, when he brought his hand back, he was holding a small black box. Jan's heart thudded. He held the box out and opened it to reveal a gorgeous diamond in a classic setting.

"So what I wanted to ask you, Jan, is this: Will you marry me and come to Baltimore as my wife?"

Jan felt like someone had splashed cold water on her. "What?"

"Will you marry me?" Bob repeated. There was such naked hope in his eyes.

"I got that part," Jan said. "But you want me move to Baltimore?"

"I was hoping you would," Bob said. Some of the hope in his eyes had been replaced by fear. "I mean, I've taken the job there, and I'd want you to be with me, of course."

Jan didn't say anything for a moment. She looked out over the water. God was in control of this, she knew. He was in control of everything. So why did things suddenly feel so out of control?

Bob wanted her to move to Baltimore for his job. But what about her job? Her life? She turned and looked back at the tearoom, dripping with gingerbread trim and lit up against the darkening evening. She saw a curtain move. Elaine had been spying, then. Jan wanted to laugh. What would she do without Elaine?

That was it though. What *would* she do without Elaine? And what would Elaine do without her? She wanted to marry Bob. She wanted it more than anything.

Well, maybe not more than anything.

She wouldn't have to choose, would she?

"I know it's not what either of us had planned. But I feel God calling me to Baltimore. I can't describe it, but I know it's what I'm supposed to do. And I want you there by my side."

"I do want to marry you," Jan finally said, turning back to Bob. The lines around his eyes relaxed. "But...the other part sort of comes out of nowhere for me. I don't really want to move to Baltimore. Do I have to say yes to that to say yes to the ring?"

Bob seemed confused. "What do you mean?"

Jan had never imagined herself in this situation. This was nothing like how she had pictured this moment. But her feelings were perfectly clear to her. He talked about feeling that God was calling him to Baltimore. Well, she felt God had called her here, to Lancaster.

"I mean, yes, I want to marry you. And no, I don't want to go to Baltimore."

"But Jan, I've already accepted the job." He seemed to be at a loss. "I have to go. And these people—they are being imprisoned for crimes they didn't commit. How can I not help them?"

Was Jan being selfish? It was noble, what Bob wanted to do. Bob always was noble. But what about her? What about the person whose life was affected most by his decision? How could he make a major decision like this without talking to her about it? She thought they'd been on the same page.

"But—do you have to go now? Maybe you can put it off for a year?" She took the box from his hands and examined the ring. The stone sparkled and danced in the evening light. It really was gorgeous.

He shook his head. "I'm supposed to start soon. And I want you to come with me."

She'd told Rose that if she put God at the center of her relationship, she'd know what He wanted, because it would be what she wanted. Jan knew, on a deep level, that she wanted to marry Bob. That God had orchestrated their relationship and brought them together. And she also knew that God had brought her here to Lancaster, to this tearoom. To this new life.

Jan set the ring box down on the deck. The chill of the evening was starting to set in. She couldn't believe it. Here she was, being offered the thing she'd wanted most in the world for the past few months. But accepting it meant giving up the life she'd come to love with all her heart. Would she resent Bob if she said yes? Would she grow bitter at having to give up this new life she never knew she'd always wanted?

"Bob, we never talked about this. I didn't realize you were actually seriously considering moving to Baltimore. I thought you were going to pass it up to stay here with me. And now, just like that, you want me to give up everything and move there?"

"You wouldn't be giving up everything." He threaded his fingers through hers and looked into her eyes. "You'd be with me. We'd be changing innocent people's lives. You'd be making me the happiest man alive."

God was in control. This she knew for certain. God had a plan, and He wanted the best for her. For Bob. Was it possible that best was not being together after all? Jan didn't know. She couldn't even begin to imagine what God had up His sleeve. She knew He'd worked bigger miracles than making sense of this mess. But right now, it felt so hard to trust.

Jan considered her words carefully. "I want that. I want to marry you more than anything, Bob. But I just—I don't know what to say."

She knew what she was supposed to say. What he had expected her to say. What all the romance novels in the world had taught her was the right way to feel at this moment.

But deep down in her bones, Jan didn't want to throw everything away for love. She didn't want to give up on her own dreams to follow him wherever he went. She loved him— madly, truly, deeply.

But maybe, she was realizing now—maybe at this stage that wasn't enough.

"This is my home," Jan said. "This is the life I want. Do you have to take the job? Couldn't we just stay here, get married, and have a happy life here, near our families? In this place we love?"

Bob opened his mouth and closed it again. He didn't seem to know what to say. The sound of the water lapping gently against the dock seemed to echo in the still night.

Then, finally, he said, "I love you, Jan. Please. Come with me."

As he spoke, Jan's hopes for the future crumbled. It wasn't just that he was presenting her with an impossible choice. It was that he was asking her to make a choice he wasn't willing to make himself. Bob wanted her to choose him over the job she loved, but he wouldn't do the same for her.

Jan had been so sure that they would end up together that she'd never even considered how she'd feel if things turned out differently. Tears sprang up in her eyes. She was more shocked than anything, though she knew the pain would come later. Bob pulled a handkerchief from his pocket—a fine linen handkerchief with his initials on it that she'd gotten him for Christmas—and leaned in to wipe her tears away with it. Jan stopped him and took the handkerchief from his hands. She could wipe her eyes herself.

"I'm sorry, Jan. I can see this is a shock to you. I shouldn't have—I should have told you sooner that I'm taking the job. I thought you'd be happy." He sounded pained, and Jan could see that he was hurt and confused. It killed her to see him like that, but she also couldn't hold back the flash of frustration. What had he thought was going to happen?

"Why don't you think about it for a while," Bob suggested. He picked up the ring box and held it out to her again. "Take this. Pray about it. And please, Jan, try to imagine it. The two of us in a cute little house on the Chesapeake. It will be nice."

Jan already had a cute house, and a lake where they could go out on his boat.

She took the ring and held it up to the light again. Fresh tears welled up. She turned from Bob and let her eyes drift out over the lake. It was so calm and still in summer evening. Lightning bugs were dancing down by the shore. The sun had slipped lower, almost completely vanished behind the trees now, and the sky was turning a beautiful deep blue.

"Please, Jan. Please understand. This is my dream job."

Even in the fading evening, the diamond cast shards of light across the worn boards of the deck.

"Yes, Bob. I know." Jan turned and gestured back toward the house. The tearoom. The business she'd built here. The life she'd built here. "And this is mine."

Jan couldn't believe it. She had never imagined Bob's proposal playing out like this. But slowly, she reached out her hand and gave the ring back.

"I love you," she said as tears spilled out of her eyes. "But if this is the choice you're asking me to make, then I'm afraid the answer is no. I can't marry you."

Jan didn't know what the future held, but God did. She didn't want to let Bob go, but she also knew she couldn't leave with him. All she could do was trust.

And, she decided, sitting there on that dock with the man she loved, the man who was leaving her, she would trust God with all her heart. He would take care of the rest.

ABOUT THE AUTHOR

Elizabeth Adams lives in New York City with her husband and two young daughters. When she's not writing, she spends time cleaning up after two devious cats and trying to find time to read mysteries.

JAN'S SUMMERY BLUEBERRY PEACH MUFFINS

3 cups all-purpose flour

½ cup white sugar

½ cup brown sugar

1 tablespoon baking powder

½ teaspoon salt

3 eggs

1 cup milk

½ cup melted butter, cooled

1 cup blueberries, preferably fresh

1 cup diced fresh peaches

Topping:

2 teaspoons white sugar

1 teaspoon ground cinnamon

½ teaspoon ground nutmeg

2 tablespoons melted butter

Preheat oven to 400 degrees. Grease or line muffin tins. In a large bowl, stir together the flour, white sugar, brown sugar, baking powder, and salt. In a separate bowl, mix together the eggs, milk, and melted butter. Pour the wet ingredients into the dry, and mix until just blended, being careful not to overbeat. Gently fold in the blueberries and peaches, and fill the muffin cups about two-thirds full.

Bake for eighteen to twenty minutes in the preheated oven or until they are golden brown and the tops spring back when lightly touched.

In a small bowl, stir together the remaining sugar, cinnamon, and nutmeg. Brush muffins with remaining melted butter and then sprinkle with the cinnamon mixture. Makes twelve to sixteen muffins.

READ ON FOR AN EXCITING SNEAK PEEK
INTO THE NEXT VOLUME OF TEAROOM MYSTERIES!

The Tea Will Tell

A breeze from one of the half-open kitchen windows stirred a corner of the newspaper Elaine Cook read, the rustling pages adding to the symphony of a quiet Saturday morning before the tearoom opened. Jan was baking, so Elaine had wandered downstairs to sit with her.

"The lake looks calm today." Jan's voice cut through Elaine's musings.

"Yep," she said, without looking up.

Jan's rolling pin made a thumping sound against the marble counter. "It would be a perfect day for a walk along the shore. We should have time before we open."

"Probably."

"Would you like to come along?"

"Good idea."

"Elaine?"

"Huh?"

"I asked if you would like to come along."

Elaine looked up to find her cousin staring at her, a small smile curving her lips. Jan lifted her hand and made a walking motion with two fingers. "Around the lake. A walk. You and me. Want to go?"

"Oh." A blush warmed Elaine's cheeks. "I'm so sorry. I was just so wrapped up in this article."

Jan closed the oven door and walked over to look. "What article?"

Elaine turned the newspaper so Jan could read the headline.

"String of Home Invasions Strikes Lancaster." Jan sat in a chair next to Elaine's. "Home invasions…as in robberies? How dreadful."

Elaine lowered the paper and eyed her curiously. "You heard that one of the homes broken into was Priscilla's, from the library, right?"

"Priscilla's?" Jan's eyes widened. "No, I had not heard that. She and I haven't had a chance to talk since the last book club meeting. She went out of town to visit some relatives, I think."

Elaine nodded. "It happened right after she got back. Lucky for her, she was working late at the library trying to get caught up from her trip when it happened. I shudder to think of the outcome had she been home alone."

"Oh, Elaine, that's so terrible. No wonder you were caught up in that article. Does it say anything else about the other homes that were broken into?"

"Only that there have been five break-ins so far," she said, handing Jan the paper. "But it does have some interesting information. See for yourself." She pointed to a picture included with the article. "The only information police are releasing is that the robber is armed and considered dangerous. That's a replica of the gun there."

Jan frowned. "How do they know what gun was used?"

"Apparently, they were able to use some video tape captured by the security system in the home of one of the other victims. The article says police are not releasing the actual photos yet because the investigation is ongoing."

The front door opened. Elaine poked her head into the hall and saw Archie Bentham step in, his cheeks ruddy and his white hair standing on end. He slipped out of his beige jacket and hung it on the hall tree next to the door.

"Good morning!" their employee called, his voice chipper.

"Morning, Archie," Elaine said. She ducked back into the kitchen. "Archie's here." This time, it was Jan who barely lifted her head.

Archie ambled into the kitchen and made his way to the coffeepot. "Smashing weather we're having."

"I hadn't noticed. I was too caught up in this article." Elaine cast a glance through the window toward the lake, where white froth danced atop the waves. "Anyway, I'm glad the weather is nice. Jan and I were thinking of taking a quick walk before the tearoom opens."

"Well, take a jacket." Archie rubbed his hands together briskly. "It *is* only September, but there's already a slight nip in the air. I wonder if this weather means we're in for a long winter. If so, we'd better stock up on ice melt."

Elaine laid her finger against her lips. "*Hmm*...I wonder if the temperatures will mean we'll have a good crowd. Labor Day is on Monday and most people will have the day off."

"We should have a respectable turnout." Archie eyed the trays of baked goods lining the counter, then joined them at the table and pulled out a chair. "It's probably a good thing you and Jan had the foresight to prepare a few extra cookies and scones."

Elaine pointed to her cousin. "That was Jan's idea. She thought we should have them on hand, just in case."

Finished with the article, Jan blew out a breath and laid the paper down. She looked over her glasses at Archie. "Oh, hello, Archie. When did you get here?"

Archie threw a puzzled glance at Elaine.

"Never mind her," she said, giving a wave of her hand. "You've heard about the string of break-ins hitting Lancaster, haven't you, Archie?"

"I have, but I haven't paid them much mind." He tapped a corner of the newspaper. "Is that what has Jan so engrossed?"

"Uh-huh." Jan smoothed her hand over the paper, then reached for her cup. "I realize we are hardly immune to crime here in our little corner of Maine, but I surely never imagined it would happen to someone as sweet as Priscilla."

"Priscilla Gates's house was broken into," Elaine explained to Archie, "along with several others."

Archie scratched his head. "That's terrible. Was she hurt? Was anything taken?"

Elaine shrugged. "She wasn't home when it happened, and I really don't know if anything was taken. I'll have to ask her next time I see her."

"Oh." Jan's mouth puckered as she lowered her teacup. "My tea is cold."

"Please, allow me." Archie rose and swept up the cup and saucer in one hand.

"Thank you, Archie," Jan said. "There are fresh cranberry scones on the counter if you'd like one. In fact, I wish you *would* sample one. I'm trying out a new recipe."

Archie dipped his head playfully in her direction. "Madam, it will be my honor."

The cousins chuckled at his antics and then Elaine waved toward the window. "What about our walk? Still want to go?"

Jan checked her watch. "It's only quarter after eight. I just put the last batch of cookies in the oven, but they should be done—"

The timer rang as if on cue, and Jan rose to transfer the cookies from the oven onto a cooling rack. "Never mind the tea, Archie. Elaine and I will be going outside as soon as I finish up here." She worked quietly a moment, then slid her hands from a pair of oven mitts and laid them on the counter. "There. That's all of them. I think we'll have time for our walk now if we make it brief."

Jan went to fetch a sweater for herself and one for Elaine. Elaine was thankful Archie had suggested it because the sun's pale rays did little to add warmth.

She jammed her arms into the sleeves of her sweater before turning for the path that led down to the shore and a dock that stretched out into Chickadee Lake. Next to her, Jan did the same, only she also buttoned her sweater up to her neck.

"Archie is right. There is a nip in the air."

ELAINE CHUCKLED. "MAYBE we'll get lucky and have one last Indian summer before the really cold weather hits."

"I hope so. This air isn't good for my skin. It gets so dry in the winter." Jan blew out a breath. "You know, Elaine, I didn't just want to go for a walk. There's something I've been meaning to talk to you about."

"Oh?" Elaine glanced at her sidelong. Jan's tone was troubled, and for her normally cheerful cousin, that was odd. "Is everything okay?"

Jan shrugged deeper into her sweater. "I'm not sure. This thing with Bob's new job in Baltimore has me in knots."

Elaine's heart sank. "So he's still bent on taking it? He hasn't reconsidered after you turned down his proposal?"

Jan's eyes widened behind her glasses. "He still says it's... it's the opportunity of a lifetime."

Her words drooped at the end, as though she'd tried desperately and failed to convince herself of them. Elaine slowed her steps. They had reached the edge of the lake. Tall rushes and trees grew here, and provided homes to a variety of fowl and wildlife. They took refuge alongside the lake, just as she and Jan had done when they bought the tearoom, but now...

She reached out to touch Jan's shoulder. "I'm sorry. I know this is difficult."

Jan sniffed and pulled a tissue from the pocket of her sweater. "It's just... I thought..." She shrugged. "Well, you know. I'd hoped Bob and I would get married. But I can't give up the tearoom, and he is set on leaving, so I will just have to make do."

Helplessness crept over Elaine like fog. She didn't like seeing Jan so forlorn, but what could she do?

"Look there." She pointed at one of the black-capped chickadees that their lake was named after. The pretty little thing was perched on one of the tall rushes and seemed content to study them, his small head tilting from side to side.

"Oh, he's beautiful." Jan pressed her hands together in delight. "No wonder the people of Maine chose those little fellows as the state bird."

Elaine smiled, struck by a sudden thought. "Well, he's not a sparrow, but I figure God's eye is on him too, wouldn't you think?"

Jan gave a slow nod.

Elaine draped her arm around her cousin's shoulder. "I think we can use the reminder."

Slowly, a bit of the tension relaxed from Jan's features. She turned to look at the bird, which chose that particular moment to soar off into the sky. "You're right, of course. And I suppose if that one tiny bird is important to Him..."

"You can rest assured that you are too." Elaine gave Jan's shoulder a squeeze, then dropped her arm. "God will find a way to work this all out. In the meantime you just have to have faith. You know I'll be praying for both you and Bob."

"I know, and I'm grateful," Jan said. Lifting her glasses, she wiped her eyes with the tissue and then pushed it back into her pocket. "Well, I suppose we should be getting back. Archie is going to wonder where we've gone."

Elaine smiled, relieved to see a bit of the spunk return to Jan's blue eyes. "So you do think business will stay steady, though most of the tourists have gone?"

She nodded. "How can it not? I've been baking all morning and I'm pretty sure I left the kitchen window open a crack. The scent should be all over Lancaster by now."

Though it was silly, Elaine took a deep whiff and nodded. "Yep, I smell it now. We'd better get back before the tearoom fills up and Archie storms off in a huff."

She offered her elbow to Jan, who took it and turned with her back toward the house.

"So you haven't told me recently, how are things with you and Nathan?" Jan eyed her slyly. "You realize that with Bob out of the picture, I'm going to take an inordinate interest in the two of you."

Elaine laughed and patted Jan's hand. "There's nothing much to tell, really." Her face warmed despite the cool morning air. "Okay, so the truth is things are progressing. I just never thought... that is, after I lost Ben, I never thought..."

She sighed, and Jan laughed. "Isn't that how it always works? When we aren't even thinking about it, and when we least expect it, that's when love happens."

Love?

Elaine bit her lip. She certainly cared deeply for Nathan, but could she call it love? She pushed the thought to the back of her mind as she and Jan reentered the tearoom.

Elaine took off her sweater and put out her hand. "Give me your sweater. I'll take it upstairs with mine."

Jan complied, and Elaine took her time heading up the stairs. She really was going to have to give this whole thing with

Nathan some serious thought. After all, dating was one thing, but to say she was in love was quite another.

Thinking about love dredged up all sorts of old memories, including her first encounter with Ben—the excitement, the tingling in her veins, the lightheaded giddiness that left her walking on air. Her feelings for Nathan were different, of course—she'd been in her twenties when she and Ben met. Was the difference in her feelings for Nathan simply that she was so much older and more mature, or something else?

By the time she returned to the east parlor, it was almost time for the tearoom to open. Rose, their other employee, was busy putting sugar bowls on each of the tables. Elaine tied a frilly cabbage rose apron that she'd found at a garage sale around her waist, then hurried to do the same in the west parlor.

At ten o'clock sharp, Elaine went to unlock the door. Within minutes, the tearoom began to fill with regulars and new visitors alike. Business was so good, in fact, that the morning passed in a blur. Thankfully, Rose and Archie were light on their feet. Rose's smile remained fixed in place as she took care of customers in the east parlor, while Archie handled the west. Elaine managed the cash register, and Jan poked her head out of the kitchen from time to time to help clear tables.

It wasn't until almost two that any of them had a chance to catch their breath. What happened to the lull that normally occurred around lunchtime? Not today. None of them had dared take a break and Elaine's stomach rumbled in protest. She drew her arm across her brow wearily. Across the tearoom, Archie lifted his hand and motioned to her. As she approached, he pointed to the hall and the kitchen that lay beyond.

"You should sit down, Elaine. You've haven't stopped or even slowed down once since we opened."

"Well, being behind the cash register helps," she said. "You and Rose did far more running than I did."

His scowl remained fixed in place as he propped his hands on his hips. "The crowd has thinned some. Have you eaten?"

Elaine hesitated and cast a long glance toward the kitchen. "Not yet, but I was just about to let Jan know that Jo Murphy called requesting two dozen ginger chews. The twins are having friends over tonight, and she doesn't have time to bake. I need to ask Jan if she has that many available before I call Jo back."

"I can take care of that. You take this into the kitchen and sit awhile." Archie held an empty teacup and saucer toward her and looked at her insistently until she took them.

"Fine, but I'll make it quick so you can eat too." Elaine turned gratefully for the kitchen. "My aching feet will never be the same after this day."

Archie chuckled. "Well then, I suppose it's good fortune for both of us that we've only a couple of hours left before we close."

"Indeed."

He patted his stomach. "Jan said she's got sandwiches made for everyone. I'm thinking about taking her up on her offer. I'm sure they'll be delicious."

Elaine's mouth watered thinking about the loaf of home-made bread she'd seen Jan taking out of the oven early that morning, but she hated making Archie wait.

She shook her head. "Tell you what, why don't you go on? I'll stay out here and wait on these last few customers. The minute they finish, I'll come in and join you."

"Elaine—"

"Archie, I insist. I couldn't enjoy my lunch otherwise." She pressed the cup back into his hands.

His eyebrows lifted as he hesitated. "What about Rose? Perhaps she could watch the front."

"I told her I would let her go early." Elaine hid a wry smile. "She has a big test coming up that she has to study for and I felt sorry for her."

Rose was in culinary school, and though she loved her classes, Elaine knew she was worried about her test.

Archie headed off toward the kitchen, and Elaine passed the time chatting with the customers who were left in the tearoom. One couple was from Texas, and had come to Maine to visit family. Another woman had traveled all the way from California and stumbled on the tearoom by accident. Elaine enjoyed listening to people explain how they'd come to arrive in Lancaster, and was filled with a satisfied sort of tired when at last she locked the tearoom door.

As though she'd been cued by the click, Jan emerged from the kitchen. Her hair stuck out oddly in various places, and flour dusted her glasses and her nose. In her hands, she bore a plate piled high with chips and a turkey sandwich that made Elaine's mouth water. "Well now, that was—"

"A rousing success?" Elaine laughed and joined Jan and Archie at one of the tables. "Please tell me that sandwich is for me."

Jan laughed and placed it in her hands. "You've earned it. We've already eaten ours."

"Thank goodness." Elaine started to sit, then eyed the few remaining tables that had yet to be cleared in the east parlor. She looked at her sandwich longingly and then back at the stacks of dirty dishes and teacups. "I suppose I should—"

"Don't even think about it," Jan interrupted. "Archie and I can clean up while you eat."

It was all the prompting Elaine needed. She dropped into the chair and took a healthy bite.

"There were a fair number of regulars here this morning," Jan said, moving to the nearest table and gathering up the teacups. "Didn't you think so, Archie? I know I saw Kit and Russell Edmonds here, and I think I spied Patti Garland. She ordered a maple croissant, didn't she?"

He nodded. "Though I thought the number of tourists was impressive too."

They continued chatting as they moved from one table to the next while Elaine munched happily on her sandwich. She picked up a chip. "And did you notice that Macy Atherton didn't have one critique this morning? She must have really liked your cranberry scones today."

She laughed and then popped the chip in her mouth, savoring the crisp snap and savory saltiness—a perfect complement to her scrumptious sandwich.

"I'll have to keep that in mind." Jan laughed and carried a tray of dishes toward the kitchen.

There was some clattering from the kitchen, and then Jan returned empty-handed. She paused in the hall near the cash register. "Say, what's this?"

She bent and picked up a brown paper bag. "It's heavy. Did someone leave it in the tearoom?"

Elaine squinted. There were no markings to distinguish the bag from any other. She shrugged. "I have no idea. Archie, did you see who left that bag?"

Across the room, Archie shook his head. "No, sorry."

"*Hmm.* I suppose I should look."

Jan pulled open the bag to peer inside. Something about the look on her face arrested Elaine's chewing mid-bite.

She swallowed hastily. "Jan? What is it?"

Jan looked up slowly, her eyes wide with disbelief. "It's..." Her gaze returned to the bag.

"What?" Not liking the pallor that had come over her cousin, Elaine persisted. "What did you find?"

Archie looked up too. "Jan?"

Jan's finger shook as she pointed. "It's a gun, Elaine. Someone has left a gun in the tearoom."

This story, by Susie Gustafson of Winter Park, Florida,
originally appeared in *Angels on Earth*.

My son was awarded two tickets to Walt Disney World in his senior year of high school. Who did he invite as his guest? Me! We spent the day enjoying the rides, especially Splash Mountain and Thunder Mountain, and had enough fun to last a lifetime.

We stayed at the theme park for the nightly fireworks and parade, and then reluctantly headed to the exit. "Mom," Chris said, "your backpack's open." I swung it around in front of me and pawed through the contents to be sure nothing had fallen out. "My wallet!" I cried. Only God knew where I had dropped it.

Chris took charge and reported my loss to an attendant in the services building. What a son I had. So I lost my wallet, I thought. A little cash gone. I'd cancel the credit cards. No problem. Nothing would ruin this day. I described my wallet for the attendant.

A woman walked up. "I couldn't help but overhear," she said. "Is this it?" She had my wallet in her hands! She'd found it by Thunder Mountain.

Chris and I talked about nothing else on the way home. Our day together in a fantasy world had been topped off by a real-life angel.

A NOTE FROM THE EDITORS

We hope you enjoyed Tearoom Mysteries, published by the Books and Inspirational Media Division of Guideposts, a nonprofit organization that touches millions of lives every day through products and services that inspire, encourage, help you grow in your faith, and celebrate God's love.

Thank you for making a difference with your purchase of this book, which helps fund our many outreach programs to military personnel, prisons, hospitals, nursing homes, and educational institutions.

We also create many useful and uplifting online resources. Visit Guideposts.org to read true stories of hope and inspiration, access OurPrayer network, sign up for free newsletters, download free e-books, join our Facebook community, and follow our stimulating blogs.

To learn about other Guideposts publications, including the best-selling devotional *Daily Guideposts*, go to Guideposts.org/Shop, call (800) 932-2145, or write to Guideposts, PO Box 5815, Harlan, Iowa 51593.

Sign up for the
Guideposts Fiction Newsletter

and stay up-to-date on
the fiction you love!

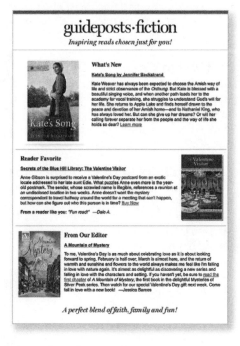

You'll get sneak peeks of new releases, recommendations from other Guideposts readers, and special offers just for you . . .

And it's FREE!

Just go to Guideposts.org/Newsletters
today to sign up.

Guideposts

Visit Guideposts.org/Shop
or call (800) 932-2145

Find more inspiring fiction in these best-loved Guideposts series!

Sugarcreek Amish Mysteries

Be intrigued by the suspense and joyful "aha" moments in these delightful stories. Each book in the series brings together two women of vastly different backgrounds and traditions, who realize there's much more to the "simple life" than meets the eye.

Miracles of Marble Cove

Follow four women who are drawn together to face life's challenges, support one another in faith, and experience God's amazing grace as they encounter mysterious events in the small town of Marble Cove.

Secrets of Mary's Bookshop

Delve into a cozy mystery where Mary, the owner of Mary's Mystery Bookshop, finds herself using sleuthing skills that she didn't realize she had. There are quirky characters and lots of unexpected twists and turns.

Patchwork Mysteries

Discover that life's little mysteries often have a common thread in a series where every novel contains an intriguing mystery centered around a quilt located in a beautiful New England town.

Mysteries of Silver Peak

Escape to the historic mining town of Silver Peak, Colorado, and discover how one woman's love of antiques helps her solve mysteries buried deep in the town's checkered past.

To learn more about these books, visit Guideposts.org/Shop